'Q g.
He plans ou-
tation. If will
find a way to ruin me.'

F He swung her
back into the shadows, up against the hedge,
and stood between Miss Ravel and the light.

'Follow my lead and keep silent,' he
murmured against her lavender-scented hair.

'Your lead?' she asked, attempting to peer
around him. Her skirts brushed his leg.
'Should I trust you?'

'Do you have a choice?' He took a glimpse
down at Miss Ravel, seeing her clearly for the
first time.

Her lips hovered a tantalisingly few inches
beneath his. Her deep blue eyes looked up
into his, trusting him to get this right and
protect her. Truly Cinderella after the ball,
missing a slipper and in need of a prince.

Richard resisted the urge to crush her to him.
Another time and in another place he would
have given in to temptation, but this closeness
was far from a prelude to seduction—it was
instead a means to prevent Miss Ravel's ruin.
He had to hope that whoever it was would
observe the niceties and simply walk on past.

AUTHOR NOTE

In the beginning there was Sophie. I wrote the first scene of this book and then thought, *Hold on—what happened before*? The 'what happened before?' thoughts led to me writing TO MARRY A MATCHMAKER, and after I'd finished writing it I considered that I could leave Sophie and concentrate on other stories. My editor agreed and thought it would be a good idea to give Sophie a chance to grow up.

Sophie had other ideas. She enlisted my daughter. My daughter was instrumental in my writing AN IMPULSIVE DEBUTANTE, and every so often Katharine would ask, 'So when are you going to write Sophie? It is all very well and good saying that she had a happy ending, Mom, but how did she get there? You must know.'

My daughter went away to university, and when we talked she'd keep on about Sophie and how she needed a proper story. Finally I asked my editor—who agreed! Sophie, of course, decided to become rather aloof because I had ignored her, and I feared I would have to write something else. Then, quite suddenly, Sophie decided she had better show up or she would not have a story!

The result is this book. I did adore writing it once Sophie and Richard decided to speak to me. I hope you will enjoy reading it.

As ever, I love hearing from readers. You can contact me through my website, www.michellestyles.co.uk, my blog, www.michellestyles.blogspot.com, or through my publisher. I also have a page on Facebook—Michelle Styles Romance Author—where I regularly post my news.

AN IDEAL HUSBAND?

Michelle Styles

First published in Great Britain 2013
by Mills & Boon, an imprint of Harlequin (UK) Limited.
Harlequin (UK) Limited, Eton House, 18-24 Paradise Road,
Richmond, Surrey TW9 1SR

© Michelle Styles 2013

ISBN: 978 0 263 89819 4

Printed and bound in Spain
by Blackprint CPI, Barcelona

Born and raised near San Francisco, California, **Michelle Styles** currently lives a few miles south of Hadrian's Wall, with her husband, three children, two dogs, cats, assorted ducks, hens and beehives.

An avid reader, she became hooked on historical romance when she discovered Georgette Heyer, Anya Seton and Victoria Holt one rainy lunchtime at school.

Although Michelle loves reading about history, she also enjoys a more hands-on approach to her research. She has experimented with a variety of old recipes and cookery methods (some more successfully than others), climbed down Roman sewers, and fallen off horses in Iceland. When she is not writing, reading or doing research, Michelle tends her rather overgrown garden or does needlework.

Michelle maintains a website, www.michellestyles.co.uk, and a blog: www.michellestyles.blogspot.com. She would be delighted to hear from you.

Previous novels by the same author:

*linked by character

And in Mills & Boon® Historical *Undone!* eBooks:

For Katharine,
who asked, begged and otherwise pleaded.

Being an author's daughter can have its advantages…
even if you still die of embarrassment
when I go looking for my books in a bookshop.

Chapter One

⟩⟩⟩⟩⟩⟩⟩⟩⟩⟩⟩⟩⟩⟩⟩⟩⟩⟩

May 1852—Newcastle upon Tyne

Why was it that some men only understood the application of a frying pan to the head? And why was it that one often met such men at balls when all one could carry in one's reticule was a hair pin?

Sophie Ravel glared at Sir Vincent Putney and took a step backwards, narrowly avoiding his outstretched hand. Perhaps this contrived confrontation of Sir Vincent Putney in a deserted conservatory was not one of her better ideas, but Sophie knew it was the only way to help one of her oldest friends avoid a fate worse than death. Tonight was the final opportunity to carry out her scheme and prevent Cynthia from being sacrificed on the altar of her parents' ambition.

'Not one step further, Sir Vincent.' Sophie raised her reticule, ready to swat his hand away.

'I have no desire to see you fall, Miss Ravel.' The oily voice grated over her nerves. 'I know how precious you are to my dear Miss Johnson. She sang your praises for weeks before we journeyed to Newcastle. Will Miss Johnson be joining us in the conservatory? Is that what she meant by a surprise?'

Sophie's eyes flew to the door. She'd been meticulous in her planning. Every eventuality covered, every solitary one except the one actually unfolding.

She should know the answer to the question, but her mind was a blank. She hated lying; avoiding the full truth was a necessity in certain circumstances.

'Miss Johnson has another matter to attend to before she can come to any conservatory.' Sophie straightened the skirt of her ball gown so that the cascades of blonde lace fell neatly once again. The tiny gesture restored her confidence. Precise planning would once again triumph and produce the perfect outcome. 'I'm sure she will appear when circumstances permit it.'

'Said with such a disdainful look.' Sir Vincent hooked his thumbs into his waistcoat. 'Despite your airs and graces, Miss Ravel, you have nothing to be proud about. I know all about your parentage and how your father acquired his considerable fortune.'

Sophie fought against the inclination to laugh. The man's accent was so entirely ridiculous, proclaiming about her parentage as if she was some brood mare.

She backed up so that her bottom touched one of the shelves. A particularly large fern nodded over her left shoulder.

'I suspect you have heard lies and half-truths.' She feinted to the left, only to be stopped when he placed his paw on the railing. 'Now, will you listen to what I have to say? Or are we going to have to play "Here we go round the mulberry bush" all night?'

He waggled his eyebrows, but did not remove his hand.

In the distance she could hear the faint strains of the orchestra as they struck up a polka. All she had to do was to calmly return to the ballroom after delivering her message. As long as she refused to panic, she was the mistress of the situation. Icy calm and a well-tilted chin. Poise.

'I regret to inform you, Sir Vincent, that Miss Johnson has other plans for this evening.' She ducked under his arm and wished she had chosen somewhere else besides the deserted conservatory to impart the news. Good ideas had a way of turning bad if not properly thought through. She should know that by now. 'Indeed, she has other plans for the rest of her life.'

'Other plans?' Sir Vincent cocked his head and Sophie could almost see the slow clogs of his brain moving. 'Miss Johnson arrived with her parents and me only a short while ago in my carriage. I know what her plans are. Her father has accepted my suit. They are watching her to ensure her reputation remains unsoiled. We are to be married come a week Saturday.'

'Her note. Miss Johnson asked me to give it to you once we were in the conservatory.'

He shook his ponderous head. 'Mr Johnson and I have come to an arrangement. He knows what is good for him. His wealth will go a long way towards restoring my family home. He saw sense in the match in the end.'

Sophie's stomach revolted. What she had considered Cynthia's fevered imaginings were utterly correct. Sir Vincent had used blackmail and threats to achieve his ends.

Since Cynthia's father had agreed to the marriage, Sir Vincent or her parents had hung about Cynthia like limpets. It was only at this ball that Cynthia stood any chance of escape. Sophie had brought the valise in her carriage. Hopefully Cynthia and her true love were now using the carriage to go straight to the railway station. The last train for Carlisle left in a half-hour. Then, at Carlisle, they would change trains and go to Liverpool, catching a boat to America leaving on tomorrow afternoon's tide. She'd left nothing to chance.

'Read the note, Sir Vincent, before you say anything we both might regret.'

He froze and his pig-like eyes narrowed, before snatching the note from her fingers. His lips formed the words as he read the note. The colour drained from his face.

'You're serious. Miss Johnson has jilted me.'

'She intends to marry someone else, someone far more congenial.'

He screwed up the note. 'We shall see about that! Her father has agreed to the match. He wants my name and status.'

Sophie rolled her eyes. What did he expect after the way he had behaved, cavorting with all manner of loose women, being insufferably rude to Cynthia and, worst of all, boasting about it to members of his club? 'I believe it is Miss Johnson's wishes that are paramount here. It is her life, rather than her father's or her mother's.'

She only hoped some day she'd meet a man who would make her want to forget her life and responsibility, but who would also be her friend. Why wasn't she deserving of a Great Romance? All of her friends had and all she'd discovered was alternative uses for hatpins and frying pans!

'You gambled and you have lost, Sir Vincent. Here is where I say goodbye.'

'We shall see about that!' He threw the crumpled note down on the ground.

'You are too late. Miss Johnson has eloped.'

'Scotland, it will be Scotland. Her father should never have come to Newcastle.'

'You will look like a fool if you go after her. Do you wish to be taken for a fool, Sir Vincent?'

Sir Vincent froze.

Sophie breathed easier. Nothing would happen to her now, but she could buy Cynthia a few more precious minutes.

'I'm no fool, Miss Ravel.'

'I'm glad to hear it.' Sophie cleared her throat. 'A notice will appear in *The Times* and a number of local papers in the morning, stating that your engagement is off. You will have to find another bride, Sir Vincent.' Sophie started towards the door. 'It is time I returned to the dance. I have a full dance card this evening.'

'This is all your fault!' He stepped in front

of her, blocking her path. 'You will have to pay, Miss Ravel. You have done me out of a fortune. Nobody does that to me!'

'My fault? I'm merely the messenger.' An uneasy feeling crept down Sophie's spine. He still stood between her and the door to the ballroom. She needed to get away from this situation as quickly as possible before something untoward happened. Carefully she measured the distance to the outside door of the conservatory with her eyes. It was possible, but only as a last resort. She'd much prefer to walk back into the ballroom rather than going through the French doors. 'And having delivered my message, I shall get back to the ball. I doubt we need ever acknowledge each other again.'

'You are in it up to your pretty neck.' Sir Vincent turned a bright puce colour and shook his fist in her face. 'You will be sorry you ever crossed me, Miss Ravel. I will not rest until I've ruined your life.'

Sophie tapped her foot. 'Cease to threaten me this instant. You have no hold over me. Let me pass.'

His hand shot out, capturing her arm. 'I am not through with you.'

'Unhand me, sir. You overstep the mark!' Sophie struggled against his hold.

'Can you afford a scandal, Miss Ravel, despite your wealth? You may wear your ice-cold hauteur like armour, but do you truly think that will save you?' His vice-like hand tightened on her upper arm.

'I am well aware of what society requires. My reputation is spotless. You cannot touch me.' Sophie twisted her wrist first one way and then the next. She had been naïve in the extreme when she had consented to elope with Sebastian Cawburn several years ago. Luckily, her guardian Robert Montemorcy and the woman who became his wife had intervened and had the matter successfully suppressed. Every night she said an extra prayer of thanks that Henrietta Montemorcy had entered her life.

'Yet you allowed yourself to be alone with a man in a conservatory. Tsk, tsk, Miss Ravel.'

Thinking about Henri redoubled Sophie's determination. She brought her arm sharply downwards, broke free and pulled the French doors to the garden open. 'This is where we part.'

As she stepped down, she heard the distinct sound of ripping lace. One more reason to loathe Sir Vincent—she had really loved her new gown, particularly the blonde lace. She didn't stop to examine the extent of the tear, but picked up her skirts and scurried out into the garden. The cool evening air enveloped her and she moved away from the light and into the velvet darkness.

Sophie pressed her hands to her eyes and tried to think. What next? She'd circle around the house and go back into the house through the terrace. Easy enough. With a bit of luck, no one would notice. She could make her way to the ladies' withdrawing room, do the necessary repairs and then plead a headache and have a carriage called. Thankfully, her stepmother had been unwell tonight and so it would be all the explanation required.

Her foot squelched in a muddy pool and cold seeped through into her foot. Another pair of dancing slippers ruined and these ones were her favourite blue-satin ones.

Behind her, she heard footsteps. Sir Vincent called her name. He was closer to the house than she. He was going to head her off before the ballroom, Sophie realised, and a cold fist closed around her insides.

She could imagine the scandal if she suddenly appeared dishevelled and escorted by Sir Vincent. She knew precisely what happened in these sorts of situations and Sir Vincent was not in any mood to be a gentleman. The whispers would reverberate through Newcastle society before morning—*the proud Miss Ravel has slipped.*

It wouldn't stop there—the rumours would spread throughout society within a fortnight. She faced the very real prospect of ruin. Despite her earlier brave words, could she be sure of her stepmother's support? Being part of society meant everything to her stepmother. Unfortunately the Montemorcys were out of the country. She was truly on her own…this time.

She turned sharply and headed out into the dark of the garden. Two could play a waiting game.

'You can be a fool, Sophia Ravel,' she muttered to herself, stepping into another puddle. Her intricate hairstyle of small looped braids combined with curls tumbled down about her shoulders. 'Would Cynthia have done this for you? Or would she have found an excuse at the last moment? How could you have forgotten the pencil incident at school!'

Sophie gritted her teeth. It was too late to worry about what-might-have-been.

Behind her, she heard the sound of Sir Vincent's heavy breathing. 'I will find you. I know you are in the garden. I do so like games of hide and go seek, Miss Ravel.'

In the gloom of a May evening in Newcastle, she could see his black outline. She was going to lose, and lose badly.

She pivoted and ran blindly back towards the house and bumped straight into a well-muscled chest.

'Where are you going?' a deep rich baritone said as strong arms put her away from the un-yielding chest. 'Are you running away from the ball? Has midnight struck already?'

Sophie's heart skipped a beat. All might not be lost. Silently she offered up a prayer that this man would be a friend rather than a foe.

'Please,' she whispered. 'You must help me. For the love of God, you must save me or else I shall be ruined.'

Richard Crawford, Viscount Bingfield, re-garded the dishevelled blonde woman in his arms. The last thing he wanted or needed was to save some Cinderella-in-distress. But what choice did he have? He could hardly turn his back on her, not after he'd heard her ragged plea.

'If it is in my power, I will help.'

Her trembling stopped. 'Do you mean that?'

'I do. Are you some escaping Cinderella, fear-ful of missing her fairy godmother's deadline?'

'Hardly that.' Her hand tried to pin one of her braids up, but only succeeded in loosening more of the blonde curls. 'I'm not running away from the ball. I am running towards it.'

'Towards the ball? That dress?' Even in the

gloom, Richard could see the rips and tears. A twig stuck to the top frill of her blouse. He pointed and hoped she was aware of the scandal which she was about to be engulfed in.

'I loved this dress.' Her hand brushed away the twig. 'Really loved and adored it. It is irreparable.'

Her lavender scent rose around him. All his instincts told him to crush her to him and hold her until her shaking stopped, but that would be less than wise. The last thing he needed was to be engulfed in a scandal and for his father to realise he was in Newcastle rather than in London. His father, the Marquess of Hallington, was in ill health. In fact, he had only now begun to recover from the last fit at the end of April. With each passing week, his father seemed to slip more and more into a jealous rage against his mother and the scandal in which she had engulfed the family, even though those events had occurred many years ago.

Richard knew he shouldn't have come to Newcastle, but equally he knew he had to vet the man who had captured his half-sister's affections. His mother was untrustworthy on this matter and he had also taken the opportunity to once again sort out his mother's finances.

He forced his arms to let the young woman

go and put her from him. 'Tell me quietly and quickly what you need and I will see what I can do about it.'

'I need to go back to the ball.'

'Looking like that? Brushing away one twig won't mend the ripped lace. You must know what will happen to you. Shall I call a carriage?'

Her hand instinctively tried to smooth her rumpled ball dress. 'Very well, then. I need to get back into the house and go to the ladies' withdrawing room where I can repair the damage. I do have my leaving arrangements in order.'

'It should be simple a matter to walk straight back.'

'Not so simple.' She lowered her voice. 'Someone is after me. He is determined to ruin me.'

Richard regarded the woman. The back of his neck pricked. He should walk away now. 'It is hard to ruin someone who does not wish to be ruined. Practically impossible.'

She gave a half-shrug. 'I was foolish and failed to consider the possibility. I fear we have not been introduced, but you must accept my assurance that I am normally considered to be extremely reliable and sensible in such matters.'

'Viscount Bingfield.' He inclined his head. 'And I am most definitely received everywhere.'

'I will take your word for it.' Her voice dripped with ice cold.

'Miss Ravel. Miss Ravel. Where are you? I will find you. You can't hide for ever. And then you will see what happens to women who try to cross me!'

Richard's jaw clenched. There was no mistaking the grating voice of Putney! The man was a bounder and a cad of the first order. He'd detested the man ever since that first term at Eton where Putney had put his hand up the maid's skirt and lied about it, causing the poor girl to be dismissed. Richard had sneaked out to see if she was all right and then the newspaper stories started. Then there was Oxford and the tragedy of Mary. Again he could not prove Putney had a hand in it, but he had encountered Putney in the street the day before he'd been called in front of the Master. Even now he could remember the furtive smile Putney gave.

'Are you trying to hide from Sir Vincent Putney, Miss Ravel?'

She gave a quick nod of her head. 'I wish to return to the ball and avoid a scandal. I've done nothing wrong. That is all, Lord Bingfield. Once back under the chandeliers, all this will cease to be anything but a bad dream.'

'In that state? Scandal will reverberate throughout the land. Your name will be on everyone's lips as they attempt to work out how this happened and believe the worst.'

She glanced down and fluffed out her skirt. 'A few repairs need to be made. I slipped in the dark. Twice. I barely know the man. I was helping a friend out and matters failed to go as planned.'

'Indeed.'

'I was helping a friend elope.' She clasped her hands together. 'My friend was engaged to Sir Vincent, but desired to end the relationship against her father's wishes. She loved an American. I merely facilitated the elopement. It went like clockwork except...' She grabbed his arm. 'Quick, Sir Vincent is coming. I need to get away from him.'

Richard reacted instinctively. He swung her back into the shadows, up against the hedge and stood between Miss Ravel and the light.

'Follow my lead and keep silent,' he murmured against her lavender-scented hair. 'We don't have time.'

'Your lead?' she asked, attempting to peer

around him. Her skirts brushed his leg. 'Should I trust you?'

'Do you have a choice?' He took a glimpse down at Miss Ravel, seeing her clearly for the first time.

Her lips hovered tantalisingly few inches beneath his. Her worried eyes looked up into his, trusting him to get this right and protect her. Truly Cinderella after the ball, missing a slipper and in need of a prince.

Richard resisted the urge to crush her to him. Another time and another place he would have given in to temptation, but this closeness was far from a prelude to seduction, it was instead a means to prevent Miss Ravel's ruin.

'With any luck Putney will walk on without even noticing anything beyond a man and a woman in the shadows. He will expect to find you alone. Foolproof.'

Footsteps resounded behind them. Every nerve went on alert. Silently he prayed this action would be enough.

Miss Ravel stiffened and shrank back further against the hedge. The heavy footsteps went on past. The nervous energy drained out of Richard's shoulders. They had done it! Miss Ravel would be safe. All that was needed was for him to step back.

His feet refused to move. Instead he lifted his hand and traced the outline of her jaw. Her skin quivered underneath the tips of his fingers and her lips parted, inviting him.

'Dear Richard, imagine! You should be in the ballroom, rather than in the garden,' a heart-sinkingly familiar woman's voice said. 'I shall have to tell your father that we met. He was asking after you at lunch last week. I had understood you were in London. Does he know you journeyed to Newcastle?'

Richard knew that things had suddenly become much worse. The most fearsome of his aunts had arrived.

He gave Miss Ravel an apologetic look and swung around.

'Aunt Parthenope, what an unexpected pleasure.' Richard made a slight bow. 'I would have called on you earlier today if I'd known you, too, were in Newcastle. I would have thought you'd be in London for the start of the Season.'

'The Season does not properly begin until after Queen Charlotte's ball. Plenty of time remains to sort out the hanger-ons and no hopers from the cream of this year's débutantes.' His aunt gave a loud sniff. 'You should have known that I always come to Newcastle at this time of year. I have done for years—to visit your grandmother's grave on the anniversary of her death. In any case, the train makes travel so convenient these days. It takes less than a day. Imagine— when I was a girl, it took more than a week by post carriage.'

'We truly do live in an age of miracles, Aunt,' Richard murmured, wondering if his mother was aware of his aunt's habit and why she hadn't warned him of the possibility.

'Why are you out in the garden, Richard?'

'Crowded ballrooms can cause claustrophobia. I wanted a breath of fresh air.' He moved towards his aunt and started to lead her away from where Miss Ravel stood, hidden in the shadows, touching his fingers to his lips before he turned away. Immediately Miss Ravel shrank back against the hedge.

'You know how it is, Aunt,' he said in an expansive tone. 'One minute, one is waltzing and the next, one needs to be away from the crowd. You have often remarked on how crowded these balls are, not like the days when you were a young girl.'

Sophie hardly dared to breathe. She could see what Lord Bingfield was about to do—lead his aunt and her party away and leave her to make her own way back to the house. It was far too

late for regrets. She had to hope that Lord Bingfield's scheme would work.

'And this is why you were out in the garden,
Nephew? A sudden and inexplicable need for
fresh air? Do not seek to flannel me. Your father did explain about his ultimatum to you at
luncheon. While I might not agree with it on
principle, I should remind you, he is a man of
his word.'

Sophie pursed her lips and wondered what
ultimatum Lord Bingfield's father had issued.
One of two things—women or gambling debts.
Possibly both. Why would the man she begged
for help have to turn out to be a dishonourable
rake, rather than the honourable person she'd
hoped? Her luck was truly out tonight.

'My father has no bearing on this matter,
Aunt.' Lord Bingfield waved an impatient hand.
'I know what he said and he must do as he sees
fit. I make my own way in the world.'

'You were always a reckless youth, Richard.'

'We should return to the ballroom, Aunt,'
Lord Bingfield said, starting forwards and
grasping his aunt's elbow so that she was turned
away from Sophie. 'I find I am quite refreshed
after a short turn. You must tell me all the news.
How does my father fare? Does his latest pig
show promise?'

Sophie flattened her back against the hedge. The prickles dug into her bodice. Silently she bid them to go.

'And your charming companion? Or do you wish to continue blathering fustian nonsense, thinking I would overlook her?' Lord Bingfield's aunt gave her nephew a rap on the sleeve with her fan. 'You do not fool me one little bit, Richard. I know how this game is played.'

'Charming companion?'

'You do know her name, I hope, Nephew. You were standing far too close to her to be complete strangers. However, with you, nothing surprises me.'

Sophie's heart sank as Lord Bingfield's aunt confirmed her growing fear. Lord Bingfield was not *safe in carriages* or indeed anywhere.

'Aunt, you wrong me dreadfully,' Lord Bingfield protested. 'Name one instance where I have behaved dishonourably.'

'I do declare it's Miss Ravel.' Sir Vincent loomed out of the darkness. In the gloom, Sophie could make out his smug grin. Her misery was complete. He intended to cause mischief, serious mischief, and she had inadvertently given him the opportunity, wrapped and tied up with a bow like a parcel. 'I am surprised that a woman such as yourself is out here in the night air, Miss

Ravel, with a man such as the notorious Lord Bingfield. What will your guardian say?'

'My stepmother is aware of where I am and who I am with.' Sophie kept her chin up. It was the truth. Her stepmother knew Sophie was at the ball, not her precise location and she had approved of the company. Her stepmother trusted her. She refused to allow Sir Vincent to imply that something untoward had happened. But it was poor luck that Lord Bingfield seemed to have a less-than-illustrious reputation himself.

'You're Miss Ravel? Sophie Ravel? The heiress who came out over four years ago?' Lord Bingfield's aunt squawked. 'It would appear, Richard, that you have taken your father's words to heart after all. Impressive.'

'Everything, I assure you, is quite appropriate, Aunt,' Lord Bingfield said. 'It would be wrong of me to allow a lady such as Miss Ravel to wander about the garden on her own. Who knows the sort of ruffian she might encounter?'

He gave Sir Vincent a hard look. Sophie's heart did a little flip. Unsuitable or not, Lord Bingfield shared her opinion of Sir Vincent. He was the only person standing between her and utter ruin.

'It was your chivalry coming to the fore, Nephew,' Lord Bingfield's aunt pronounced.

'All is now clear. I had feared you had decided to take after *your* mother's side of the family.'

A muscle jumped in Lord Bingfield's cheek and his hand clenched in a fist.

'I believe Miss Ravel wishes to return to the ball, now that this little misunderstanding has been cleared up,' he said in glacial tones.

'Has it?' Sir Vincent asked in a weasel-like tone. 'You were in a close embrace! Did you see it, Lady Parthenope? It was quite clear from where I stood. And I know what a stickler you are for propriety and how everyone at Almack's looks to your judgement.'

'You were standing rather close to my nephew, Miss Ravel,' Lord Bingfield's aunt pronounced. 'Young ladies need to be wary of their reputations at all times.'

'Your attire is a little more dishevelled than a simple turn about the garden would suggest. How did you manage to tear your dress?' Sir Vincent continued with a smirk.

Sophie winced. Lord Bingfield's aunt would be someone of importance. Seeds of doubt and suspicions, that was what Sir Vincent intended. Little by little until she had no reputation left.

Her stomach churned. There was no way she could explain the current state of her attire away.

She gave Lord Bingfield a pleading look as she searched her brain for a good excuse.

'I do take offence at having Miss Ravel's attire discussed in such intimate terms, Putney,' Lord Bingfield said, stepping between her and Sir Vincent. His stance looked more like a pugilist preparing to enter the ring than a man at a ball.

Sophie released a breath. Despite her earlier fear, Lord Bingfield had kept his promise. He was protecting her.

'Why?' Sir Vincent stuck out his chest. 'I merely state what everyone will be thinking when they spot Miss Ravel.'

Lord Bingfield cleared his throat. 'Miss Ravel is doing me the honour of considering my proposal and, until she has time, discretion is the best option. You did not see anything untoward and I would refrain from mentioning something you might live to regret.'

Chapter Two

L ord Bingfield's words circled through her brain. A proposal! What sort of proposal did Lord Bingfield have in mind? Sophie's reticule slipped from her grasp and she made a last-second lunge to rescue it before it tumbled to the ground. At the same instant, Lord Bingfield reached down and caught it. Their fingers touched and a faint tremor went through her. He gave a slight nod and she remembered his earlier words—*whatever happens, follow my lead.*

She stood up and clutched the reticule to her chest. She had little choice. It was either go along with Lord Bingfield's scheme or face certain ruin at Sir Vincent's hands. She had to go against her hard-learnt habit and trust an acknowledged rake. All she had to do was ensure she refrained from making any rash promises to him. Easy if she maintained her poise and dignity.

'A proposal? Do tell, Nephew.' His formidable aunt rapped her fan against her hand. 'I am all ears.'

'It was the sort of proposal that I have longed to hear ever since I first encountered your nephew,' Sophie said in a loud voice. 'You do not know how happy it made me to hear his words. Perhaps it was a little rushed, but the location was so romantic. My heart simply soared.'

She glanced over at Lord Bingfield and saw that his eyes were dancing. They were as one on this plan. Her heart thudded.

'Are you going to give him your answer?'

'I think such a proposal merits careful consideration. Often a young woman has been led into folly by making too hasty a judgement one way or the other,' Sophie retorted. A sense of thrilling excitement swept through her. For the first time in a long time, she felt as though she was living rather than merely existing, trying to be good and attempting to maintain a poised cold dignity in all her dealings with men. The realisation shocked her.

'I am grateful that you are giving my proposal any consideration in light of my past,' Lord Bingfield said.

Sophie tilted her chin upwards. 'I have learnt that one's past is never a guarantee of one's future.'

'You appear to be a highly sensible young lady, Miss Ravel, despite being out in the garden alone with my nephew,' Lady Parthenope pronounced. 'A word to the wise—even if you are overcome with heat, it is always best to keep your chaperon in sight. To do otherwise is to invoke comment. However, on this happy occasion I must forgive the tiniest lapse of judgement.'

Relief swept through Sophie. Lady Parthenope was practically purring her approval. Her reputation might survive.

'I know your nephew has honourable intentions, your ladyship,' Sophie said firmly, fixing Lord Bingfield with her eye.

'I was unaware you were acquainted with my nephew. That is all, Miss Ravel. I must do more to further our acquaintance,' Lady Parthenope said.

'Come, come, Aunt.' Lord Bingfield put his hand on his aunt's sleeve. 'Do I need to send you a note every time I meet a suitable unmarried lady? Every time I wish to make a proposal of a sensitive nature to said lady? If that is to be the way of the world, I want no part of it.'

'It would be helpful, Richard.' The elderly woman gave a sniff. 'Your father was very tedious at our luncheon.'

'Nor was I aware that you shared a close friendship with Lord Bingfield, Miss Ravel,' Sir Vincent said. 'The things one learns at balls. It puts our earlier conversation in a very different light. I do hope you remember every word of our previous encounter.'

A faint prickle of alarm ran down Sophie's back, but she forced her lungs to fill with air. Sir Vincent's threat was hollow. She was safe. Lady Parthenope had pronounced judgement. Despite the slight hiccup of Lord Bingfield being notorious, he had behaved impeccably.

'Where did you think I was going to, Sir Vincent, after I delivered Miss Johnson's note? I do hate being late.' She made a curtsy which bordered on the discourteous. 'I did say that I had a prior engagement. I failed to mention Lord Bingfield before because, quite frankly, it is none of your business.'

Sir Vincent's mouth opened and closed several times.

Lady Parthenope suddenly developed a cough and Sophie struggled not to laugh after she caught Lord Bingfield's eye. Her heart suddenly seemed much lighter. Tonight's events were not going to be a catastrophe after all.

After tonight, she would not push her luck. She had to remember that adventures only became exciting in memory. During an adventure, one was often out of sorts and uncomfortable. Adventure should happen to other people, not to her if she wished to keep her reputation. Ice-cold calm and dignity while she waited to meet the man whom she could love. Friends first, but only after he'd proved himself worthy—it was the only way to have a great and lasting romance. She had seen the formula work with Robert and Henrietta and now Cynthia.

'Sir Vincent may escort me in,' Lady Parthenope said after she recovered from her coughing fit. 'His mother and I were at school together. And, dear Miss Ravel, you may take your time as long as you come to the right decision quickly. It is blindingly obvious to me that nothing untoward happened here. You must not presume the worst, Sir Vincent. There again, your mother possessed that unfortunate habit. It obviously runs in the family.'

Lady Parthenope swept towards the house with a bleating Sir Vincent on her arm and the rest of her party trailing in her wake. Sophie waited until the noise had abated, feeling the cool night air on her face. She had survived.

Lord Bingfield held out his arm. 'Shall we go, Miss Ravel? I take it you have had time to consider my proposal. My nerves shall be a-quiver until I hear your answer.'

'I doubt your nerves ever quiver, Lord Bingfield.'

'You wrong me.' He put his hand to his forehead. 'I may be the type to weep at dead daffodils.'

'Are you?'

He stood up straighter. 'Thankfully, no. I can't remember the last time I wept at anything. Shall we go in before we invoke more comment?'

Sophie placed her hand on his arm. Her body became instantly aware of him and his nearness. His proximity to her was doing strange things to her insides and her sensibilities. Had she learnt nothing in the past four years? Rakes oozed charm and women forgot propriety when they were near them. The best defence was to be calmly aloof.

A tiny prickle coursed down her spine. Even when she had considered an elopement in her youth, she had not felt as though she wanted Sebastian Cawburn to kiss her, not in the desperate deep-down way that she wanted Lord Bingfield to kiss her when they had stood so close earlier.

'Thank you for rescuing me,' she said, trying for the poised voice she'd perfected after the Sebastian débâcle. Failed miserably as it came out too breathless for her liking. 'Your idea of an unnamed proposal was particularly inspired. I hope… It doesn't matter what I thought. It is finished now and my reputation is safe. From what Sir Vincent said earlier, I believe Cynthia will be safely married soon to the man she has chosen. It is important to choose a congenial life's partner rather than have one chosen for you.'

'I agree entirely,' he said, helping her around a muddy puddle. 'A close call, but I feel it was easily accomplished in the end. There should be no repercussions. Who would dare gainsay Lady Parthenope's pronouncement of innocence?'

'Will your aunt be cross when she discovers we have no intention of marrying each other?' Sophie asked in an undertone. Her body was immediately aware of the way his gloved hand curled about hers. He frowned and let go of her hand.

'She will get over it. Being a disappointment to my aunt appeals. Someone has to be and my cousins have thus far all proved to be sterling examples of moral rectitude and sobriety.'

Sophie forced a smile, but her heart gave a little pang. Lord Bingfield was by far the most interesting man she had met in years and the most unsuitable. A poised demeanour had to be her armour. Never again would she return to that frightened girl, cowering behind a door. 'You were truly a shining knight.'

'I've no love for Putney and a soft spot for beautiful ladies in distress. It was no trouble. Think no more about it.'

They reached the doorway to the house and in the sudden light, she saw Lord Bingfield clearly for the first time. His dark-brown hair curled slightly at his temples, framing his burnished gold eyes. His mouth was a bit large, but hinted at passion. It was the sort of face to make a woman go weak at the knees and forget her solemn vows.

Sophie fought against an inclination to prolong the encounter. There was no future for her and Lord Bingfield. She had given up on notorious men years ago. The adventure had finished and she and her reputation were safe.

She stopped beside the ladies' withdrawing room. 'The adventure has ended.'

'Should you ever require a knight again, fair lady, let me know.' He raised her hand to his lips.

The light touch sent a throb of warmth coursing through her. It would be easy to believe in romance, rather than chemistry. Against her better judgement, she wanted to believe he could be a shining knight and protect her from harm, rather than destroy her utterly.

'You see, I did accept your proposal of protection from Sir Vincent. It was a truly honourable proposal.'

'My pleasure and you understood the proposal.' He gave a half-smile and inclined his head. 'You do know I have no intention of marrying despite what my aunt might believe or my father might dictate.'

'And you do know I have no intention of behaving badly,' Sophie said, clutching her reticule close to her chest. Her earlier instincts had been correct. Lord Bingfield was the sort of man who was *not safe in carriages*. He had saved her reputation, but she knew how that particular game was played. Some day she hoped she'd meet someone who would make her heart soar and fulfilled all the criteria she had agreed with Henri on that fateful day. A friend before a lover. Someone of honour and whom she could love with the right pedigree for her stepmother. Other people had found love—why shouldn't she?

A small dimple showed in the corner of his mouth. 'Have I asked you to?'

'No, but I suspect you entertain hopes. It falls to me to quash them.' She pinned him with her best I-am-a-formidable-person look. 'It is always best to be perfectly clear about such things.'

He threw back his head and laughed a deep rich laugh, utterly real and inviting rather than the arched one he'd used as he confronted Sir Vincent earlier. It warmed her all the way to her toes. Sophie started, surprised that the sound could affect her in that way. 'The day I lose hope is the day I die.'

She concentrated on the flickering light of the chandelier in the entrance hallway, rather than the dimple in the corner of his mouth. She had to keep her wits about her and not indulge in some flight of romantic fantasy. He had given her an explicit warning about his intention to avoid marriage.

Naïve women chose to ignore such words of warning, believing that they were special or unique. It was what a rake traded on. Soon without meaning to, the woman had crossed all manner of bridges and boundaries. That was when a rake struck, showing his true colours. Sophie had learnt this lesson the hard way. A rake meant what he said all the times, and most definitely when it was said in a light-hearted or jesting fashion. And when things didn't go as they wished…

'We are at an impasse,' she said, inclining her head. 'For my determination is every bit as strong as your hope.'

'Shall we risk a polka? Surely you can spare a dance for me?' He held out his hands and his smile became even more beguiling. 'I did save your reputation and I never ask a second time.'

Sophie swiftly shook her head, banishing the image of them swirling to the music together. It would be very easy to give in to the temptation and dance in his arms. And from there? Each little step would lead her further down a path she'd sworn never to go on again.

'Here we part. I shall bid you goodbye. We part as friends.' She held out her hand and allowed a frosty smile past her lips.

He ignored her hand. 'Until we meet again, Miss Ravel.'

He paused and his gaze travelled slowly down her, making Sophie aware of the way her hair tumbled about her shoulders and her torn dress. Perhaps not quite the ice-maiden look she had hoped to achieve. He gave a long slow smile. 'As we are no longer strangers.'

'How could you do it, Richard? You are insupportable. I declare you get that from your father!'

Richard shaded his eyes with his hand. His head throbbed slightly and he reluctantly bid the dream of Sophie Ravel, naked in his arms, goodbye.

After he'd left last night's ball, he'd spent time at the Northern Counties Club, playing cards and trying not to think about Miss Ravel and ways to meet her rather than returning to the house he rented for his mother and half-sister.

As his aunt had pointed out yesterday and the gossip in club confirmed, Sophie Ravel was a highly eligible heiress, rather than a young widow in need of money or the neglected wife of an aged and jaded aristocrat in search of an afternoon's amusement. But he also knew the gossip was wrong on one important point. Miss Ravel had the reputation of a fearsome ice maiden—beautiful to look at, but brimming with virtue and utterly lacking in passion. The woman he'd nearly kissed last night had simmered with passion under her frosty exterior.

Only if he wanted to stick his head in the

parson's noose should he be having anything to do with her. Several of his dalliances had reached the scandal sheets in recent years—more for the women's indiscretions after they parted than his actions, but it was enough to make him wary. He refused to be the instrument of any woman's ruin.

The certain knowledge of his past notoriety had caused him to drink more than was good for him last night. How his father would laugh. He'd always predicted that his son would one day regret being in the gossip columnists' sights and the day of reckoning had arrived.

He winced. He might not have deserved the scandal sheet's attention when he was at Eton, but he'd certainly deserved it a few years ago when he'd attempted to forget his part in Mary's fall from grace, her forced marriage to a man she loathed and her untimely death. Then, after that, he'd run through a number of bored wives and widows, ending each affair on his terms and walking away without a backward glance. And he did make it a point of honour never to ask a woman twice for something.

It was only a chance encounter with his half-sister eighteen months ago which had led him from the path of self-destruction.

'Richard, are you going to speak to me? I

know you are awake.' A tall woman stood sil-
houetted in the doorway. His man lurked behind her.

Richard shook his head. Myers had always
been a soft touch where women were concerned.
He focused on his mother instead of his valet.
The sooner this contretemps in a teacup was
sorted, the sooner he would get back to his
dream.

'Mother, what are you doing waking me up so
early?' Richard sat up and stretched. He glanced
at the small ormolu clock on the bedside table.
'I thought you would find this time of day ex-
ceedingly early for civilised people.'

He waited for her to make her excuses and
withdraw.

'I left you to sleep for as long as I dared,'
his mother said, straightening her cap. 'Luckily
your sister remains in ignorance of last night's
events. I only pray we can keep it that way. Her
head cold last night turned out to be a blessing
in disguise after all. I dread to think what would
have happened if Hannah had been at the ball.'

Richard's heart sank. His mother had obviously heard the wrong sort of gossip. Silently he
bid goodbye to a morning's rest. He would have
to sort out whichever mess.

'What promise have I broken?' Richard retained a leash on his temper. His mother enjoyed her dramatics. 'At least do me the courtesy of hearing the full accusation.'

'You obviously haven't seen the morning papers. It is in all of the local ones. It is sure to be in the London ones by nightfall. Your father will know you are here! He is far from stupid and he will know your reason for coming to Newcastle.'

'I'm a grown man, Mother. My father doesn't dictate or control my movements. There are numerous reasons why I might have travelled to Newcastle, none of which involved yourself or Hannah.'

'He will ruin any chance of Hannah's happiness out of sheer spite. You know what he is like when he is in one of his rages. How could you involve yourself in scandal at this juncture?'

Richard pressed his palms against his eyes. He did know what his father was capable of and how, each time, the fits of anger appeared to last longer. Most of all he feared the gentle father he loved would remain a raging mad man, incapable of coherent thought. The doctors told him that there was nothing they could do except lock him up, and Richard was not prepared for that to happen.

'Mother, as I went to bed in the not-so-early hours of the morning, I have not seen the papers.

Whatever you are seeking to blame me for, I am innocent.' He held out his hand. 'Pinch me. See, I am here in my bed, alone.'

'At least tell me that the woman in question is an heiress, this redoubtable woman of yours. Your father might understand your need to chase her up here if she was eligible. Your being single must be a worry. I know how relieved he was when I produced you as the heir. All your father has ever cared about was having the line continue and those blasted pigs of his.'

He pressed his lips together, considering the first part of his mother's statement. He could explain away Newcastle on chasing an heiress. His father would accept that, rather than going into some apoplectic rage over the fact that his son had regular contact with the one woman he hated more than life itself. His father's mental state and health were far too fragile to risk that. He loved both parents and refused to bow to his father's insistence that he choose a side. Once his father's health improved, he would explain properly. For now, a small amount of subterfuge had to be used. Two parts of his life kept separate.

'What do the papers have to do with it?' he asked.

'Myers, the *Newcastle Courant* for your master, if you please.'

Richard nodded to his valet, who gave a bow.

His manservant brought the *Newcastle Courant* as well as one of the more popular scandal sheets, freshly ironed. He turned to the gossip page of the scandal sheet and pointed. Richard gave him a curious look.

'It has the best wording, my lord. The *Courant* used a bit more veiled language. I thought it best to take the precaution of examining all the papers. I like to be prepared for all mention of my gentlemen.'

Richard scanned the paper and winced. *Has the scandal-prone Lord B—been captured at last by the redoubtable Miss R—? Turtledoves were cooing last night. A wedding is devotedly hoped for but, given Lord B—'s form, not expected.*

Scandal-prone indeed! The last crim. con. trial had not been his fault at all. His name should never have been mentioned. The Duke of Blanchland admitted that later. He'd been the innocent party, attempting to assist a woman, driven to distraction by her errant husband. The Duchess had never been his mistress. He had already bedded her sister. He had his code.

He folded the offending paper in half and glared at his mother.

'Preposterous nonsense, Mother. You shouldn't

believe things that you read in the papers. Surely you learnt that long ago!'

His mother slapped her gloves together. 'I won't have it, Richard. Not when Hannah is about to be married. They will drag up the whole contretemps between your father and myself… and the issue of Hannah's parentage. And if your father comes up here, there is no telling what he'd do. He swore revenge. I won't have my innocent child suffer!'

'And this has nothing to do with Hannah. In any case, your late husband adopted his daughter. It was all sorted in the end. My father did behave well on that.'

'He never paid back my dowry and he ensured I had to lead a life of economies.'

'It was your father who negotiated the settlement. The money was spent in part on refurbishments that you ordered.'

'Do you know this redoubtable Miss R?' His mother slapped her hand down on the paper. 'For the life of me I can't think of any acquaintances with the last name of R who would warrant the sobriquet of "redoubtable". There is Petronella Roberts, but she has spots, and Sarah Richards fills out her ball dress in all the wrong places.'

'Sophie Ravel—yes, I know her. I would have used the word ravishing rather than redoubtable.'

Richard put his hands behind his head and con-jured up Miss Ravel's delicate features. Her gen-erous mouth had held the promise of passion, if a man could find a way to unlock it. 'Even Aunt Parthenope declared there was nothing scandal-ous in our behaviour.'

His mother went white. 'Parthenope was there?'

'My aunt attended the ball last night. Appar-ently my grandmother is buried in Jesmond. She visits the grave every year.' He glared at his mother. 'You never said.'

'She is sure to write to your father, giving a report. Even if he misses the papers, he will know you have been in Newcastle. Parthenope is like that—full of spite disguised as doing good. When she is at her most charming, she is also at her most deadly.'

'You overreact, Mother.'

'Richard, this is important. It is your sister's future. Hannah has an excellent chance to have a glittering marriage. Could you use this Miss Ravel as an excuse to stay, rather than dashing off to London this afternoon?'

Richard tapped his finger against the scan-dal sheet, the beginnings of an idea forming. Pursuing Miss Ravel without interference from either parent and seeing if there was passion underneath the ice she presented to the world was tempting, but…

Richard folded the paper in half again. 'What puzzles me is how quickly the papers have acquired the story.'

'Someone is always willing to sell a good story.' His mother gave an exaggerated sigh. 'Poor girl. It is the women I feel sorry for. The men can survive, but a woman, well, she always has the whiff of a scandal hanging about her skirts.'

'I will sort it out before it becomes an inferno, Mother.'

'I trust you to do the right thing, Richard.'

'I am surprised you even need to say that, Mother. I know my duty. The necessity of doing it has been beaten into me since childhood.'

'Did you have a pleasant time at the ball, Sophie? You said very little about it last night. You were back far earlier than I expected.'

Sophie's hand froze in the act of buttering her toast. It made no sense for her stepmother to be asking further questions about last night. She'd given an account when she came, an account in which Lord Bingfield did not feature as there was no point in alarming her. Her stepmother seemed well satisfied then, but now she regarded

Sophie with razor-sharp eyes. Her stepmother waved a newspaper in Sophie's direction. 'I do read the papers. Every item.'

'The papers? Why should they say anything about me?' Sophie asked, genuinely perplexed. Lady Parthenope had declared that the little incident was entirely innocent. She'd left it to Lord Bingfield to explain to his aunt that they would...alas...not be marrying.

'It is what I want to know.' Tears shimmered in her stepmother's eyes. 'I trusted you, Sophie, last evening and allowed you to go to the ball without a chaperon. When you were younger, you used to be involved in harum-scarum affairs and I despaired. After Corbridge, you changed. Perhaps you became a bit too stand-offish, but I retained hopes of you fulfilling your father's dying wish and marrying into society.'

Sophie attempted to ignore the nasty prickle at the back of her neck. 'Do what? What have I done? I behaved perfectly properly all evening. You knew about Cynthia's elopement and approved.' Sophie carefully kept her mind away from how she'd nearly kissed Lord Bingfield in the dark. Wanting to kiss him and actually kissing him were two separate things. She had behaved properly and they would never encounter each other again. 'Show me the papers. I need to know what I have been accused of.'

Her stepmother held out one of the worst scandal sheets. Sophie's eyes widened. 'The redoubtable Miss R? Do I look redoubtable to you? I am the least formidable person I know. Really, Stepmother, I'm surprised you read such things! All they print are lies and tittle-tattle.'

'How else can I find out what is going on in Newcastle, let alone in the rest of the country?' Her stepmother dabbed her eyes. 'Who is this Lord B who has captured your attention? Were you too ashamed of me to introduce us? I know I used to be in service, but that was long ago before your father fell in love with me.'

'Ashamed of you?' Sophie stared at her stepmother in astonishment. 'I love you and whomever I marry had best love you as well or he will not be the man for me. Now that we have cleared that up, I want to know about your plans for your new bonnet.'

'Sophie, stop confusing the issue with bonnets. The item in the papers. I shall not be deterred.'

'You know it is a pack of lies, don't you?' She put her hand over her stepmother's. 'As if I would consider marrying without consulting you first. Honestly, Stepmother, sometimes you read too many penny-dreadfuls. When have I ever kept any of my friends from you? And I would never marry anyone who was not a friend first. I learnt a painful lesson three years ago.'

'But there is a kernel of truth.' Her stepmother's cap trembled. 'I know how to read your face, Sophie. You can never hide things from me, not things which truly matter. Who is this Lord B? Would Robert and Henri approve?'

'Lord Bingfield,' Sophie supplied. Her stepmother conveniently forgot the times when Sophie had kept things from her, including the precise truth about Sebastian. 'He assisted me after Cynthia's elopement. I doubt the entire proceedings would have gone as smoothly if not for his assistance. I was introduced to his aunt, Lady Parthenope, who is great friends with three of the Lady Patronesses at Almack's. However, that is as far as it went. Someone has an overblown imagination and is making mischief.'

Sophie waited for her stepmother to ask about Lady Parthenope's dress or what she had said.

'Almack's is far from the power it used to be and I won't be distracted.' Her stepmother frowned and Sophie's heart sank. Her stepmother was worse than a dog with a bone about this snippet of gossip. 'Why didn't you tell me about Lord Bingfield immediately?'

'Because you would have jumped to the wrong conclusion like you are doing now, and I was tired.' Sophie crumpled the toast between her fingers. The last thing she needed after her broken sleep was to be quizzed about Lord Bingfield. Every time she closed her eyes last night it seemed she remembered how his breath had fanned her cheek or how he had nearly kissed her. The encounter was nothing to him, but she couldn't forget it. About three o'clock, she had decided that she'd been foolish and arrogant to reject his offer of an innocent dance. She should have danced with him and been done with it. She never dreamt about any of the men she danced with. The knowledge did not make her any happier.

'You were thinking about me and my health.' The ribbons of her stepmother's cap swayed their indignation. 'Sophie! Do you think I was born yesterday?'

'Given how you are reacting now, is it any wonder? You are seeking a romance where there is none.' Sophie was unsure who she was trying to convince—her stepmother or that little place inside her which kept whispering about Lord Bingfield's fine eyes. 'Besides, I doubt Lord Bingfield's ultimate intentions towards me were honourable. He inhabits the scandal sheets, after all. Remember The Incident and why I had to hurry up to Corbridge? I've sworn off men like that.'

Her stepmother's eyes narrowed. 'You had better hope it is a proper proposal from Lord Bingfield. People have long memories, Sophie. Your name will now be tainted from the mere association with his. Did you think about that last night when you were so busy accepting his trifling assistance? You know what your father wanted for you—a marriage into the higher echelons of society—and you have jeopardised that.'

'You are talking fustian nonsense.' Sophie tapped her finger on the scandal sheet. 'How many papers?'

'I have sent the butler to check. I should think most of them. Lady Parthenope sent me a note. She has invited us to take tea with her.' Her stepmother's hand trembled with excitement as she reached for the letter. 'She wants to vet us. That's what this is. You know what they say about her door-keeping at Almack's. I shall need a new bonnet!'

Sophie bit her lip. 'You can always refuse.'

'One does not refuse Lady Parthenope, Sophie, and stay within the bounds of polite society.' Her stepmother folded her hands in her lap and gave a smug smile. 'I've been after an invitation for years. You will pass muster without a problem. My stepdaughter will become a member of the aristocracy, even if she will forget me.'

'Stop spinning fantasies and nothing is finalised.' Sophie slumped back against the chair. She would have to tell her stepmother the full unedifying story. It was the only option. 'But there are, and will be, no impending nuptials to Lord Bingfield. I'm quite decided on that point. It happened—'

'There is a gentleman to see you, Miss Ravel.' The footman came in, carrying a silver platter with a single card, interrupting Sophie's story.

With a trembling hand, Sophie picked it up. Richard Crawford, Viscount Bingfield.

She stood up and absurdly wished that she was dressed in something more up to the minute than her old blue gown. She ruthlessly quashed the notion. Lord Bingfield and last night's escapade needed to be consigned to the past. The papers this morning proved it. Scandal dogged his footsteps.

'I will see Lord Bingfield in the drawing room.'

'I shall come with you, my dear.' Her stepmother started to rise, but Sophie put a hand on her stepmother's shoulder.

'That is far from necessary, Stepmother. If I

need assistance, I will shout. I have access to a poker and am not afraid to use it.'

'Sophie!'

'The truth, Stepmother.' Sophie narrowed her eyes. 'Allow me to do this or I shall write to Lady Parthenope, explaining that I have rejected her nephew's suit and therefore neither of us will be able to take tea with her.'

Her stepmother covered her eyes. 'I shudder to think what Robert—or Henri, for that matter—would say, but very well, my dear, you may see him on your own. On pain of death, do not close that door and I will be in earshot. Your father wanted the best for you and I am determined you shall have it, even if I have to beg Lady Parthenope on bended knee for a voucher to Almack's.'

'My father would expect me to sort out this mess. Despite what you or Henri or Robert might think, I am perfectly capable of sorting this tempest in a teacup out. I am an adult and, according to the papers, redoubtable.' Sophie raised her chin. 'I will simply tell him no.'

Chapter Three

Richard stood in the middle of the Ravels' overly ornamented and chintz-hung drawing room, trying not to knock over any of the porcelain shepherds, china ladies or vases filled with wax flowers of every hue imaginable. The entire drawing room was a riot of pink tassels, lace doilies and small tables strewn with knick-knacks, all in the most fashionable but horrendous taste. His frock-coat had narrowly missed one china pig and a precariously balanced bowl of waxen fruit already as he paced, waiting for Miss Ravel to put in an appearance.

What sort of woman was the redoubtable Miss Ravel? The woman he rescued last night had not seemed in any way formidable, but badly in need of protection. The gossip from the club said that she was aloof, an ice maiden, but he kept remembering the way her eyes had flashed when she rejected his offer of a polka.

His head pounded worse than ever. All the way here, he kept going over in his mind the possible scenarios and becoming angrier. Who else could have linked their names and informed the papers? He also knew that he had to make Miss Ravel understand that he had never made a proposal of that sort.

He had expected more from Miss Ravel. He regarded a particularly nauseating shepherdess who was more strangling a lamb than cuddling it. He knew next to nothing about her except that her ball gown had fetching sophistication and she had been in trouble. Hardly the stuff to build a relationship on. It was far better to get his painful interview over and get back to leading his life.

The lady in question strode into the drawing room. The simplicity of her blue dress contrasted sharply with the overly fussiness of the room. Richard drew in his breath sharply. His dreams had not done her features justice. A certain forthrightness about her jaw warred with the frankly sensuous curve of her bottom lip. Her waist appeared no bigger than his handspan.

Her quick backward glance at the door to ensure it remained wide open, rather than shut, was telling. She appeared determined to observe proprieties, even if no one else was in the room with them.

'Lord Bingfield,' she said, dropping a perfunctory curtsy and her lips curving up into a smile, but she failed to hold out her hand to be kissed. Truly redoubtable this morning. 'An unexpected development.'

'You have seen the papers?' he asked, surprised. 'I could hardly avoid calling on you after such item was printed. It would mean neglecting my duty. I may be many things, Miss Ravel, but I have never been a cad.'

'We both made our positions quite clear last evening.'

'I understand the item in question may have made some of the later London editions. My father—'

'This would be the father who doesn't know you are in Newcastle?' She gave a superior smile. 'I can remember what your aunt said. I'm far from stupid, Lord Bingfield. However, if your being in Newcastle was going to cause problems with your parent, you should have been open and honest about it.'

'My reasons for being in Newcastle are private.'

She raised a delicate eyebrow. 'I will allow you to keep your reasons private. I merely mentioned this as plans have a way of going awry.'

'Have you seen the item?'

'My stepmother informed me of it.' She gave a small cough. 'Apparently your aunt has written to her, inviting her to tea. My stepmother is transported with excitement at the thought of taking tea with the great Lady Parthenope.'

'How charming.'

Her eyes flashed blue fire. 'I won't have my stepmother mocked, Lord Bingfield.'

He inclined his head. 'I was referring to my aunt, rather than your stepmother. I had not anticipated this development.'

'Your aunt began it.'

'Aunts are a law unto themselves, Miss Ravel, particularly my aunts. They can be wildly unpredictable. It is part of their charm.' Aunts were a law unto themselves, but he'd never expect his aunt to take it this far, making contact with Miss Ravel's relations before any nuptials were publically announced. There again, his aunt prided herself on her ability to ferret out people's most discreet indiscretion and remembering snippets of gossips. It was why she proved such an effective gatekeeper for Almack's. Currently slow torture would be too good for her, in Richard's opinion. He'd suggest it to one of his cousins. 'I hope your stepmother will not be too disappointed when you explain why she must not accept this invitation.'

'My stepmother has longed for such an invitation ever since she first married my late father. She wishes to mingle with the truly genteel.' Her neat white teeth worried her bottom lip, turning it the colour of ripe cherries. There was something innocent about her. Despite her age and reputation of being formidable, she seemed soft and gentle and in definite need of protection. 'It was one of the reasons I was sent away to school for a time.'

'My aunt is haughty rather than genteel. Her rudeness and sense of entitlement can be shocking at times.'

'No matter how I explain that it doesn't matter, my stepmother persists.' Miss Ravel shrugged a shoulder. 'My stepmother must do as she pleases, but I have disabused her of any notion that we are considering an alliance. I leave it to you to inform your aunt.'

'Did you have anything to do with the item in papers? Are you responsible for it?'

'The appearance of the item is a mystery and most vexing.' Her eyes flared. 'Why on earth would I want to endanger my reputation by linking my name with yours? I am well aware of what happens to women who become entangled with men like you.'

'A simple yes or no to the original question will suffice.' Richard fought to control his temper. Miss Ravel made it sound as though he was some sort of affliction to be avoided at all costs. He had never knowingly ruined a woman. 'We shall go at it another way. Do you know your enemy, Miss Ravel?'

Her blue eyes met his. 'Then, no, if you must know, I did not contact the papers. And until today, I didn't consider that I had an enemy. Sir Vincent must be more persistent than I thought. He has ignored your aunt's pronouncement of total innocence. Why would he do such a thing, except that he knows the merest hint of your name will soil my reputation?'

The tension rushed out of Richard's shoulders. Her assessment was the same as his. 'Thank you. I believe you. Forgive me for doubting you, but I had to know.'

The fire went out of her eyes. 'You are apologising.'

'Sir Vincent and I have previous history. He is a formidable enemy.'

'Indeed.' She passed a hand over her eyes and sank down on to the pink-damask sofa. 'I have made an enemy who intends to use underhanded means to win.'

'He has succeeded before. I am determined to stop him. This time.' Without bidding, the image of Mary's face floated in front of his eyes. He would have done the decent thing and married Mary before he was sent down from Oxford, despite the pain it would have caused his father. If he'd done that, she'd never have been forced into that marriage, would have never run away and met her death in that canal accident. He forced his mind away. He had to concentrate on the now and saving Miss Ravel. He knew what she was up against. Miss Ravel was an innocent.

'Putney means to ruin you, Miss Ravel. I've seen him do it to other women years ago and this time I will stop him.'

'Ruin me? How?' she said with a hiccupping laugh. 'We have witnesses that you made an honourable proposal. Sir Vincent can't harm me.'

'There are several scandal-mongers lurking outside your house.' He gave an apologetic smile. 'When you have been notorious, you learn to know their type. I sent them on their way.'

'They are watching the house? Still?'

'It is entirely possible,' Richard admitted.

Miss Ravel walked over to the drawing-room window and closed the shutters with a bang.

'You should have told me about them before you started accusing me of informing the papers. My stepmother will be beside herself. My former guardian will have apoplexy. I would never have allowed you in if I'd known.'

'I went to my club after I left the ball. I hadn't seen the papers or I would have been here earlier...'

'But they will know you were here.' She put her hands to her head. Her face had gone pale. 'Don't you see? The scandal will be all the greater. The scandalous Lord B has called on the redoubtable Miss R...or possibly the not-so-fearsome Miss R...but wilful and headstrong.'

She clasped her hands together as if she was trying to keep them from trembling. Richard fought against the inclination to take her in his arms and hold her until the trembling stopped. She was right. His coming here had made matters worse, but he could not have just left her to face the coming storm alone. It was not in his nature.

'It had to be done. Your post could be watched. The gutter press is called that for a reason.'

'I shall have to quit society.' Miss Ravel began

to pace the room. 'My stepmother will be displeased, but it will have to be done. She still harbours hopes of a glittering marriage for me. I'll leave for Corbridge in the morning.'

'The scandal hounds will follow you. Putney will ensure it. Running will only encourage them.'

She put a hand out to steady herself. 'This is positively the last time I assist in anyone's elopement. The consequences are far too grave.'

'Listen to me, Miss Ravel, before you panic utterly.'

'I never panic.' she shouted. 'This is my life you have ruined. All you have to do is leave this room. No one has any expectations of you.'

He raised an eyebrow and her cheeks infused with colour. He quickly calculated the odds and knew the risk was worth taking. He would have done everything possible and he could leave her with a clear conscience. He would also have fulfilled the vow that he made at Mary's graveside. Putney would never use him to ruin another woman. 'I have expectations of my behaviour. It is my expectations which are important here, not someone else's.'

'What do you suggest?' she whispered, clasping her hands together so tightly the knuckles shone white.

'It is nothing that either of us wanted, but I can see no other practical solution, one which allows us both some measure of honour.' He went down on one knee. 'Will you marry me, Sophie Ravel?'

Sophie stared at Lord Bingfield in astonishment. He had gone down on one knee with one hand clasped to his breast and was looking up at her with an intent expression.

Her mouth went dry. It was a proper proposal. He was truly proposing. Lord Bingfield, despite his scandalous reputation and his vowed intent never to marry, was doing the decent thing and properly proposing marriage. Her stepmother's drawing room filled with its waxen fruit, china dogs and vases full of wax flowers had a distinct air of unreality.

'You are silent for once, Miss Ravel. Have you been struck dumb?'

Her shoulders relaxed slightly. She refused to believe in fairy tales or instant love. He was doing this for his own purposes and not to save her.

She had learnt her lesson the hard way years ago. Some day she would find a man whom she could love and whom she wanted to share the remainder of her life with, but until then she kept her head. Bingfield expected her to refuse. Of course he did. Then he could say that he'd done the decent thing, but alas, the lady had been unwilling. She gave a small smile. She understood the game now. She fought against the temptation to whisper 'yes', simply because he must expect a 'no'.

'Am I supposed to give this serious consideration?' she asked, tilting her head to one side and allowing her lashes to sweep down. 'Or am I supposed to refuse outright, send you on your way with a clear conscience that you have behaved with propriety? It might solve your problem with your code of honour, but it will not solve mine.'

His eyes hardened to stones. 'That is not for me to say. I merely asked the question in the proper manner. It is for you to answer when you have considered it. Simply know I will not ask the question twice. Being coy will get you nowhere.'

'You do not know me well enough to feel any finer feelings.'

'I never pretended any finer feelings, Miss Ravel. I asked you to marry me. You would hardly want me to be dishonest. The proposal suits my purposes for the moment. I will abide by your answer.'

The words served to puncture her entirely.

Sophie frowned at the unexpected disappointment. It shouldn't matter what Lord Bingfield thought of her, but it did. A tiny piece of her had hoped that somehow she'd been wrong and he'd fallen instantly in love with her. She had thought that the romantic part of her had died in that inn on the road to Scotland along with the rest of her girlish dreams, but apparently it hadn't.

'Is this some sort of a joke, Lord Bingfield?'

He slowly rose to his full height. Sophie was aware of the power in his shoulders and the way they narrowed down to his slim hips. Her body remembered how close they had stood last night. Her cheeks grew hot. He might not have any finer feelings for her, but she knew she wanted him to kiss her and that was not going to happen.

'I would hardly go down on one knee unless I was serious.' His lips turned down and his eyes became shadowed. 'In light of today's papers, do you think Putney will stop?'

'He needs to be exposed.'

'Others have tried and failed. I refuse to be used as an instrument of your ruin by the likes of him. Equally I refuse to be labelled a cad and have it whispered that I ruin eligible women for sport. Years ago, I made a vow that I would not be used by him to ruin any woman.' He gave her a resolute look. 'Marriage is the right and proper thing to do in these circumstances. If I had not asked, it would have weighed on my conscience. It is now up to you to make a decision. I will abide by your choice.'

Sophie stared at the ceiling. The proposal might be real, but he didn't expect her to accept it. Not truly, not given in such a manner and after last night's exchange. But did she need the protection of a marriage to save her reputation from Sir Vincent? All she needed was an engagement. Her heart thudded.

'You suggest a fake engagement until the newspapers lose interest and I can jilt you? Putney is sure to move on when he realises that I am no soft target.' She pursed her lips, considering. It made complete and utter sense. It would buy her time until the Montemorcys returned and she could get proper advice. She turned around and faced Lord Bingfield, adopting her best social smile. 'A false engagement should stop comment. Whoever is doing this expects you to run and to leave me ruined, but this way Sir Vincent Putney will be left exposed. Marriage is not the answer, an engagement is.'

His brows knitted together and he seemed genuinely perplexed. 'A false engagement? One is either engaged to be married or one is not, Miss Ravel. I don't deal in fakes and deceptions of that nature. Attempting to cozen society is fraught with difficulty.'

'It is in the novels my stepmother likes to read. They are all the rage.' Sophie gave him a breezy assurance, but her insides twisted. He made it seem as though she dealt in deception regularly. She didn't. Sometimes it was easier to give an impression of a certain behaviour for the greater good, that was all. 'We don't actually have to marry. Once the furore has died down and Putney is unmasked or quits the neighbourhood, we can part…amicably. Legitimate engagements are ended for all sorts of reasons.'

'I meant a marriage if it came to it. I knew the risks when I asked. And if you had refused, I would have told the various journalists that my heart was broken by the redoubtable Miss Ravel.' He inclined his head. 'I will not pretend instant undying love. I have seen enough of love to know it leads two people who are wholly unsuited to each other to do stupid things. Love has little place in marriage. We might have suited if you had desired it.'

'We obviously have different views on the subject. I would never have such a cold-blooded thing as an arranged marriage. A happy marriage needs a firm foundation of love.'

A half-smile flickered across his face. 'Despite your formidable reputation, Miss Ravel, you are a secret romantic. Love only complicates things and makes people profoundly unhappy in my experience.'

'I demand certain standards from any prospective bridegroom.' Sophie drew herself up to her full height. 'Standards which you sadly lack.'

'However, I will consider your wish of a fake engagement and evaluate the risks. We might be able to play Sir Vincent at his own game.'

His mouth twisted as he spat the word fake. Deep-seated anger at the injustice of the whole situation flooded through her. She was trapped in a situation not of her making and had found the perfect solution if only he'd agree. She was being honest and forthright, whereas if she'd accepted his offer he would have found a way to make her jilt him. And his idea of telling the press she'd rejected him would make them more interested in her, rather than less.

'Consider!' Sophie put her hands on her hips. 'It is the perfect solution. Surely you must see it. There will be no need for further scandal. We will quietly part at the end. There will be no hurt feelings or accusations as we both know from the outset that the marriage will never happen. Honesty on both our parts from the start.'

'You know nothing about me!'

Sophie crossed her arms. He was like any other rake, solely interested in himself. 'I know enough.'

'I had not considered a limited engagement, but it would serve the same purpose, I suppose.' He gave a long sigh. 'My father will be disappointed when the longed-for engagement ends, but he generally is with me these days.'

'You are a fortune hunter. It was why your aunt was so pleased to see you with me.'

Sophie backed away from the window. Her stomach knotted. She should have guessed. And she had handed him the perfect opportunity. Just once she wanted to be wanted for herself rather than for the fortune her father had amassed. The walls seemed to close in on her and she wished her corset wasn't as tight. Here when she walked into the drawing room, she'd been so pleased with the way the slenderness of her waist contrasted with her new crinoline. It was always the way—either look good or be able to breathe. Next time she'd remember that breathing was important when dealing with people like Lord Bingfield, particularly Lord Bingfield.

'Miss Ravel, jumping to conclusions is never good.' His ice-cold voice filled the room and cut through her panic. 'My fortune is quite secure. The estate is well funded thanks to my mother's dowry and eventually it will be mine. My father cannot change that. Do you wish to see the accounts? He merely wishes me to marry and provide an heir.'

Sophie pinched the top of her nose. She could hardly confess about her past mistake with Sebastian. Just thinking about that made her feel unclean. 'I have met fortune hunters in the past. They are a known hazard for heiresses. One has to be cautious. You can be left without any fortune at all.'

'So I understand.' His mouth twisted. 'There are ways to protect women if one acts before marriage. You must take your time and get the right settlement. It saves heartache, as my mother found out to her cost.'

'Your mother is still alive?'

'My parents are divorced. The settlement was not in her favour. They were in a unique situation, as I am sure you are aware. It was all in the papers at the time. My mother was for ever banished from polite society.'

Sophie hung her head. She had done it again— jumping to a conclusion when the truth was precisely the opposite. It made sense now why he had acted so quickly to protect her. 'I didn't know. I have no idea who your parents are.'

'Truly?' He raised an eyebrow and his features seemed carved from stone. 'You surprise me, Miss Ravel. My parents' divorce was the subject of great scandal. The account of the crim. con. trial went into several editions. A best seller, or so Putney informed me when we were at Eton.'

'It happened a long time ago. The world moves on,' Sophie replied evenly. Her stomach clenched and she knew that she had to get this right. If she said the wrong words, he could decide not to help her. 'Scandal is not branded on people's foreheads. A person's true character is of far more relevance than any perceived scandal.'

'Other people may beg to differ. Ever since I was at Eton, the press have been interested in my doings. First because of my parents and then...'

She fixed him with her eye. It was obvious the sort of reputation he must have. He probably made Sebastian Cawburn look like an angelic choirboy. 'Because you decided to give them what they wanted.'

'I was determined to live my life as I pleased rather than looking over my shoulder for their approval. They have printed lies in the past and continue to twist my life so they can sell more papers. Once I had my head around that fact, I found it much easier to accept. Regardless of what the papers might say, there are certain lines I do not cross. Once I make a vow, I do my utmost to keep it. You must remember that, Miss Ravel.'

'I am not interested in other people's opinions and I am interested in how a person behaves.'

A light flared in his eyes. 'You are a unique individual, Miss Ravel.'

'I like to think so. Do you agree to my scheme?' Sophie held out her hand and willed him to take it, sealing their pact. 'Once I jilt you, you can nurse a broken heart for ages. The papers will be sympathetic. Your father will have to give you time to grieve. We are simply being honest with each other at the start, rather than playing games. Neither of us will get hurt. We have much to gain.'

He gathered her hands in his and she noticed how good it felt to touch him. Her body went rigid. She did not have to act on the attraction. Desire burnt itself out quickly. Desire was not the same as lasting love. 'We could have made a great team, Miss Ravel.'

'Sophie!' Her stepmother's outraged tones came from the open door. 'What is going on here? You are holding hands with a strange man! Where has your sense of propriety gone, my girl?'

Sophie slipped her hands from Lord Bingfield's. Her stepmother would have to choose this moment to come into the drawing room. Nothing had been settled. 'Going on, Stepmother? Everything is utterly innocent.'

'Hornswoggle! I have seen that look in your eye before, young lady. You had better not think to twist me around your little finger.'

'Allow me to introduce myself, Richard Crawford, Viscount Bingfield. My father is the Marquess of Hallington, Mrs Ravel.' Lord Bingfield recaptured her hand. Sophie gave a little tug, but he didn't let go. 'Your stepdaughter has done me the honour of becoming my fiancée in light of the news reported in today's papers.'

Sophie struggled to fill her lungs. He had done it, despite his misgivings. They were embarked on the deception.

'Sophie!' Her stepmother went white and then red.

'You had best sit down, Stepmother.' Sophie let go of Lord Bingfield's hand and led her stepmother to the pink-damask sofa. 'You have had a shock.'

'Then it is true, my dear child? Not some nonsense?' Her stepmother fumbled for her reticule and her smelling salts. 'You are going to marry this stranger? You could have told me that was the reason why you needed to meet him alone.'

'I had no idea he would offer, Stepmother.' Sophie took the reticule, retrieved the vial and waved it under her stepmother's nose. 'I didn't want to get your hopes up. An engagement is the best solution in the circumstances. The gutter press appear determined that we court.'

'I regret that subterfuge was necessary, but we didn't wish for the press to become interested with regards to your stepdaughter's innocence.' Lord Bingfield bowed his head. 'Alas…'

'I completely understand,' her stepmother said, her face alight with eagerness. 'The press must be such a bother for you, dogging your footsteps. You seem to be a great favourite of theirs.'

'Most of the stories they print about me have no bearing on reality, my dear Mrs Ravel. I do have my code of honour.'

Her stepmother gave a long sigh.

Sophie rolled her eyes. A few well-chosen words and her stepmother melted. She regretted the necessity of keeping her stepmother ignorant of the true arrangement, but her stepmother had never been able to keep a secret. And it was necessary to stop Sir Vincent once and for all time. But the sooner this deception was over, the better.

'I had never considered what the people in the scandal sheets must feel and how cautious they have to be.'

'You read the scandal sheets?'

Her stepmother put her hand to the side of her mouth and leant forwards. 'Sophie disapproves.'

'Does she?'

'What a truly noble thing you have done. They were all wrong about you and how you break women's hearts. I never believed the story about you, that Russian countess and her husband, the one who committed suicide rather than compete with you.'

'I am grateful.' Lord Bingfield inclined his head. 'The situation was not how the press portrayed it. I met the countess after her husband died, and introduced her to her new husband. We remain friends.'

Sophie stared at him. Precisely how much of a favourite with the gutter press was he?

'Lord Bingfield, you must partake of some tea or perhaps something stronger.' Her stepmother straightened her cap. 'I know how fond you gentlemen are of something a little more potent. I am dying to learn the truth behind some of the latest scandals.'

Sophie attempted to signal over her step-mother's head, but Lord Bingfield simply gave a superior smile. 'I would be delighted to spend time with you, Mrs Ravel, but I never discuss the latest tittle-tattle for obvious reasons.'

'I shall leave you two now,' her stepmother said at the end of a very long cup of tea. 'Sophie has been glowering at me ever since the teapot arrived. I, too, remember what it is like to be young. I am so pleased you decided to do the decent thing, Lord Bingfield. I do worry about Sophie. Her future happiness has been a source of sleepless nights and now it is all settled. The late Mr Ravel must be beaming down from heaven. His Sophie will be a marchioness. He'd never thought his daughter would climb so high, but I knew she would.'

'I am sure he is, Mrs Ravel.'

Her stepmother turned a bright pink and hurried off. Lord Bingfield closed the door firmly behind her. He loomed larger than ever. Sophie retreated a step.

'The die is cast and the deception has begun,' she said, adopting an ice-cold tone. 'There was no need to close the door. We can take our leave in full view of any passing servant.'

'There is every need.' The gold in his eyes

deepened. 'I want to know why you believe you have only your fortune to offer in a marriage.'

'What I have to offer is none of your business!' Sophie crossed her arms. Her stomach tightened. In suggesting the false engagement, she'd just given Lord Bingfield an iron-clad opportunity for a seduction! She'd simply have to insist that certain boundaries weren't crossed. 'I was merely seeking to understand why you were insistent we have a real engagement. You have no regard for me.'

He took a step closer. 'Are you saying that you are indifferent to me?'

'Yes.' Sophie stuck her chin in the air. 'Yes, definitely.'

'Liar.'

She went still. Her heart raced and her mouth became parched. She wet her lips. 'I do not make a habit of lying, Lord Bingfield.'

'Richard.' He reached her and put his hands on her shoulders. 'I am your fiancé now. You need to think of me as your true betrothed or Putney will create an even bigger scandal. Remember that. This might help you. Think of it as an *aide-mémoire*.'

She was aware of him in the same heart-thumping way she'd been aware of him the night before. She concentrated on the chintz curtains behind his left shoulder, rather than on his mouth. 'What are you intending on doing?'

'Demonstrating…Sophie.'

Her name sounded like a soft caress, sliding over her jangled nerves and soothing her. A warm pulse went down her spine. No one had ever used her name in quite that fashion before.

His hand tilted her chin so she looked into his eyes of pure gold.

She had only time to blink before his mouth descended, slowly, like a tiny fluttering of a breeze and then increasing intensity. Sophie told herself that she should keep her body still or scream. She should do something besides enjoying the kiss, but she discovered she was powerless to do anything else.

She closed her eyes, savoured the sensation and swayed towards him.

He let her go and stepped back. 'Point proved… Sophie.'

This time her name was anything but a caress. Her cheeks grew hot and she rubbed her aching lips furiously. 'It proves nothing except you, like any self-respecting rake, know how to kiss.'

He picked up his hat. 'I will pick you up tonight.'

'What is happening tonight?' Sophie asked, her hand freezing in mid-air. The hard part of this engagement was not going to be pretending to be attracted to him, but keeping the attraction at bay. After insisting on the fake engagement, she could hardly back down now. When it was all over, she wanted to walk away with her head held high, knowing she had withstood the cynical seduction of a rake.

'You and I will go to the Assembly Rooms tonight. You will demonstrate your waltzing skills to me. We want people to talk.'

'Are we announcing the engagement?'

'Not yet.' He leant forwards and his breath caressed her cheek. 'Everyone needs to see how besotted we are with each other. You can do besotted, Sophie, can't you?'

Chapter Four

Sometimes it was better to know than not to know, Sophie decided as she fastened her earrings, the final detail in tonight's dress. In the grand scheme of things she would have liked to ask Richard Crawford more about himself and to have set the precise boundaries for their relationship, but she didn't have time.

She glanced at her stepmother, who was already dressed in her evening finery and hovering behind her, making comments. 'You will tell me what you know about Lord Bingfield from the scandal sheets.'

'You should ask your intended about what the scandal sheets have printed over the years, if you want to know. If you had read them before now, you wouldn't have to ask me. You must do the decent thing and wait for Lord Bingfield to tell you.'

'Stepmother!' Sophie turned on the stool and motioned for her maid to leave the room. 'You may tell me what is bothering you.'

'It is difficult to understand why you have kept your cards so close to your chest. How well do you know this Lord Bingfield? He does have a reputation for sweeping married women off their feet. There was that Russian countess with the dead husband and a duchess more recently. Possibly there have been more.'

Sophie stood up and fluffed out the upper tier of her skirt. Married women. Women of experience. Not unmarried heiresses. He had not lied about that. He had his code. 'It is what an engagement is for. A chance to get to know the gentleman in question. I have not married him… yet. If I decide we will not suit, then I have the chance of changing my mind. The item in the newspaper left me few alternatives, Stepmother. Once the gutter press get hold of you, they keep hold. You can remember what Robert said after The Incident.'

'Sometimes I feel like you are keeping secrets from me. We used to share everything, Sophie, when I first married your father.'

'You are the one keeping secrets now, Stepmother. You love gossip. Generally I have to block my ears. Tell me something about Lord Bingfield and his family, please. Help me to understand why the press are so interested in him.'

Sophie waited as a variety of emotions warred on her stepmother's face. If her stepmother would not supply the information, she would go to the Lit and the Phil and spend time looking at old papers to see if she could discover the scandal.

'Very well, I shall tell you about his parents,' her stepmother said when Sophie had given up hope. 'Lord Bingfield's parents were involved in a massive scandal about twenty years ago. The marchioness ran away with her lover and there was a huge crim. con. case. It was absolutely fascinating and a best seller. Of course they say the marquess never recovered from it. And the marchioness…well…she was never received in polite society again. When Lord Bingfield entered society, everyone was naturally curious, and he didn't disappoint.'

'It must have been awful for Lord Bingfield,' Sophie said. 'He was a child, the innocent victim of two people's complicated lives.'

'He certainly hasn't been shy about courting scandal in his adult life,' her stepmother remarked tartly. 'He must have a list of mistresses as long as your arm. Women seem to forget the sense they were born with around him. There are things which have to come from the other person, my dear, rather than from reading a newspaper.'

'You know the newspapers do print lies. Robert has told you enough times.' Sophie tilted her chin upwards. Her stepmother's revelations were proof enough that she needed to be cautious.

'Sophie, are you sure you want to marry this man?' her stepmother asked in a rush. 'With Robert and Henri out of the country, I feel I must say something. Refuse to be rushed. You can have a long engagement. You don't need a special licence, an ordinary one will do.'

'I thought you always wanted me to marry by special licence.'

'Only if the man is suitable for you.' Her stepmother gave a long sigh. 'I don't know what is wrong with me. This morning when Lord Bingfield was here, I was transported with happiness for you, but I have spent all afternoon staring at Mr Ravel's portrait and wondering—is this the sort of man your father would have approved of? Is being in the aristocracy worth your ultimate happiness?'

Sophie concentrated on her bare hands, rather than looking at her stepmother's face. Her stepmother only ever spent time talking to her father's portrait when she felt overwhelmed. It was tempting to confide in her, but the arrangement would only make her more agitated. And could she trust her stepmother to keep it a secret? Her stepmother had the habit of gossiping with friends. It was far more important to catch Sir Vincent and destroy him. She'd confess later. Her stepmother would understand. Far better to beg forgiveness, than request permission in this case.

Sophie glanced at her stepmother's kindly face and swallowed. Or at least she hoped her stepmother would understand.

'I know what I am doing. And it was in all the papers, Stepmother. You know what happened to the Neville girl. She was banned from court and that was fifteen years ago. Once the gutter press get hold of you, they do not let go.'

'Do you know about his finances? Such men can be dreadfully let in the pockets. You remember Lord Cawburn. He tried to rush you and it was only through Henri's intervention that your reputation emerged unscathed. Now, this business with the newspapers… Could he…? That is to say, Lord Bingfield has much to gain.'

'Lord Bingfield is not trying to rush me. We are engaged because the gutter press demanded a robust response. There is little point in denying the rumour as Lord Bingfield was prepared to do the honourable thing. I refused to do anything irrevocable without a proper settlement.' Sophie patted her stepmother's hand.

Everything would work out if her scheme was allowed to happen. There had to be a simple way of trapping Sir Vincent and then saying goodbye to Richard Crawford before she started liking him too much. They were allies only because they faced a common enemy, not because they shared a mutual understanding or finer feelings.

'You have eased my mind.' Her stepmother took her mother's single pearl and undid the clasp before fastening it around Sophie's neck. 'I hope you are not doing this just to please me. All I have ever wanted for you is to be happy.'

A tiny prickle of fear went through Sophie. What if they didn't succeed in trapping Sir Vincent? She pushed it away. They had to win. 'And if I can't do that within society?'

'Your father worked his entire life to ensure his daughter would be gentry. You won't dishonour your father's memory.'

'Trust me, please. I am all grown up. I've survived three seasons since Lord Cawburn without incident.'

'It is what makes this situation so strange. I don't understand how you could have met a man such as Lord Bingfield without me knowing.' Her stepmother stepped back. 'There, pretty as a picture. I do wish your father had lived to see you triumphant and in love.'

Sophie straightened her blouse. With her favourite pair of earrings, and the cream ball gown with cascades of lace, she was armed for battle.

Sir Vincent was not going to get away with his scheme and he wasn't going to be allowed to wreck anyone else's life. She simply had to figure out how to feed him information which would incriminate him before she did truly become besotted with Richard Crawford. She had to remember that above all things she had to keep her heart safe. Men who were *not safe in carriages* were best handled at arm's length, rather than offering up her lips at the earliest opportunity. Boundaries were required and it was up to her to set them.

She reached for her tortoise-shell fan and ignored the way her lips ached in memory of that kiss. Kissing complicated matters. They might be posing as an engaged couple, but it did not mean he had any finer feelings or regard for her. She was a means to an end.

One last glance in the mirror told her everything she needed to know. The dress was passable, but she looked far too excited. And she was excited, excited about the possibility of beating Sir Vincent, rather than seeing Richard Crawford.

'Shall we go? I feel capable of achieving great things tonight.'

Richard drew in his breath as Sophie walked down the stairs. Tonight she was the perfect epitome of a redoubtable ice princess rather than a woman in distress. Her blonde hair was immaculate and the bodice of her ball dress skimmed the tops of her breasts. A single pearl nestled in the hollow of her throat. But for all her finery, he could see the nerves underneath—the slight hesitation on the last step, the pinched way she held her mouth and the way she clutched her gloves until her knuckles shone white. Sophie was less certain about tonight's piece of play-acting than she wanted to be.

He had a great longing to throw her over his shoulder, and take her somewhere where he could protect her. But tonight was necessary for more than one reason. Not only would he demonstrate to Putney that seeking revenge on Sophie in this manner was doomed to failure, but he would also provide the perfect excuse for any visit to Newcastle. His father would understand the need to pursue an heiress far better than Richard's need to be part of his mother and sister's life.

'You look exquisite,' he said when Sophie reached the bottom of the stairs.

'It is last Season's dress and the sleeves didn't alter as well I wanted them to, but I like the shape of the skirt too much.'

'You sew your own clothes?' Richard struggled to think of a woman of his acquaintance who would admit it. The last one was probably Mary. His mind moved firmly away from that memory. He was not going to start liking Sophie Ravel. He only became friends with women after he no longer desired them. To allow a woman into his heart and his whole life was to invite her to abandon him. It was not going to happen to him as it had happened to his father. He was the one who left first, before his heart became involved.

'Only alterations. I want perfection and my stepmother ensured my accomplishments included both fine sewing and the making of clothes.' Her smile lit the hallway. 'One has to be practical. A dress can easily be made over into the latest fashion. I never want to disappoint.'

'You won't do that.' He reached into the pocket of his evening coat. 'But you are missing one thing.'

She glanced down. 'I believe I have everything. Slippers, reticule, fan and gloves.'

'A ring.'

Her cheeks flamed. 'I…I hadn't considered it necessary. Not for tonight.'

His heart gave an odd wrench. It was ironic. Normally he was the one who put limits on his relationships with women, but this time it was Sophie. He'd seen the ring at the jewellers and knew it would be the one thing to give her confidence. 'How else will people know we are engaged?'

'A notice in the papers?' Her laugh rang hollow.

Richard held on to his temper. He wanted to murder the man who had made her so distrustful. She should try trusting him. He wanted to prove to her that he could solve their difficulty.

'Hold out your finger and stop being awkward. It will remind you that you belong to me if you are tempted to waltz with any divine dancer. No flirting with any other man.'

She held out her hand and he slipped on the ring, a pearl flanked by two sapphires. She twisted her hand back and forth. 'It is very pretty and it fits. I never flirt, Lord Bingfield. It goes against my nature.'

He allowed the remark to pass. He had seen

a glimpse of the passionate woman underneath her frosty exterior and wanted to see her again. 'I saw it in a jeweller's window this afternoon and guessed your size. Sapphires for your eyes. It suits your hand.'

'It is elegant rather than showy.' Sophie tilted her chin upwards. 'It is the sort of ring I would have chosen…if asked.'

'I will remember for the future.'

'You mean you don't intend for her to have the family jewels?' Mrs Ravel asked with a suspicious glance at the ring as she came to stand guard over Sophie. 'I would have thought the fiancée of a viscount deserved something better.'

Richard gave a quick glance at Sophie, who shrugged. She had obviously failed to confide in her stepmother about the false engagement as he'd expected her to do after he left. Intriguing.

'Engagement rings have an unfortunate past in my family. With your stepdaughter, I thought it best to break with tradition.' Richard made a bow. 'Should Sophie wish it, she may of course exchange it for another.'

'And the family jewels? I presume there are some. There again, the family jewels are always the first to go. Several women I know were palmed off with paste.' She tapped the side of her nose. 'You can always tell.'

'Honestly, Stepmother! I explained that Lord Bingfield is not let in the pockets.'

Richard controlled his temper. The pair had obviously dealt with a fortune hunter before. Could he be the one responsible for Sophie's caution? A stab of jealousy went through him. He wished… Richard pushed the thought away. He never speculated on a woman's past. Ever.

'Kept in a vault at Hallington, awaiting the next marchioness. After we are married, the jewels can be reset to her taste. My father has always been clear on that.'

'Admit it, Stepmother, you simply wanted to boast that I was wearing a family heirloom. Personally, I am pleased Richard has shown some restraint and taste.' Sophie flashed a smile. 'How perfect to be able to wear it tonight. I believe I shall keep my gloves on to start with. It will make the revelation of our engagement all that more sensational if the need arises.'

'My thinking entirely.' Richard's shoulders relaxed as they shared a conspiratorial smile. Tonight was about laying the foundation of the trap for Putney and ensuring Sophie remembered whom she belonged to at the moment, rather than proclaiming the engagement to everyone. Patience was required. He could risk liking Sophie as he knew what the outcome would be. He could stop this before it went too far.

'I'm pleased we are as one on this.'

Her level blue eyes met his. 'We are.'

The Assembly Rooms blazed with light and sound when Sophie arrived with Richard and her stepmother.

With each turn of the carriage wheel, the ring grew heavier on Sophie's finger. It became harder and harder to keep up a light conversation. There were so many things she wanted to say to Richard about the necessity of boundaries, but her stepmother was there. And her stepmother was sure to pick up any attempt at subterfuge. Her head pained her and she wished she'd found an excuse not to attend, rather than trying for this pretence.

'The first dance must be mine,' Richard murmured as he handed her down from the carriage. The simple touch of his gloved hand on her elbow did nothing to calm her nerves. If anything, it heightened her awareness of him and the way her body reacted when he was near. 'We must begin as we mean to go on. Besotted, Sophie, not looking like a death sentence hangs over your head. You were the one to suggest this. For it to succeed, people need to believe in the romance. We met and fell instantly and irrevocably in love. Right now you appear more ready for a funeral.'

'I thought you liked my dress,' she said in dismay. Besotted indeed! There was no possibility of allowing her heart to rule her head. What she was feeling was attraction and desire towards a distinctly unsuitable man. She didn't have to act on that attraction. This engagement was about saving her reputation, not destroying it for ever.

'I do, but it is your expression I worry about and I was sure you would break your fan in the carriage. You clutched it far too tightly and you chose to sit as far away from me as possible, practically hugging the door.'

Sophie pressed her lips together, hating that he had noticed her discomfort. She could hardly confess to being wary of him. It would only mean making it easier for him to seduce her. 'It is difficult to fit two dresses in the same carriage.'

He laughed. 'If that is what you want to believe you may, but I prefer to trust my instincts.'

Sophie forced her features to relax. Her stomach was in more knots than the first time she had attended a dance. It amazed her that Richard had noticed anything and had thought to ask.

Her stepmother had sailed on, seemingly oblivious as her earlier misgivings proved groundless.

There were so many pitfalls to this current
plan. She wished she had actually thought it
through thoroughly before she suggested it.
But it was this or ruin. *Or accepting his offer
for real.* She ruthlessly quashed that little voice.

'We need to speak. Urgently,' Sophie whispered back. 'There is so much which is unsettled
between us. Ways other people, particularly Sir
Vincent, can expose us.'

'It must be a waltz. Waltzing is more convenient for speaking than a polka.'

She refused to consider how he knew such
things. If they waltzed, she'd be in his arms, Sophie realised with a gulp. 'I thought you never
asked a woman twice. I refused you last night.'

'Last night I asked. Tonight I am telling you.
I trust you know the difference.'

'A quadrille won't do?' she squeaked.

'Not for a prolonged conversation.' A faint
dimple shone in the corner of his mouth. 'There
is always bound to be a quiet card room where
we will not be disturbed.'

She didn't want to think about going to a card
room with him. She could remember all too
clearly what had happened when she went into

that deserted card room with Sebastian. Never again would she be like that!

'I have had enough of card rooms, thank you. In any case my stepmother will think it odd if we simply disappear at the first opportunity. She knows about the promises I gave my guardian years ago and how I have endeavoured to keep those promises.'

'A waltz or the card room, Sophie.'

'The first waltz, it is. I believe it will go a long way towards the besotted impression.'

His entire being stiffened and didn't appear to hear her last teasing remark.

'Is there a problem?' she asked, peering at the young lady and stylishly dressed older woman who seemed to have caught Crawford's eye. The young lady was beautiful in that dark sort of way that Sophie knew she could never be. There was a faint exoticism about her features. The older woman was clearly her mother.

He shook his head and cupped his hand under her elbow, definitely turning her away from the pair. Her body reverberated from the touch. 'It was simply someone I thought I recognised. A mistake.'

'Another one of your conquests?' She laughed and tried to concentrate on the poster advertising the visit of Charles Dickens that coming

August. She should have expected it, but it still hurt. Once a rake, always a rake. She had no right to expect anything from him. This entire engagement was spun-sugar pretence and artifice, rather than truly solid and secure love. 'I don't mind. There is no finer feeling between us. Indeed, I have no interest in you beyond securing my reputation.'

Her heart thudded that it was a lie. She was certainly aware of him. And he had been perceptive enough to realise that she was nervous. She simply didn't want to start liking him. There had to be reasons to keep her heart safe. Soon enough, he would revert to type. She had to keep remembering that he was the worst sort of rake, the sort of man whom the gutter press loved. It was only because he wanted to conduct a private war against Sir Vincent that her reputation stood any chance of survival. He had not done this because he cared about her or her prospects.

'Most definitely not one of my conquests. Nor ever likely to be.' The light in his eyes flared gold. 'And, Sophie, when we are together, I will not look at any other woman. I promise. It is not the way I was made or brought up.'

'It can happen.'

'And it causes tremendous heartache for other people.' He stared down at her. 'I have witnessed the consequences firsthand. Many times. And I have never knowingly caused a woman to break her vows, but it has always been a matter for her, rather than for me.'

Sophie swallowed hard. She could hardly confess she had asked her stepmother about the scandals he had been involved in. 'But you do know the women.'

'After a fashion.' His brows knitted. 'I had not expected them to be here tonight. It changes nothing. Until our association ends, I am yours.'

'Once the first waltz starts, you can come and find me if you wish to speak to them now,' Sophie said brightly, forcing her mind away from the way her heart wanted to believe his words. Underneath he would be the same as any other rake—selfish and solely concerned with his own pleasure. 'There is no need to introduce me. There are a number of other people I need to speak to.'

Sophie silently prayed the waltz would be soon. Otherwise it was going to be torture waiting to speak to him and hoping that they had their story correct. But staying close to him was another sort of torture, undermining her resolve to keep aloof from his seductive technique.

A smile transformed his features. 'Our luck appears to be holding. I believe I can hear the first strains now. There is no need to greet distant acquaintances.'

She allowed him to lead her into the middle of the dance floor. While some of the other rooms had gas lighting, the main ballroom still had its magnificent chandelier lighting system.

He placed his hand on her waist, holding her a bit more tightly than strictly necessary. She pointedly twisted her waist to gain a little space.

'I have been civilised, Miss Ravel. You will come to no harm.'

'Everyone is watching us.' She swallowed hard and attempted to ignore the fluttering in her stomach.

'Everyone will have read the papers. They want to see what happens. Abject devotion.'

'From you or me?' Sophie gave a pointed smile. She was on firmer ground here. 'Abject devotion fails to agree with me, Lord Bingfield. Never has done and I have no plans to start. Remember, I am redoubtable.'

'I never believe anything I read in the press.'

'You should believe that. I have spent years ensuring I do not have pointless flirtations.'

'What a pity.' He clasped his hand over hers. 'I shall take comfort in the fact that you are far from indifferent to me. Your body must remember what happened the last time I held you in my arms.'

Sophie ground her teeth. 'A gentleman would refrain from mentioning that kiss.'

'It was utterly delightful.' He gave an unrepentant smile. 'That is better. Your cheeks have colour. Far better for giving the impression of being besotted.'

Besotted indeed! The one thing this engagement was not going to become was a way for him to seduce her. She knew the boundaries. The kiss would not be repeated. She refused to slip slowly but inexorably along that path again towards an illicit room in a rundown inn.

She cleared her throat. 'The dance has begun.'

He began to move and she discovered that he was an expert dancer. She had danced with some very good dancers before, but Richard moved differently. It was more like floating on a cloud or having her body move as one with his. It would be easy to forget everything and simply enjoy the sensation of being in his arms.

'We need to come up with a story,' she said and ignored how his hand had moved to fit her waist far more snugly. 'Something to test Sir Vincent.'

'I doubt that will be necessary.'

'We need to prove that he is our mutual enemy.'

'Proving is nothing. What we need to do is ensure that he will not continue with his scheme. And he needs to learn that he should not try that sort of behaviour with anyone else.'

'I take it you have a plan.'

'I promised to protect you.' His hand moved around to her back. 'Trust me to do so and not abandon you to the winds of fate. You are far from alone, Miss Ravel. Relax and enjoy the dance. Look me in the eyes as if you never want to look anywhere else.'

'And if someone asks how we met? I can hardly tell them the truth.'

He missed his step, but recovered. 'I had not considered it. Have you been away from New-castle recently?'

'Carlisle,' Sophie answered with a faint smile. 'I trust you know where that is.'

He cleared his throat. 'I meant somewhere in the south.'

'We went to Liverpool in late March as a new design of tea clipper was being launched and I wanted to see the hull. I know everyone says that steam will replace the sail, but there is some-thing so glorious about the way the sails fill.'

'I shall take your word for it. I had never considered the design of a hull before. All I want to know is that a ship will get me from one port to another, safely, if I am forced to take it.'

'Much of my fortune comes from shipbuilding, Lord Bingfield.' Sophie breathed easier. Speaking of shipbuilding kept her mind from the way he moved or the shape of his lips. Feigning being besotted was one thing, actually being so was another problem altogether. 'I was brought up to have a keen interest. The board of directors may run the day-to-day business, but it is the lifeblood which brings all the good things in my life. It is important not to take such things for granted, but to understand and to be able to question.'

His smile became genuine. 'I knew you were more than a pretty face.'

'Do you like ships?' Sophie asked quickly.

'I am invariably seasick. It doesn't matter if it is a rowing boat or a tea clipper—once I am on the water, my stomach heaves. Always has done. I suspect it always will.'

'You do get used to the sea in time. Lots of people get over it and are never troubled again. A long sea voyage would do the trick. It did with me when I was seven. We went to the West Indies and I was so sick to begin with, but then I recovered. My father told me even Admiral Lord

Nelson was seasick on occasion. Somehow it made it easier to bear.'

'I shall take your word for it since you argue so passionately. Some day maybe I will test your theory.' His eyes crinkled at the corners. A bubbly sense of excitement filled her. 'But for now Liverpool with its shipbuilding will have to do. The timing is reasonable and plausible. I do hope you did attend some sort of gala or a ball while you were there and your trip wasn't entirely business.'

'Do for what?' Sophie frowned, trying to remember precisely what she had done. It was disappointing that Lord Bingfield wasn't interested in ships and more than slightly disconcerting that she had hoped he would be. She shouldn't want any connection with him, but she did. She trod down heavier than she should have and narrowly missed his foot. It was only Richard's skill as a dancer which kept them upright. The heat in Sophie's cheeks increased.

'We went to the theatre. It was an amusing comedy that my stepmother was desperate to see. I cried off the launch ball because I had twisted my ankle at the shipyard. Is it important?'

'For where we met? Yes.' His eyes crinkled at the corners. Sophie hurriedly glanced away.

'I'd have hardly liked to have met you in a ship-yard or on a railway platform. The theatre is a splendid choice. Plenty of time to spy people from a box and arrange a meeting. I take it you are adept at fan language despite your pretensions towards formidability?'

He was going to imply she had arranged a meeting with her fan. Typically arrogant. Sophie started to pull away, but his hand tightened on her waist, holding her against his body.

'Why is this necessary?' she asked.

'I must have had a reason to come to New-castle to see you and see if the spark we both felt was something more. And your stepmother most blatantly had not met me before.' He gave her hand a squeeze. 'Our meeting yesterday was hardly a chance one. You were enchanted by my persistence and overcome with desire. I had completely rearranged my life to be with you and you were utterly captivated. The press always do love a romance.'

Sophie concentrated on taking the next few steps, rather than considering the desire part of his statement. She hated that a tiny part of her wanted to believe in the tale which he had spun. She wanted to believe that he would rearrange his life for her. 'It does make sense. As a personal rule, I dislike being enchanted about anything. I have learnt, Lord Bingfield, that it is best to examine faults thoroughly.'

He gave a bark of laughter. Several people turned to stare at them. 'You might wish to pretend you are practical, but you possess the soul of a romantic, Miss Ravel. I see straight through you. You long to be swept off your feet. Otherwise why assist in an elopement?'

'I much prefer being practical to starry-eyed. I gave up endangering my heart years ago.'

'You are unlike any woman I have met.'

'I hope that is a good thing. I like the idea of being an individual.'

'Never doubt that! You, Sophie Ravel, are a one-off. You have even given me a hankering to test your theory about seasickness with a voyage to the West Indies, but only if you were with me.'

'That won't happen.'

'A pity. A sea voyage with you could have been intriguing.' A dimple played in the corner of his mouth. 'You won't even consider a trip across the Channel? You and I together? You could hold my hand.'

Sophie glanced down. It would be so easy to allow herself to slip a bit more under his spell. She gave her head a shake and tried to remember all the reasons why he was not a good prospect for marriage. 'Liverpool and the theatre in late March is where we met. Stop trying to cloud the issue with talks of voyages which will never happen. I want to save my reputation, not throw it away by giving in to the determined seduction of a man like you.'

'Relax.' His breath caressed her ear. 'You see, everything is sorted. You don't have to worry about a thing. All you have to do is to enjoy the waltz. Nothing will happen on a dance floor. I gave you my promise.'

His hand firmly pressed against her back and she became more aware than ever of the way he moved.

It was only a dance, but Sophie could feel her self-control ebbing away. With each step, she seemed to be more encased in a dream bubble of romance which she wanted desperately to believe in.

It wasn't real. She had made a mistake like this before, confusing the excitement of being noticed by someone who was older and more experienced than she was with real romance. She knew she wanted her romance real and true, like Robert and Henri shared, something which had grown over time rather than hitting her suddenly. What she felt for Richard Crawford was far too sudden to be real and substantial. It was another illusion and this time she refused to be taken in.

Sophie concentrated on taking another step, rather than looking him in the face. She had to hope that his scheme worked quickly, otherwise Sophie knew all of her resolutions would be for nothing—she'd start believing in the romance. And she knew precisely where that led—straight to her barricading herself in a room at some run-down coaching inn.

What was worse, this time, this time there would be no expectation of marriage. It would only be an affair as she had refused his proper offer of marriage and he would never ask her again. On that point, she knew he'd keep his word.

Chapter Five

The cool night air bathed Sophie's flushed face as she stood out on one of the little balconies which fronted the Assembly Rooms' first floor. After the waltz finished, Richard had abandoned her in search of refreshment, but Sophie knew everyone had seen their little display of being besotted with each other.

The trouble was she knew that she could not keep it up. It would be far too easy to slip into the habit of dancing with him and being held far too closely. Her body still thrummed with awareness of how he'd placed his hand on the small of her back and how his fingers had curled about hers.

Richard Crawford was precisely the sort of man she could easily lose her heart to, but he had one fatal flaw—he was *unsafe in carriages* and she'd be wrong to forget that. She recited the vows she had made in that inn bedroom; only they seemed to be of little substance.

Sophie pressed her hand to her forehead. When he left her, Richard whispered in her ear that they would dance a polka later. And every fibre of her being looked forward to it. It was wrong of her. This was a temporary arrangement, not something that was going to last the rest of her life.

A marriage needed to be more than physical desire. Sophie firmed her mouth. She'd been right to refuse his reluctant proposal. She wanted a steady love borne of friendship, rather than will-o'-the-wisp desire masquerading as something more.

'Enjoying making a spectacle of yourself?' The overly oily voice grated over her nerves and the stench of Madagascar hair oil washed over her. Sir Vincent had discovered her refuge.

Sophie counted to ten and composed her features before she turned. She wished Richard had confided his plan to expose Sir Vincent, but he hadn't. The next few minutes were up to her. Richard would simply have to go along with whatever happened. 'Sir Vincent. Imagine encountering you here. I had not thought to see you again so soon.'

'Lord Bingfield won't marry you. You are simply making my job easier. I wonder where your recklessness will next take you. It is amazing that you have enjoyed such a spotless reputation until now.'

Sophie deliberately widened her eyes and adopted her best naïve débutante voice. 'Why wouldn't Lord Bingfield marry me? He has offered to protect me.'

'He is not the marrying sort.' Sir Vincent shook his ponderous head. 'Other ladies have deluded themselves in the past and been terribly disappointed. Can you risk being more exposed in the press? They are already highly intrigued by you. I do hope you have no secrets in your past.'

'Did you supply today's item of tittle-tattle?'

He gave a slight cough and adopted a pious expression. 'People will speculate and I was unable to resist confirming what I knew. Unlike some, the press trust me.'

Sophie rolled her eyes heavenwards and struggled to keep her temper. 'Will the press speculate? That does surprise me no end. Gossip is endemic in Newcastle and always has been, Sir Vincent. It is such a shame when it proves to be false or people spread malicious rumours. It is amazing how quickly the gutter press can turn on one of their trusted sources.'

'Your friend's parents inform me that their daughter was caught on the road to Edinburgh and they hope hourly for her safe return.' He blew on his nails. 'But I have gone against the idea. Who wants an unwilling bride? Perhaps one of their other daughters will suit.'

Sophie gulped hard. 'You mean to have one of Cynthia's sisters?'

'Yes, one of them might be suitable as Lady Putney. There again, they all might bear the taint of their eldest sister's conduct. What a pity you assisted in ruining another person's life. Possibly several young persons' lives. You must seriously reflect on your behaviour, Miss Ravel. Someone must stop you before you ruin anyone else's life.'

Sophie's stomach clenched. It was a deliberate lie. She had received Cynthia's postcard in the second post. The couple had made it to Carlisle without mishap. She would not put it past Mr Johnson to offer one of his other daughters, but she doubted that he would enforce it, not after Cynthia had made her dramatic bid for freedom. Mr and Mrs Johnson did love their children.

'Do you enjoy theatricals, Sir Vincent?' Sophie asked, making sure her voice flowed like honey. Her insides churned, but she refused to give way to panic. Somewhere in that crowded ballroom was Richard Crawford and he had behaved perfectly correctly. He refused to be used by this man. The thought gave her confidence. 'Plays and the like?'

'Not overly.' He gave a smug smile. 'Sometimes the actresses are worth watching, but I only go to the theatre to be seen. The true spectacle happens in the stalls.'

'A pity. You would have made the exact prototype of a pantomime villain.' Sophie clenched her fan tighter and sought to control her temper. This time she would walk away and not lose her head or panic. She would find Richard and demand they carry their engagement a step further—only an announcement in the papers would end the speculation.

Even Sir Vincent in his arrogance must know where that particular line of polite society was drawn. Sophie's head spun. That was it. She had to find a way of getting him to cross that line in full view of everyone. Expose him and his pathetic attempts at blackmail. And she had to do it now.

Behind Sir Vincent, she could see the crowds of people standing on the edge of the ballroom.

A few steps into the room and this conversation would be overheard. Sophie's stomach clenched. She didn't have time to wait for Richard to appear. Long ago, she'd given up on any errant knights coming to her rescue. She would have to execute the entire operation herself.

Sophie judged the distance. Too much in the open and he'd never react. Too far into the balcony and no one would hear or react. It had to be just right. Without giving herself time to think, she edged towards the ballroom.

'You dare to insult me!' Sir Vincent took a step towards her, blocking her exit and obviously intent on forcing her more fully on to the balcony.

'Why would I do that?' Sophie's mind raced and she attempted to remember the way he had lost his temper last night. She ducked under his arm. 'Could it be because you are a pompous fool? Why would anyone in their right mind wish to be married to someone like you? I know Cynthia's younger sisters and they feel exactly the same way about you. They think you a pompous braying fool.'

She was out from behind the curtain now. The ballroom teemed with people and music. Everyone had their back to her and her personal duel with Sir Vincent.

Richard was nowhere to be seen. She was

truly on her own. Silently she prayed that she had done enough. Her heart thudded in her ears.

'No one calls me that!' Sir Vincent parted the curtain and emerged red-faced and spitting with anger.

'I just have! Now I must bid you adieu, Sir Vincent.' She made a curtsy which bordered on the insulting. 'Pray remember I am not some snivelling scullery maid or a naïve débutante. I do have friends, so stay out of my way. Do not attempt to blacken my name again!'

He reached out and grabbed her arm. 'We are finished when I say we are.'

'Unhand me!'

'Not until we have finished our discussion.' He started to drag her back towards the balcony.

'Someone help me. Please.'

A fist connected with Sir Vincent's jaw and he staggered backwards against the heavy curtain and fell down. The curtain tumbled with a loud thud and rip which resounded through the room.

'You have insulted Miss Ravel for the last time, Putney.' Richard's voice held none of its usual warmth.

He had arrived! Precisely at the right moment. Sophie's heart did a little flip.

Richard towered over Sir Vincent. 'When a

lady asks you to let go, you do so. I demand an apology!'

'What right do you have to intervene?' Sir Vincent rose to his feet and adopted a pugilist's stance. 'Hit me again and see if I am slow to respond. Fight like a gentleman, Bingfield.'

Richard's voice held a note of barely controlled fury. 'I claim the right of any gentleman to act when a lady is accosted.'

'We were merely conversing. I demand satisfaction. You have impugned my character for the last time, Bingfield.'

'I can see the marks of your hand on her elbow, Putney. I heard Miss Ravel beg for help. I suspect the vast majority of the gathering heard her plea. What man among you would fail to assist a woman in need? Are you a molester of women, Putney? Is that the reputation you seek to defend?'

Sir Vincent went a violent colour of puce and foam speckled his mouth.

Sophie saw a crowd had gathered around them and the orchestra had stopped playing. In the silence, she made sure her voice could carry. 'Sir Vincent threatened me and grabbed hold of my arm. He refused to let go. I feared for my person and my reputation. Lord Bingfield rescued me.'

'I couldn't help overhearing the conversation,' an elderly lady piped up. 'That gentleman grabbed hold of the lady in a most unbecoming manner.'

'That's precisely right,' said a well-upholstered man. 'This gentleman acted bravely in rescuing the lady.'

Various other people in the crowd murmured their agreement. Sir Vincent stood there with an increasingly panic-stricken look on his face.

Sophie pointed towards the large double doors on the other side of the ballroom. 'Depart, Sir Vincent, and reflect on your behaviour. It falls far short of what civilised society requires.'

A small round of applause rippled throughout the room.

Sir Vincent glanced over his shoulder and slowly lowered his fists. 'I will remember this, Bingfield.'

Sophie held out her hand to Richard. She started towards the dance floor. 'Shall we go, Lord Bingfield? I fear the incident has quite spoilt my evening and here I was having such an enchanting time. Perhaps another dance with you will restore my mood.'

'Putney's behaviour was not what I would have wished for, not tonight of all nights, but I could hardly allow your plea for help to go unanswered.' A faint smile touched his lips. 'Another waltz will suit admirably, Miss Ravel.'

'He won't marry you, Miss Ravel. You will have only yourself to blame when it ends in tears,' Sir Vincent called out, halting their progress. 'You should look to your own reputation before you start smearing others. Do you know how many women he has cozened and fooled? How many women he has ruined?'

Richard's entire being stiffened as his hand became a clenched fist. Sophie knew what she had to do to prevent a brawl breaking out. Richard might want to beat him into the ground, but she had a better means of destroying him once and for all.

The moment had come. Silently she thanked his foresight of getting her a ring. Her stomach clenched slightly. Finally the time had come to triumph. She peeled off her glove and raised her hand so the two sapphires twinkled in the candlelight.

'If he has no intention of marrying me, why did Lord Bingfield give me this ring?' Sophie asked, twisting her hand to and fro so everyone could see it. 'And my behaviour this very evening? You must forgive the extravagant display earlier, but how often does a woman accept a proposal from the man of her dreams?'

Sir Vincent spluttered, but no sound came from his throat. The gathered crowd, however, gave a long collective sigh.

She put her hand on Richard's arm and forced her feet to move away from the scene where Sir Vincent was now surrounded by various people intent on getting their penny's worth in before he was hustled out of the ballroom. It would appear he was not as well liked or thought of as he'd boasted.

A great crowd of people surrounded them, blocking Sophie's view. The men wrung Richard's hand, offering congratulations, while the women all wanted to admire the ring. Everyone said how delighted they were with the outcome. One or two of the ladies confessed that it was the most romantic thing they had ever seen and wasn't Lord Bingfield the epitome of a hero. Sophie found it harder and harder to mouth the words about how much in love they were and how sudden and totally thrilling it was.

Her head started to spin and she gave a helpless look at Richard. He appeared to understand instantly and ushered her away to a small antechamber, the very model of a solicitous fiancé. Her heart did a queer leap as her body instantly responded to his touch and she knew her cheeks flamed worse than before.

Once they were away from the crowds, he removed his hand. Sophie sank down on a chair and waved her fan frantically, hoping Richard would think it was speaking to all the well-wishers, rather than his touch, which had caused her high colour. The cool breeze did much to restore her equilibrium.

'My knees threatened to give way out there. The number of people who wanted to congratulate us was simply astonishing. I didn't anticipate there would have been so many interested in my ring. The news of our betrothal seems to have spread like wildfire. The redoubtable Miss Ravel has captured the Rake.'

He stood with his back to her, making it impossible for her to tell his true feelings. 'Interesting and dramatic tittle-tattle has a way of doing that. Particularly when you announced things in the way you did.'

'I've recovered from my faint,' Sophie said firmly. She refused to apologise for her actions. Surely Richard had to see they were positively inspirational. 'The crush overwhelmed me. So many people demanded to see my ring that I struggled to breathe.'

'Your timing was impeccable both in leaving the crowd and earlier when we left Putney,' he said, turning around to look at her. His eyes glowed with a sort of admiration. 'Well played, Miss Ravel. Very well played indeed.'

'Yes, I was rather proud of the way I handled Sir Vincent, particularly the final flourish.' Sophie leant forwards. 'I simply had not accounted for how many people were listening in.'

A smile tugged at the corner of his mouth. 'I quite like the thought of being someone's dream, although it gives me a lot to live up to.'

Sophie primly folded her hands in her lap. Perhaps her word choice had been extravagant, but it had utterly crushed Sir Vincent.

'A figure of speech, that is all,' she said, meeting his gaze full on. 'I never thought you would hit Sir Vincent.'

'I saw the opportunity and seized it. The punch was long overdue.'

Sophie pressed her lips together. She had to remember that Richard had his own reasons for wanting to hit Sir Vincent. It had nothing to do with her and her troubles, but what had passed between the pair years ago. He had no finer feelings for her. She was simply the means to the end of exacting revenge on Sir Vincent. Because he had made a vow. She was a duty rather than a pleasure.

Drawing a steadying breath, she stood. It was imperative to keep her wits about her and not to start believing in the romantic fantasy she had spun for various female acquaintances in the crowd of well-wishers. She knew precisely the sort of man Richard Crawford was and she'd be a fool to forget it.

'My father used to say that opportunities are to be used, rather than lamented about later. You make your luck. Thankfully everything went the way I hoped. Sir Vincent is utterly destroyed.'

'With a little assistance from me.'

She smiled up at him. 'Some very welcome assistance. I couldn't have done it without you. Cynthia's parents will hear of tonight's events. They may not be so quick to offer one of their daughters up as Sir Vincent predicted. A fantastic victory.'

'Do you play croquet?'

'On occasion.' She tilted her head and regarded his features. 'It is the latest craze. We brought a set back from the Great Exhibition. I spent last summer in Corbridge perfecting my technique. I used to play cricket and was quite handy with the bat. It felt good to be hitting a ball again.'

'I suspect you give no mercy to your opponents.'

'I enjoy winning, but I don't grind my opponents in the ground like some.'

'We must play some time.'

'It might be a pleasant way to pass the time.' Sophie hesitated. The time had come to end their fake engagement and put temptation beyond reach. 'I must warn you, Lord Bingfield, that what I said last night remains true. I have no intention of giving up my reputation, even for a man like yourself who did save me. I fear we must soon part.'

His finely chiselled features frowned. 'Do you wish to go home?'

'Now that tonight's performance has ended?' Sophie stopped and replaced her glove, covering up her ring. She had only worn the ring for a short while, but she would be sorry to give it back.

'I am at your disposal.' He inclined his head. 'Most women would be overwhelmed by what just occurred. No one will remark when we leave.'

Sophie froze, considering. Did he mean that he wanted her to stay or that he thought a woman of delicate sensibilities would have to leave the ball immediately? Her backbone was made of far sterner stuff, but she could see how leaving would make matters easier. 'Before you hit him, Sir Vincent as good as admitted to me that it was he who had informed the papers. I doubt he will try that again. Should he attempt to ruin me, I can point to tonight's events as a reason why his poison should not be believed. Our engagement is finished. I can leave on my own if you wish to stay.'

She waited for his agreement. His frown increased.

'Your actions do mean we are tied to each other for a while longer.' A tiny smile played on his lips. 'Becoming engaged to your dream man meant you forgot your sensibilities. Your words, not mine. Consider what will happen if you jilt me tomorrow. Consider what the press will say then. Will you be known as a flighty heiress?'

Sophie gulped. She could see the headline now. 'They were a figure of speech, an added flourish.'

'Added little flourishes can have grave consequences, Miss Ravel. Perhaps you should think before you act.'

She bowed her head, acknowledging the truth in his words. 'I can hardly jilt you tonight or any time soon. I shall have to wait until the furore dies down.'

'It may take weeks or even months.' His eyes glittered amber. 'The episode has ensured that the engagement will be on everyone's lips tomorrow morning. Various members of the gutter press were in the crowd. Our engagement will be the lead item in the gossip columns throughout the land. "The Redoubtable captures the Rake" has a certain resonance. Prior to your intervention, I had thought "Lord exposes caddish behaviour" or, better still, "blackmailer".'

Sophie winced. He had exposed a fatal flaw in her actions and had stated very clearly that he could not wait to be rid of her. Only now they were shackled together. Her doing, not his. All of his actions had been designed to take revenge on Putney and he had nearly succeeded in provoking a duel. Now, she had inadvertently prolonged the time they had to spend together.

'It was the killing blow. I could not be certain your scheme would work,' she argued.

'You failed to think. Emotion carried you.' He looked down at her. 'It carries you still. Luckily, I still possess my faculties. We will have to spend more time in each other's company, pretending that our engagement is one of the great love stories, or we shall be exposed as cheats.'

Sophie put her hand on her stomach and tried to stop her insides roiling. She would have to dance with him again. She would have to pretend to be besotted. And there would be no expectation of marriage if she gave in to his charm. 'I would like to return home now. Will you please find my stepmother and make the necessary arrangements? We can discuss how long our engagement must continue at a later date. My head pains me too much to think straight.'

Richard struggled to control his temper as the carriage stopped outside Miss Ravel's house. There were things which needed to be said between Sophie and him, but Mrs Ravel sat squarely between them. Mrs Ravel kept up a steady stream of conversation, seemingly oblivious to the stony silence from Sophie.

It was far from his fault that the engagement had been announced in the way it was. That was entirely her doing. There again, it had prevented him from beating Putney into a bloody pulp.

The sight of Putney's hand restraining Sophie had filled him with a primitive anger. He had wanted to murder him for daring to even look at Sophie, let alone touch her in that fashion. His actions had nothing to do with the past and everything to do with Sophie.

'There is no need to see us in, Lord Bingfield,' Sophie said, alighting from the carriage before he had a chance to hold out his hand and help her down.

'There is every need,' Richard retorted silkily, managing to swallow his annoyance. Despite her public declaration, in private, Sophie made it all too clear how she felt about him. 'I could hardly allow my fiancée or her stepmother to make their way home without being there to ensure their safety.'

What made it worse was that he had to accept all the congratulations, knowing that the woman beside him could not wait to be rid of him.

He had never considered that he was like his father and would lose his reason over a woman, but now it seemed he had. His feelings tonight made a mockery of his proposal. No finer feelings. He definitely wanted to hold Sophie in his arms again and feel her lips tremble under his. He wanted to unlock the passion he glimpsed again tonight when they had waltzed.

Sophie pointed. 'We can easily make it to our door, Lord Bingfield. You can see the door from where you are standing.'

'Sophie!' Mrs Ravel exclaimed. 'Where are your manners tonight? First you insist on leaving before I finish my hand at whist and now you seek to dismiss your fiancé like a lackey.'

'The upset at the Assembly Rooms has quite turned my brain.' Sophie inclined her head. 'I merely meant Lord Bingfield did not need to feel obliged. He has done so much for us tonight.

It would be wrong for us to presume further. I didn't want to put him to any trouble.'

'I am sure it is no trouble, Sophie. Is it, Lord Bingfield?'

Richard silently blessed Mrs Ravel. Sophie's earlier caution in confiding in her stepmother had resulted in him gaining a valuable ally, one which he intended to exploit fully. Everything was fair in this battle between him and Sophie's fears. He intended to win and unlock her passion. He wanted to see what she'd be like when she forgot herself.

He could not remember when a woman had intrigued him as much. She made him forget about his family and his reasons for being in Newcastle.

'It is not an obligation, but a pleasure,' Richard added smoothly.

Mrs Ravel shook her head. 'I do wonder about young people these days. Not an ounce of romance in their soul. You two may say your goodnights in the drawing room. I am quite weary and will take myself off to bed. I do trust you, Sophie. Lord Bingfield, if Sophie failed to inform you—tomorrow and every Thursday is our At Home.'

'I am grateful for the intelligence, Mrs Ravel.' Richard gave Sophie a hard look. If she thought

she'd get rid of him that easily, she had another
think coming. He intended to exploit the situation to his advantage and see what the woman
Sophie tried to hide was like. 'Sophie and I obviously have had other things on our minds. I'll
make a note of it, but I can't make any promises.'

Sophie marched ahead of him into the drawing room, her skirt slightly swaying to reveal
her slender ankles. She stopped to turn up the
gas lamps, bathing the room in a soft light before facing him with her arms crossed and blue
eyes glowing like star sapphires.

'What was that little demonstration with my
stepmother in aid of? A goodnight in the carriage would have sufficed.'

Richard assessed her with half-closed eyes.
She was attracted to him and he would get her
to admit it. Tonight. 'You haven't informed your
stepmother of our arrangement. I would hardly
wish for her to think ill of me. It would be impolite to miss an At Home simply for lack of
knowledge. It might cause speculation. I believe
there has been more than enough speculation
and gossip recently. If you are not careful, people will begin to look at your waistline.'

She flushed scarlet. 'That…that is an impossibility.'

'You were the one who uttered the words

about our impulsive marriage, not I. Women who have found their dream man often forget their sensibilities.'

She gave a decisive nod and removed her gloves. 'My stepmother has gone upstairs. There is no need for you to linger. Or indeed for you to appear at the At Home at all. We can slowly drift away. It will provide an excuse for me jilting you. Ultimately you can forget some important function. Isn't that what men like you do? Selfishly put their own needs above others?'

Her words stung. Women had flung the words at him before, but generally when he ended the association.

He recalled the gossip of the Northern Counties Club about her icy behaviour. Was it him or all men? He clenched his fist and wanted to murder whichever man had sown the seeds of distrust.

'There is every need,' he said smoothly, plucking a stray thread from her shoulder. 'Your stepmother said your next At Home was tomorrow. For your sake, I need to be there.'

Sophie slapped her gloves against her hand. 'What is your prediction for my stepmother's At Home? They are not very well attended. The great and the good often have other calls to make.'

'It will be full to bursting with well-wishers, people who have grudges and simply the curious, all wanting to know about the great romance and when our next appearance as a couple will be. The polite ones will only stay fifteen minutes, hoping to see us together in their allotted time, but the curious will find an excuse to linger and see if your unknown bridegroom-to-be puts in an appearance or if it was all fustian nonsense.'

A faint line appeared between Sophie's perfect brows and the tapping stopped as she considered his words. 'I sincerely doubt it. True, people will speculate of course. I will concede your point—in light of tonight's events the At Home will be more crowded than usual. I will have the footmen put out extra chairs. But no one will want to meet you or send invitations for the both of us.'

'I shall rearrange my plans.' He paused, watching her digest the news. 'My friends will understand why I have decided to linger in Newcastle for an indefinite period. There was an expectation I would attend a house party in Hampshire next week.'

There was no need to tell Sophie that he had written declining the invitation, before he went to see her this morning and proposed marriage.

The woman who had invited him had expected him to continue to grace her bed. After meeting Sophie, such sport with another woman held no attraction.

He simply refused to allow Sophie to have a hold over him. This wasn't about love or romance, but satisfying his curiosity. When it was over, he'd walk away with his heart intact and the knowledge that he'd solved the puzzle of Sophie.

'I've no wish to interrupt your plans and be a bother,' she said, turning towards the fire. 'You were right earlier when you said I didn't think. You must go if that is what you wish to do. If invitations do come, the disappointment of you not attending will make it easier to explain the breach when it comes.'

'If we have a breach too quickly, Putney's words will be remembered,' he reminded her. 'I did make a vow that I would not be used as an instrument of your downfall. With each new scheme you propose, you make it easier for him. I am the one with experience. You are a novice.'

She covered her mouth. 'I hadn't considered...'

'Next time do. It is not just your reputation at stake here, but mine—'

'Won't the woman mind?'

He shrugged. 'I was looking for an excuse to end it. The affair was pleasant while it lasted, but she had begun to bore me. I dislike being bored.'

Her cheeks coloured at the remark. 'I...I hadn't thought. I know very little about such matters.'

His shoulders relaxed. Sophie was truly innocent and unlike his normal sort of woman. In her company, he'd been exasperated, amused, bemused, but never bored.

'I gave you my word that I would not pursue another woman while we are together,' he said. 'When I am interested in a woman, my interest stays on her. When it is finished, it is done, with no regrets or backward glances on my part. But I always inform the woman first.'

He clamped his mouth shut. He never allowed regrets. Leaving was far better than being left. And he knew while there might be a few tears, it was always hurt pride, rather than actual feelings. Since Mary, he'd never permitted himself to fall for an inexperienced woman.

She dipped her head and did not meet his eyes. 'Other people have. The woman can be the last to know.'

Silently he once more cursed the man who had made her so wary. He wanted to run him through for causing Sophie to doubt her charms and power. And an unexpected surge of jealousy went through him. She should not be comparing him to such a cad.

He went over to her and raised her chin so that she was staring directly into his face. She did not pull away.

'I am not other men, Sophie Ravel,' he said in a soft voice. 'Why should I want to pursue other women when the world thinks I am engaged to you?'

'Because...' Her tongue flicked out, moistening her lips and turning them to the colour of ripe cherries. 'Because we are not truly engaged.'

'I would hardly dishonour any fiancée in that way, particularly not one I'd sworn to protect. Whatever you might think of me, know I keep my promises.'

Giving in to temptation, he bent his head and tasted her lips.

This time, they trembled under his and parted slightly, inviting him to prolong the kiss. Before deepening the kiss, he brought his arms about her, pulling her close so that her body collided with his, just as he had longed to do ever since they had waltzed together. It fitted perfectly— her curves meeting his hard planes in exactly the right places. She melted further, opening her mouth wide so that he delved his tongue in. He tasted. There was something so right about her taste, something that had been missing from his life. He hadn't known he needed it until that instant and the longing frightened him.

With the last vestige of self-control, he raised his head and put her from him. He drew a ragged breath and resisted the overwhelming urge to take one more taste.

She looked up at him with uncomprehending eyes as her chest heaved. And he knew what he was destined to dream about tonight—Sophie naked in his arms. This was desire and nothing more. His shoulders relaxed. He understood desire.

Once he'd solved the puzzle of her, it would fade. He touched her cheek, enjoying its petal softness.

She looped a strand of hair about one shell-like ear, making a pretence of icy fortitude. 'What…what was that about?'

'There, that is how I say goodnight to my fiancée.' He inclined his head. 'Remember that the next time you wish to make an accusation about my habits, or believe yourself unworthy. You are my fiancée and I refuse to expose you to ridicule.'

Chapter Six

The last place Sophie wanted to be was at her stepmother's At Home. Crowded At Homes generally made her feel as though she was some exotic beast on show for the masses and this week was worse than usual.

She had lost track of the number of people who just happened to call, most with congratulations about the engagement. And those who had not bothered to read today's editions were soon apprised of the fact by others in the room. As she had predicted, 'The Redoubtable captures the Rake' was the lead item.

Everyone wanted to meet the prospective bridegroom and hear the thrilling tale of a whirlwind romance which had turned into the engagement of the Season, if not the year!

Richard had been right. Their engagement was now an established fact. She couldn't cancel it without seeming flighty or, worse still, a liar. She was well and truly trapped in a scheme of her own making. Worse, he had not put in an appearance.

She found herself watching the door and the clock, but the minutes were slipping by. The At Home would end without an appearance from him.

She wanted to run and hide and not face the humiliation of his non-show, but she felt guilty for even thinking of the idea. A Ravel always met her social obligations. The fact had been drilled into her at a young age when she'd hidden behind a curtain rather than meet one of her father's business associates. So she smiled and asked after various children and elderly relatives and hoped no one else noticed that Richard wasn't there and she had declined to give a time or date for the engagement party which her stepmother loudly proclaimed would be happening soon.

Sophie forcibly turned her gaze from the front door, tilted her head and graciously enquired after a neighbour's son who was cutting his first tooth. If she concentrated on other people, then maybe she'd forget the deepening hole inside and all the doubts and what ifs.

'Lady Parthenope will be arriving momentarily,' her stepmother's latest butler declared in an overly theatrical fashion. 'Her carriage has been spotted.'

Her stepmother went red with pleasure. Sophie excused herself and hurried over to her stepmother, putting her hand on her stepmother's sleeve. 'Is there some reason that Lady Parthenope has come to call? I wasn't aware you are intimates.'

'I sent her a note, dear, after you refused to allow me to go to her tea,' her stepmother explained with the sort of smile which could light up a thousand ballrooms. 'It seemed the right thing to do. She is dear Bingfield's only female relation in the neighbourhood. I wanted her advice on the engagement party. I do hope she gives me a moment to compose myself before she finally appears. I declared I'm all at sixes and sevens. It is worse than waiting for the Queen.'

'Her advice on the engagement party?' Sophie put her hand on her stepmother's sleeve. Composing herself for Lady Parthenope would have to wait. She needed to know precisely the full horror of what her stepmother had done.

'It needs to be an event of glittering magnitude. There again, perhaps the aristocracy do things differently. I do want to be guided, my dear, and Henri is away in Europe. People have expectations.'

'You have written to Henri!' Sophie's heart sank. She had hoped to present the entire episode as an amusing anecdote when Henri and Robert returned with their two young children, but her stepmother had closed that door.

'I thought she'd want to know.' Mrs Ravel peered around her and motioned to the footman to move several tables and chairs. 'I do think it bad of Lord Bingfield not to call. I had wanted a chance to quiz him about it as well. After all, it will be his engagement party, too.'

'You sent Lord Bingfield a note about the party?' The complete horror of what her stepmother had done penetrated Sophie's brain. Any engagement party would make things worse. They would have to be there as a couple in love. She might even start depending on him to be there. But she had no idea of how to stop it. Her stepmother's juggernaut would flatten everything in its path.

'First thing this morning while you were showing your new maid your clothes. Is there any reason I shouldn't? Sophie, have you entirely forgotten your manners?' Her stepmother waved a hand. 'And invitations have been arriving all morning along with an unsigned postcard from Liverpool. You and Lord Bingfield will be much in demand, I am happy to say, but where is he? It is most vexing.'

'Lord Bingfield will call when he has the time.' Sophie concentrated on the teacup. Cynthia arriving in Liverpool was the best news she had had all day. She had to remember that Cynthia's love was true. She and her intended had known each other for months before they eloped. Sophie knew she had to hang on to the thought, rather than dreaming about Richard and his goodnight kiss. Desire did not make a love match. Desire did not mean she actually liked him. *It didn't mean she disliked him, either*, a little voice whispered.

She narrowed her eyes. 'How many others did you happen to ask for advice about this engagement party?'

Her stepmother counted on her fingers. 'Fourteen, maybe seventeen. It depends on who you count. Miss Smith and her sister were visiting Mrs Butterworth when I happened to mention the engagement yesterday. They were the ones who suggested a party. It is not as if I am spreading lies, Sophie. You are going to marry

Viscount Bingfield and will eventually be a marchioness.'

'An engagement has been agreed,' Sophie corrected. 'There is a difference. You know how many engagements were broken last year.'

'Hornswoggle. Last night anyone with half an eye could see how entranced you were with each other when you waltzed. And then your declaration after Lord Bingfield punched that dreadful toad Sir Vincent Putney. It made my heart thrill. Romance truly does live. Your father would be fit to burst.'

'You shouldn't have done it, Stepmother, without consulting me.'

'Mrs Butterworth was overly proud last year when her eldest daughter married a baronet. You being married to a viscount will be just the sort of setdown she needs. You will take precedence. My stepdaughter, one of the higher-ranking peers, just as your father always dreamt.'

'But I would have preferred to have been consulted about this party first. You have no idea whether Lord Bingfield wants a party or not.'

'It is why I want to speak to him.' Her stepmother patted Sophie's hand. 'People always speculate. In any case, most of the people here I didn't mention the party to, but everyone is asking about it.'

'I wonder why that is.'

'It will have to be a glittering affair. Your father did love a good party. Imagine if Lord Hallington attended. A living marquess in this house!'

'We haven't agreed on the settlement yet.' Sophie lifted her cup to her lips. This entire affair seemed to have taken a life of its own. She had to begin to sow seeds of doubt or her stepmother would take to her bed for weeks when Richard and she broke it off. And what better place with all these people attending the At Home? Sophie raised her voice slightly. 'I shouldn't have even shown my ring last night. It was wrong of me. Premature. My father would be appalled at my lack of prudence. Perhaps Robert Montemorcy, my former guardian, should be consulted before this goes further.'

Sophie glanced about the room which was now filled with an expectant hush, awaiting Lady Parthenope's arrival. Seed sown, her job was done.

Her stepmother gave a little frown. 'I suppose you are right. I will put the party off until later in the year.'

'Once it has been announced officially, then we can plan the party, properly with Henri. You know what an expert she is with such things.'

Sophie nodded towards the door. 'You must go greet Lady Parthenope. It would not do to keep her ladyship waiting.'

Her stepmother's ribbons trembled. 'What shall I say to her?'

'Hello?' Sophie offered with a faint laugh, but her stepmother's agitation only increased.

Lady Parthenope swept into the room and nearly knocked over a table of china pugs as the entire room fell silent and teacups were poised halfway to the lips. Sophie watched fascinated as her stepmother warred with two emotions— the desire to protect her china collection and the pride that so illustrious a personage should visit her house. In the end, pride won out. She hurriedly waved towards the china-dog table, which the butler moved without saying a word, and the background of a busy At Home recommenced.

'I shan't beat about the bush,' Lady Parthenope said after she had greeted her stepmother. 'Is it true you intend to give a party to celebrate your engagement to my nephew? I would have thought informing a family circle would be the first order of business before you announced to all and sundry, but what do I know about young people these days? The manners are all so different from when I was young after the war.

Then things were done in a certain fashion or not at all.'

'It is something you will need to consult with your nephew about—why he asked before getting your permission to marry,' Sophie replied and was pleased the words came out far more assured than she felt inside. 'I would hardly like to break a confidence. You must understand that, Lady Parthenope, and these matters, much as we hope otherwise, are often fraught with inner peril. My stepmother is perhaps over-eager with the plans for a party, but they are far from well advanced.'

'Humph,' Lady Parthenope said with a glacial frown. She turned and began to greet the other women, asking after various relations or mutual acquaintances.

Sophie noted with no small amount of admiration that the woman appeared to know how to greet everyone graciously. She had to wonder if Lady Parthenope had always been like this or if she had ever hidden behind a curtain. No, she decided, Lady Parthenope belonged to that special breed of woman who was always sure in any social situation.

'I see you wasted no time, Aunt, in making your acquaintance with my intended's family,' Lord Bingfield said as he came into the room.

His frock-coat was immaculate and he seemed to fill the drawing room. She noticed the way his hair curled about his temple and how the cut of his coat showed off his hips. Their eyes locked and a slow smile spread over his face.

Realising she was staring, Sophie hurriedly set down her teacup, managing to slosh the liquid on to her hand. Painfully obvious. The sudden heat jolted her back to reality. She winced, knowing her cheeks must be flushed. She was behaving worse than some débutante who was only a few weeks into her first Season. She was a veteran of four and knew better than to respond to men like Lord Bingfield. She had made so many mistakes in their short acquaintance.

'Someone had to, dear boy. Your father is hardly likely to travel to the north. And the less said about your mother's side of the family, the better, in my opinion,' Lady Parthenope pronounced.

'Finally you appear, Lord Bingfield. Sophie has been counting the minutes,' her stepmother cooed, much to Sophie's surprise and annoyance.

Her stepmother made it sound as though she had nothing better to do than to moon over him. Things were problematic enough with Lord Bingfield getting ideas about how she might feel about him. Her stepmother's triumphant look did nothing to calm Sophie's nerves.

'My pleasure, Mrs Ravel.' He bowed low over her stepmother's hand. 'I regret the slight delay, but what does that matter as I am here now? I am at your disposal, Mrs Ravel. Who would you like me to meet first? Your friends all appear charming and I don't want to get the order of precedence wrong.'

His smile spread over the entire gathering. Her normally poised stepmother turned a shade of red, highly akin to beetroot, while a gaggle of her stepmother's friends gave barely concealed sighs. His voice was the sort that warmed your toes, oozing superficial charm.

Sophie frowned and concentrated on the alabaster vase containing a bouquet of wax flowers. She'd be wrong to forget that it was superficial, pretty to look at but having no real substances, and the fact that this was all an act. She knew precisely what happened when the charm faded and the rake in question was turned down.

Her temple throbbed slightly. She refused to go back to that inn. She had ceased to be that carefree girl years ago. Real and honest love took months, if not years, to develop and he had been quite honest about not having finer feelings for her. She was not going to believe in the romance of it all. She had to be the practical one and search for other opportunities to sow seeds of doubt, so that when the end came, it would not cause her stepmother to take to her bed for weeks.

Richard accepted a cup of tea from her step-mother and came over to her. Her nerves pulsed with warmth. She found it impossible to forget the way his mouth had tasted when he'd kissed her last night.

She concentrated on the spill and tried to think of something else beside him and the way his shoulders filled out his frock-coat.

'Do you need a handkerchief, Miss Ravel?'

His heady scent of balsam mixed with a sub-tle spice wafted over her, tickling her nose. And she inhaled deeply, savouring it, but then recol-lected where she was, sat up straighter and fixed him with her eye.

'Everything is under control. I knocked the cup a little. I am fully capable of cleaning up my own messes.'

'I would hate to think anything untoward hap-pened to your delicate flesh.' He came over and took her hand. His brow furrowed as his palm brushed her ring finger before releasing it. A subtle caress. 'You are wearing the ring.'

Sophie fought against the temptation to flee.

He knew precisely what he was doing. He had played this sort of *double entendre* game with countless other females. It would be wrong of her to think otherwise. 'I felt it best. Everyone wanted to see it. Even if it is tempting fate to wear it.'

'Fate?' A dimple played in the corner of his mouth, reminding her that her dreams had been full of that mouth and the way it tasted.

'Nothing has been settled until certain agreements have been reached,' she said decisively, banishing the thought.

He raised her hand to his lips. The tiniest touch, but enough to make her stomach flutter and the heat rise on her cheeks. She tried to tell herself that every woman had that sort of reaction to him, but it didn't make it any easier.

'It will be settled to our mutual benefit,' he said, releasing her hand. 'You have my word on that. From now on wear it with pride and stop worrying.'

The room chose that moment to fall silent. Sophie winced and knew the colour in her cheeks flamed higher.

'You see, Sophie,' her stepmother crowed. 'What did I say! Settlements can be easily achieved when a couple is in love.'

'I apologise.' Sophie gestured about the room. 'It was quite unnecessary of you to call.'

'We must disagree. It was completely necessary. I gave my word.' He inclined his head. 'If you would manipulate public opinion, Miss Ravel, the public do have to have something to talk about. It is far better that they discuss our engagement, rather than anything else about either of us.'

'You make it sound like you are an expert.'

His eyes glinted like hard glass. 'I had to learn. You were the one who increased the stakes.'

'I will remember it for the next time and bow to your expertise.'

'You may run along, then,' he said, touching her sleeve. 'I still have to greet a variety of other ladies, but my duties here must be short.'

'And do what?' Sophie put her hand on her hip. How dare he order her about! 'The At Home is in its dying throes. I suspect once this lot have finished, we will not get any more callers. My stepmother has the tea and coffee under control.'

'Grab your hat and cloak, of course. Unless you wish to have more gossip in the papers. I have a new pair of horses and a carriage up from Tattersalls. I want to put them through their paces in the northern air.'

'Do you drive?'

'I leave that to others but I do know the difference between a good carriage horse and an unsuitable one.' A dimple played in the corner of his mouth. 'Unless you are frightened to be seen with me?'

'I welcome it.'

Richard stood in the hallway. He struggled to remember when he'd last enjoyed himself so much. Gently tweaking Sophie Ravel's pretence of cold hauteur so that she was forced to reveal her inner passion was his new favourite sport. He wanted to explore her layers and find out more. He looked forward to it. He could not be sorry that circumstances forced them to spend time with each other.

'Have you written to your father, Richard, informing him of your proposed alliance?' his aunt said, coming into the hallway.

'You are departing so soon, Aunt Parthenope?'

'One stays precisely fifteen minutes. Always. I know the timing exactly. One should never be seen to regard a clock.' His aunt sniffed. 'You are leaving too soon.'

'I will bear that in mind.' Richard pointed towards the drawing room. 'The crush was overly heavy. I'm waiting for Sophie.'

'The girl is perfectly acceptable if one's taste is for icy blondes, but the stepmother...' His aunt lowered her voice. 'Have you seen the décor? Your father would turn puce. Far too much china. Far too much chintz. Her manner is far too fine.'

'Mrs Ravel is a perfectly charming lady. Sophie knows her own mind about decoration and fashion, just as she knows her own mind about me.' Richard forced a smile over a tremor of horror. He did not want to think about his father travelling to Newcastle and the complications that it would bring.

His relationship with Sophie had nothing to do with his family. She belonged to another part of his life, separate and distinct from his duty towards his family.

He had taken the time to move into a well-appointed set of rooms on Granger Street this morning. Luckily, for once, his mother had agreed with his caution, although her reasoning differed from his.

'My father will adore Sophie once he meets her. Does he have plans to travel here?'

'Who knows what your father will do?' His aunt made a disapproving noise. 'He is a law unto himself, but I have every reason to think that he will not set foot in Newcastle. I, myself, have tried to persuade him for years to visit our mother's grave, but he has always refused. His pigs must come before everything. I swear he uses them as an excuse to avoid doing his duty.'

'My father is a man of steadfast devotion to his pigs.'

His aunt fixed him with a stare and he had to wonder if she had guessed his true reason for being up in Newcastle. 'I shall have to write to your father about this fiancée of yours. You understand why it is necessary, I hope. The best that can be said for her stepmother is that she is no conversationalist.'

'You do that. It will not change the outcome, Aunt.' Richard nodded towards the stairs. 'Here comes my intended, Aunt. I would hate to think you had caused her one moment of distress.'

His aunt put her hand over his. 'Any wife of yours should be a credit to our family and its standing. You must not allow love to cloud your judgement.'

'We are agreed on that. Love will never do that.'

Richard went towards Sophie, who looked absolutely fetching in her dark-blue leghorn bonnet and matching cloak, truly a breath of fresh air and peace in his turbulent life.

She did not have any side in his parents' war. He'd learnt a long time ago that explaining about his family only made him feel uncomfortable and awkward rather than contributing anything meaningful. He saw no reason to break the habit with Sophie.

'Where are these horses?' Sophie asked with a pretty smile after his aunt departed.

'Waiting outside. Will you be bringing your maid?' he enquired, wondering how much further he'd push her today. She would melt.

Sophie hesitated, understanding what he was asking. It would be prudent to have someone else there to prevent things getting out of hand, but it would also mean speaking in front of her. She could hardly explain about the party débâcle with someone listening in.

'We are an acknowledged couple.'

He tucked her hand into his arm. 'So I am given to understand. I promise to be on my best behaviour.'

'My maid hasn't been with us very long and she has a pile of mending to do.'

'I understand entirely now. Do you go through servants easily? I only ask because your butler appeared quite new.'

He made it seem as though she was careless. 'My stepmother does demand the best, but normally I keep my maids unless they marry. My last one ran away with the underfootman from two houses down. Jane has only been with us for two weeks.'

'And you have no idea if she is reliable,' he said, handing her into the smart carriage.

'Precisely.' Sophie turned towards him. 'I have no idea if she can be tempted to tell her story to the papers. Such things have been known to happen.'

'With great regularity.' The dimple showed in the corner of his mouth. He stretched slightly and his arm came around the back of the seat. Sophie sat straighter.

He gestured to the coachman, who started off abruptly and she was jolted back against the seat and his arm, which instantly tightened about her. She gave him a sideways glance, certain he had arranged the incident. His hand squeezed her shoulder, sending a warm pulse through her before he removed it.

'I'm pleased with your foresight,' he said. 'What did you want to speak to me about? What has agitated you? You were positively clinging to that teacup with a death grip.'

Sophie gulped. He had noticed! It made it

worse that he'd noticed. She could almost think he cared. She pulled her bonnet forwards so that it covered her face. 'Was I that obvious?'

'Only to me. My aunt takes unholy glee in making people agitated and upset. It provides her chief amusement.' He put his hand over hers and squeezed it. 'You appeared perfectly in control to everyone else, I am sure.'

Sophie swallowed hard and withdrew her hand from his. She concentrated on looking out the carriage window. Every time they met, she found a reason to like him more. He said precisely the right thing to reassure her, but how hard was that? Men like him did these things for one purpose only—seduction.

'I need to apologise for my stepmother and her engagement-party scheme,' she said before she lost her nerve or he developed the wrong idea about why she'd agreed to come without a chaperon. 'She had the idea fixated in her brain. I had no idea she entertained the notion…until it was too late.'

'And you haven't told her the truth.'

'How could I!' Sophie turned slightly and faced him. He had to understand about her stepmother and her kind heart. 'I planned to say something this morning, but my stepmother was preoccupied with the At Home arrangements. I want to let her down gently, Richard. My step-mother means well. She made this promise to my father on his deathbed…and she sees this as a gold opportunity to fulfil it. My father… my father made his own fortune. He wanted his daughter to live like a princess.'

Richard said nothing for a while and Sophie listened to the wheels of the carriage turning, hating that she'd confessed about her father's naked ambition.

'My aunt has obviously written to my father,' he said when her nerves were at breaking point. 'We will have to instruct our various men of business to begin drawing up the settlement.'

Sophie blinked hard. 'Excuse me?'

'During the At Home, you made some re-marks about settlements.'

Sophie fiddled with the lace edge of her glove, rather than meet his eyes. Her posturing at the At Home seemed ill conceived now that he was here, questioning her on it. 'I thought it a kinder way of sowing doubt. I don't want my stepmother to be too disappointed…when it ends.'

He raised an eyebrow and Sophie knew what he had tactfully not said. The only way she could keep her stepmother from being disappointed now was to actually marry him. She wished she had considered her stepmother's reaction before embarking on this adventure.

'You are reluctant to tell your stepmother the truth, particularly in light of her extreme reaction.'

She gave a hesitant nod.

'Then there is only one course of action. You must instruct your man of business straight away. The matter of settlement must be seen to be being addressed. I shall instruct my solicitors.' He named a very well-known London firm. 'My father always uses them. He would think something amiss if I didn't. I will trust you to make the appropriate outrageous demands.'

She stared at him in wonderment. He actually had the perfect solution to the problem, one she'd never ask, assuming he'd reject it out of hand. She swallowed hard and attempted to puzzle out the implications. 'You intend to keep your father in ignorance as well?'

'You would hardly want him replying to your stepmother when she writes to him.' He paused and gave her a hard look. 'And you know your stepmother will...if the letter isn't already in the post. My father is not a man to mince words, Sophie. Neither will he see any reason to lie.'

Sophie closed her eyes. She could readily picture the scene when her stepmother received a terse reply from Richard's father. The blow would destroy her. Utterly and completely. 'It is very kind of you. Unexpectedly kind.'

He raised her hand to his lips. 'I told you that I'd protect you. Why do you harbour so many doubts about my intentions?'

'Because I do.'

Sophie sat up straighter and tried to ignore the way the warmth crept up her arm. Somehow it felt right to have his hand holding hers. And that was very wrong. No good could come of this carriage ride if she allowed liberties.

'I will instruct my solicitor.' She concentrated on taking steadying breaths as the warm tingling feeling increased. It was in moments like these that a woman was most in danger. If she kept her wits about her, she'd survive. She gave her hand a slight tug, but only succeeded in dislodging her bonnet. 'My old guardian is out of the country with his family and will need to look it over before it is approved, of course. My stepmother will understand the delay. It will buy us time.'

'Who was it?' he enquired softly, not letting her hand go. Instead he put his other arm along the back of the seat, almost as if he held her in his arms.

'Who was who?' Sophie edged towards the carriage door.

He released her and leant forwards to straighten her bonnet. 'Who made you so wary of men? Of me?'

Chapter Seven

'You are talking nonsense. Absolute and complete nonsense.' Sophie searched for her reticule and wished she had thought to bring more than a hatpin with her as Richard's question echoed round and round in her brain. He wanted to know why she was terrified of men. It wasn't all men. It was men who were unsafe in carriages.

The carriage suddenly seemed claustrophobic and tiny, and a complete mistake. How could she have thought for one instant she'd be safe with someone like Richard?

Sophie struggled to breathe. The last thing she wanted was to confess about that dreadful night, particularly here in Richard's carriage. The consequences to her reputation could be dreadful if he realised the sort of person she truly was. All the vile words Sebastian called her on that night echoed in her mind.

What if she was truly like those words? What if it wasn't the man, but her? What if she caused men to be unsafe in carriages?

'I have no idea why you said this! I am not wary of men.'

Richard said nothing in reply. He simply looked at her with a steady expression in his eyes. 'Why, Sophie?'

Suddenly it came to her—the logical answer, the perfect answer. Air rushed into her lungs. There was no need for a confession. He need never know what sort of person she was underneath her cold exterior. Bluster and outrage had always served before. She could turn the conversation to his failings.

'Why shouldn't I exercise caution? Everyone knows about men who are *not safe in carriages* and the untold damage they can wreak on a woman's reputation. She might never recover while the man simply moves on to the next unsuspecting soul.' Sophie stabbed a finger at his chest. 'You, Richard, are most definitely *not safe in carriages.* Had the desire to protect my stepmother's feelings not preyed on my mind, I would have refused. I should have refused. We have settled very little and now I wish to return to my home. Immediately.'

Sophie hated the tremor in her voice and that she wanted him to do something to prove once and for all that he was the sort of man she knew he must be.

'You want to believe the worst in me.' Richard's golden gaze peered into her soul, but he kept completely still. 'What have I done? How have I behaved improperly towards you? All I have done is to try to preserve your reputation, rather than seek to destroy it or entice you into bad behaviour.'

Sophie straightened her shoulders and forced an uneasy laugh. 'You have a certain well-deserved reputation. Your exploits are favourite fodder for the scandal-mongers. There is little smoke without fire, as my father used to say. Oh, you might say it is lies, but how much is half the truth?'

'I have never denied my less-than-angelic past, but it is more than that.' He ticked the points off on his fingers. 'You are skittish. You maintain this façade of icy hauteur because you are terrified of any man paying you attention. When you forget, you are full of feisty wit. Someone made you that way. What was his name? You owe it to me for saving your reputation.'

Sophie's mouth went dry. He had guessed. Richard had seen her for what she was—petrified of becoming what Sebastian Cawburn predicted she was. She should have thought. Crawford had a vast amount of experience with women. He had saved her from Sir Vincent's machinations. She owed him the truth.

'Sebastian Cawburn. Lord Cawburn,' she whispered, staring straight ahead, rather than looking him in the eye.

'That old lecher! You are comparing me to him?'

At the exclamation, Sophie rapidly glanced at him. An expression of extreme hurt flickered across his face so quickly that Sophie wondered if she had imagined it.

'Sophie. We are nothing alike. I can't stand the man.'

'Not comparing, exactly,' Sophie admitted. Her grip on her reticule caused her hand to hurt. She should have guessed Richard Crawford would be acquainted with Sebastian. They travelled in similar circles. 'You both enjoy a certain reputation, to put it bluntly. It terrifies me that I might be attracted to someone like him again. That I am destined to repeat my mistakes.'

She closed her eyes and tried to control the trembling in her stomach. There, she had finally said the words out loud. Finally admitted her attraction to him and the impossibility of it going any further.

'Sophie, you wound me. I am nothing like that man.' Richard leant forwards and raised his hands in supplication before her. It hurt more than he liked to admit that Sophie equated him with Sebastian Cawburn. He wanted her to see him for who he was, not who she thought he was.

She simply sat there with her eyes closed.

'He cheats at cards,' Richard continued. 'He maintains two mistresses. He had to flee to the Continent to escape his creditors three months ago. I've done none of those things. Nor will I ever do such things. Believe me, please!'

She cautiously opened her eyes.

'I'm sorry. I can't help it. I refuse to repeat my mistakes. I made a solemn vow.'

'When...when did it happen to you? When did you encounter Cawburn? Tell me that much.' He swallowed hard and tried to control his frustration. Shouting at her would make matters worse, but he wanted to know how she'd become mixed up with Cawburn and what he'd done to her. A primitive urge to do violence to the man filled Richard. Somehow, he'd harmed Sophie. 'Help me to understand why you might be comparing us.'

'It was my first Season. I was naïve.' Sophie raised her chin and he could see tears shimmering in her eyes. She clenched her fists before continuing. 'Lord Cawburn can be very charming when he wants to be, but when he doesn't get his own way, he is…he becomes a violent monster.'

Sophie pressed her hands to her eyes, making a sudden decision. She had to tell him everything, then he'd see why their relationship was doomed and why she refused to act on her attraction to him. He was sure to turn away from her in disgust. It would hurt a little, but better to be hurt now than to be led inexorably towards another room in a seedy inn.

'Go on.' He put his hand on hers. His voice was soothing as if he were speaking to a nervous horse. 'Whatever happens, know I won't be angry with you. I want to understand. It was during your first Season you had the misfortune to encounter Cawburn…'

'I believed his promises. The ones I wanted to, rather than the ones I thought he said as a joke. I should have paid more attention to those ones.' Sophie slowly withdrew her hand from his. He made no attempt to recapture it. He simply looked at her with burning gold eyes that bored deep into her soul.

'It was very flattering,' Sophie said when the silence became too great to bear. 'I was his angel put on the earth. It was exciting to have someone that experienced interested in me. Before that I was Sophie, the one with the awkward hair who could never remember to start on the correct foot during the quadrille. It all went to my head. He kept arranging for us to meet at various balls and entertainments. When my stepmother discovered us in a deserted card room, holding hands, my guardian objected to the match and brought me away, but that only increased my desire for Lord Cawburn. He bribed my maid and sent clandestine letters, declaring his undying devotion. He followed me north. We eloped together at his insistence.'

'But you didn't marry.'

'My guardian and Sebastian's cousin, Henrietta, caught up with us the next day.' Sophie gave a hollow laugh. 'We hadn't even reached Scotland. The carriage had broken down. Trust me to pick someone who couldn't even organise a proper elopement.'

She waited to hear his sarcastic laughter at her youthful folly. Her heart thudded as the only sounds were the turning of the carriage wheels.

'There has never been a whiff of scandal,' he said finally. 'I have never heard that Cawburn eloped with anyone. Not that I don't believe you, but I am at a loss to explain how such a thing was kept out of the papers. Cawburn has never breathed a word of it, either, not even when he was completely pie-eyed after a Derby win. And he is the sort of repellent individual who regularly boasts about his conquests to anyone who might listen. How did you manage it?'

Sophie's shoulders sagged slightly. He believed her story, rather than accusing her of lying. Or worse.

'That was Henri's doing,' she said, leaning forwards. Richard had to understand how grateful she was to Henri Montemorcy. 'She is marvellous at arranging things like that. I shall never know what she said to Lord Cawburn. We've never spoken about it. Henri married my guardian soon after. That part was very romantic. It made me realise the importance of true love versus flattery.'

A primitive surge of anger swept through Richard. Sophie had gone through hell and she'd had to rely on Cawburn's cousin. 'You spent the night with Cawburn. It is an intriguing little fact. I am surprised your guardian didn't insist on a marriage.'

'Henri sorted it out. In the excitement of her marriage to my guardian, my indiscretion was overlooked, just as Henri predicted. Henri is marvellous. She has been so helpful in showing me how to behave correctly.'

'Your guardian's wife must be very good at arranging things.' Richard struggled to contain his anger and frustration. Cawburn had not suffered at all for his part in this. 'Most things like that appear within the first months, if not days. How long has it been since it happened?'

'Nearly four years.'

'Four years! My God, she is better than good. I'd never have thought Cawburn would keep quiet that long. Of course, if he said anything now, who would believe it?' His eyes narrowed. 'Why is it that your guardian did not force the marriage? Even if his brain was love-addled, he had to have appreciated the risks to your reputation.'

Sophie winced. And Richard knew his words had come out too harshly.

'I spent the night barricaded in an inn's upstairs room. I hit Lord Cawburn with a frying pan when he decided to take liberties and, once he left, I pulled a chest of drawers, a trunk and the bed against the door. I sat up all night with the frying pan in my hand. Lord Cawburn came up twice to shout at me through the keyhole, but I refused to open the door until Henri appeared.'

The muscles in Richard's shoulders relaxed. Sophie remained an innocent. He had thought he'd have to go and make sure that Cawburn suffered a slow and painful death, but he'd allow him to live. He would simply use his influence to ensure Cawburn had a frosty welcome when he next turned up in London.

Silently he vowed he'd demonstrate that she was wrong in her assessment of him. He wanted to show beyond a shadow of a doubt that he could never do what Cawburn had done to her. He put all thoughts of seduction from him. Sophie needed a friend, not a lover.

'You hit Cawburn with a frying pan. Thoroughly deserved.' Richard banged his hand on his knee and barely stopped himself from hugging Sophie. Trust her to sort out Cawburn. 'What did he do after you hit him once? Did he take the hint that you were no fragile flower and run?'

'It took three goes, but he went. It is lucky that I know how to play cricket and how to hit the ball hard.'

He laughed out loud.

Sophie smiled back at him. Relief flooded through her. Somehow it made it easier to talk about it. Henri and Robert had never wanted to discuss that night. After they left the inn, Henri told her it was unnecessary as nothing had happened. But it had and Sophie couldn't forget it. Sometimes she woke up with a pounding heart, reaching for the frying pan, trying to get it from her bag and finding her bag empty. 'Three times, but I succeeded in the end.'

He instantly sobered and the fury returned to his face. 'It should have taken him one, but it should never have to come to that. He should have accepted your no. You did say no, Sophie, before you started swinging your frying pan?'

'I screamed it!'

'Good girl. That's what I like to hear.' He patted her shoulder. The tiny gesture of approval sent a pulse of warmth throbbing through her. Richard agreed with her actions. 'But why did you have a frying pan? It is not the usual sort of equipment one carries on an elopement. Are you a keen cook?'

'When we first met, Henri had warned me that her cousin might have difficulties in understanding no. She thought a hatpin wouldn't do, but he might need a frying pan applied to his head. I think she was joking when she said it, but I couldn't be sure. When Sebastian insisted on eloping, I took the frying pan as precaution. I might have been a naïve débutante and inclined to believe flattery, Richard, but I am far from stupid.'

'And what happened afterwards? Once you were rescued? Did no one tell you that it was Cawburn to blame, not you? Did your friends explain that you were young and unused to the ways of rogues and cads?'

Sophie looked at her hands. All sorts of things had been said, but she knew they were easy words. The shame at what she'd done and how she'd behaved rose in her throat. 'Henri told me that I was to forget that it had ever happened. My life was supposed to go on as before. No one would ever know, but I knew. And I have made sure that I am never in situations like that again…until the other night. I thought I was safe. All I was doing was delivering a note from Cynthia. It was the work of a moment. I had no interest in Sir Vincent as a man. Sir Vincent seemed so…so…'

'Infused with gentlemanly virtue?' Richard supplied with a bitter twist to his mouth.

'Exactly, but he wasn't. He…he called me the same sorts of names and threaten—'

A shudder went through her. Her throat worked up and down, but she knew if she continued, she'd break down in tears. She refused to cry, particularly not in front of Richard.

Without a word, he gathered her into his arms and rested his head on top of hers. Unlike the other times he had held her, this time had a quality of caring and comfort to it. The gentleness of his touch made her feel secure. Safe in a way that she had not felt for years, not since the inn. She laid her head on his chest and listened to the steady beat of his heart.

'What did he say to you?' he asked, gently stroking her back. 'Cawburn, I mean. I can guess, but I need to know, Sophie. Can you tell me, please?'

'He turned very nasty and called me all sorts of names. A hell-cat, a she-devil. He said that I had led him on. It was all my fault and that he'd never behave like that around a true lady. I had shown my true breeding—a common whore.'

A single tear trickled down her cheek. She sat up and wiped it away with furious fingers. He silently passed her a handkerchief. She dabbed her eyes and regained control.

'I have made a mess of your shirt front. You must realise that—'

'Hush. They were all lies.' He tilted her face so he looked her directly in the eyes. 'All wicked lies, Sophie, from a cowardly scoundrel. You are the epitome of a lady. You were young. He took advantage of you. Cawburn bears all the blame.

You were and remain the innocent victim who used all the means at your disposal and some brilliant ingenuity. Did he say anything else? Threaten you?'

She gave a brief nod. He might believe that, but she had to wonder, particularly given how much she'd enjoyed Richard's kisses yesterday— was she truly a bad woman who simply played at being good? 'Finally he said that we would have to marry and he'd spend all my money. He'd enjoy seeing me reduced to poverty and dressed in the meanest rags.'

'You can see what a liar he was.' He ticked off the points on his fingers. 'You didn't have to marry. And he most definitely has not spent all your money. You have a sterling reputation and are admired by many people, while he was forced to flee to France to escape his creditors… and I know of at least one incident where he cheated at cards. He was caught red handed and denied it with very great bleats, accusing everyone else, until I drew the card from his boot.'

'You did?'

'A man who will cheat at cards will cheat and lie at anything, and most particularly in love. Think of that the next time you are tempted to believe anything else he said. The reason you enjoy such a good reputation is because you are a good person, Sophie. Everyone is allowed one mistake.'

'It was because of Henri… It was all her doing.'

He shook his head. 'I have never met this Henri, but I know you. No one wields that much power. She might have kept it quiet for a little while, but your subsequent actions ensured silence. You haven't hidden or stopped doing what you pleased. You simply stopped some of the lies he told you. It is time you stopped believing the rest of the filth.'

'I still have nightmares,' Sophie confessed.

'Always with him. Never with me starring in his role.' He pinned her with his gaze. 'You are not frightened of me, are you, Sophie?'

Sophie bit her lip. She could hardly confess to the sort of dreams she was having about him! And how for the past two nights, she had woken with his name on her lips and a deep longing to have his lips against hers. It was trying to make those sorts of dreams real which led to her utter destruction.

'Only with him,' she managed. 'I haven't known you very long.'

'I will never give you a reason to have a nightmare.'

'Thank you.'

'Is there any dream you have given up because of him and his lies?' he asked into the silence which had filled the carriage. 'Something you could do to prove to yourself that he no longer has power over you?'

'I used to enjoy drawing. I was going to be a great painter. He had promised to take me to the Alps so I could paint.' Sophie tried to swallow the hard lump which had formed in her throat. 'I…I had always dreamt of going there on my honeymoon. I wanted to paint the mountains. I read somewhere that the light was good. People used to say that I was quite accomplished. Afterwards, I found it difficult to hold my brush or pen without the feelings of shame and remorse washing over me. Drawing became torture, something I did before. It was like my life was divided into two parts.'

Her limbs started to shake as she struggled to keep control and not allow those feelings to swamp her.

He pulled her back into his arms. 'Hush, now. Your friend didn't put a frying pan to Cawburn's head. You did. And you are safe now. You can go to the Alps and paint if you want to. You don't have to wait for a wedding trip. You can travel, Sophie. It is easy. All you have to do is buy a ticket and go. You mustn't allow a creature like that and his self-serving lies to rule your existence. You allow him to win by doing that. And that is nothing you want.'

She breathed deeply and allowed the crisp masculine scent to fill her nostrils. She'd shed all the tears she needed to over that man and what he'd done to her innocence. Richard was right. She had to start living again. She breathed deeply one more time, made a memory and then sat up.

'Thank you. I will get some new paints when I next go to the shops.' She looped a strand of hair behind her ear. 'The trip might have to wait a while. Perhaps after our engagement is done, I might need to get away to recover. My stepmother might agree. She has always wanted to take the waters.'

A half-smile touched his lips. 'There, better already.'

'Much better.'

'Good.'

His hand stroked her cheek. A warm tingle pulsed through her. He was going to kiss her again. She closed her eyes, parted her lips and hoped.

Rather than kissing her, he gave a great sigh before rapping the carriage roof. The carriage turned around almost immediately.

'Where are we going?' Sophie asked, her eyes flying open as a pang of disappointment went through her. No kisses today. Despite his easy words, he felt she was tainted in some way.

'Back to your home, but I want you to do something for me, Sophie.'

'What is that?' she whispered.

'Give me a chance to prove that I am as far removed from the sort of creature that Cawburn is. I do understand the word no and that when a lady says it, she means it.' He raised her hand to his lips. 'Will you do that for me, Sophie? Judge me for me, rather than considering me to be like Cawburn?'

'I...I will try.'

The box of paints with its bright colours neatly arrayed stared up at her. She fingered the aquamarine and then the crimson red. Gorgeous rich colours which made her soul ache to use them. She pulled her hand away before the temptation overwhelmed her.

'You have given me oil paints?'

'They seemed more appropriate than water-colours. You are not some milk-sop miss content with a pastel-coloured life, but a vibrant being who requires true colour to match her view of the world,' Richard replied. 'Or that was my thought.'

'I know how to paint with oils. I used to pre-fer them, but watercolours seem more ladylike.' Sophie gently closed the wooden box, before she gave in to the urge to start painting there and then. Oil paints were for people who led reck-less and chaotic lives, rather than ordered ones.

'Sophie, you are a lady whether you paint in oil or water. It is how you act. Your stepmother will confirm it.' He tilted his head. 'Where is Mrs Ravel? I have a present of wax fruit for her.'

'She has a dress fitting.' Sophie gestured to the piles of old magazines, penny-dreadfuls and fashion plates. 'I'm sorting through these and trying to decide which to keep and which to throw away. I hadn't thought you would call. There is no At Home on a Friday.'

Rather than living in hope of Richard calling, she had chosen to wear a faded rose-coloured gown with a high-necked collar and her loos-est corset. Her hair was drawn back in a simple knot, rather than being artfully done. Sophie absurdly wished she was in the dark-blue gown which set off her eyes and that she had used curling tongs to make sure her ringlets framed her face.

She squashed the thought. It did not matter

what he thought of her looks. They were thrown together by circumstance. She was not going to act on any feelings of attraction towards him. He might have been the perfect gentleman yesterday, but could she trust him today?

'Is there something wrong with a man calling on his fiancée?' He glanced about the small sitting room which her stepmother and she used in the evenings when they were not entertaining. 'This room is far more pleasant than the drawing room. Cosy and more you.'

'No, nothing is wrong. And I like this room better with fewer china ornaments to knock.' Sophie picked up a brush and toyed with it, twisting it about her fingers. 'I will make sure my stepmother gets the fruit. It is good of you to remember her.'

'I have brought some paper as well as a variety of pencils,' Richard said, holding out another parcel. 'In case you didn't have any. I wasn't sure about the size of canvas you might require, but the man at the shop will drop off a selection later today.'

Sophie tilted her head to one side, eyeing the parcel with suspicion. 'I don't understand. Why are you giving me these things?'

'Have you forgotten what we spoke about yesterday? You promised to try drawing again. As you said you stopped four years ago, I reckoned you would not have paints, pencils or drawing paper.' His eyes glinted gold. 'Finding excuses is a terrible thing.'

'Spoken like someone who knows.'

'There are things I avoided until I was forced to,' he admitted with a studied shrug.

Sophie caught her breath and waited.

'I am not here to speak about my failings,' he said finally. 'Know I have many. Are you going to draw?'

'And I do intend to after I have finished with the magazines. But these are far too much, Richard.' Sophie gave the paintbox a wistful stroke. The tubes were new and unclotted. When she had looked this morning at her old oil paints, she couldn't even squeeze the tube, the paint was so old and cracked. Her brushes were matted and glued. The thought of going and buying more had been beyond her and she'd put it off for another day.

'What is the harm in spoiling you? Do you like them?'

'Very much,' Sophie admitted. 'I am puzzled why you have given me all this.'

'Can't a man give his fiancée a present?'

'It is nothing that others will see,' she explained. 'I'm hardly likely to bring it up in conversation, either.'

'And what of it? You will know I gave it to you. Sometimes it is not about creating an impression, Sophie, but doing the right thing.' He shrugged. 'After our conversation yesterday, I wanted to encourage you. To paint.'

She knew he was talking about more than that. He wanted her to stop allowing The Incident to rule her life. Rather than fearing it, a sort of reckless excitement filled her. It was an unexpected challenge. 'You are very kind.'

'Some day you might get to the Alps and want to paint, but you won't have practised for a long time. You need to practise now, so you are ready. The wax fruit are in case you need a subject. But I thought your stepmother was more the wax-fruit type.'

'I will definitely go...one of these days.' Privately Sophie vowed that she would go once they had ended. And she would paint meadows filled with flowers with snow-capped mountains towering over them. It would be a way to ease the pain in her heart. She froze and buried the thought. She liked Richard and enjoyed his company, but nothing more. They could never be real friends. There was far too much between them. After this false engagement ended, she'd never see him again. They would be strangers. The thought depressed her. 'Yes, I will definitely go.'

'Then you will accept the gift? I give it to you as a friend. I do consider you a friend, Sophie. I hope you will come to consider me as a friend.'

A friend. Sophie's heart thudded.

'Can a man and a woman ever be friends?' she asked lightly.

'I like to think you are. We share a secret.'

Friends for now, strangers in a few weeks. She'd miss him. 'How could I refuse when it was given in the interests of friendship?'

He stood there without moving and she wondered if he expected a kiss. She carefully placed the box down on the table with the drawing paper and pencils next to them, making a show of straightening them, but all the time watching him out of the corner of her eye.

'I shall start a painting today to show you I'm serious,' she said to cover the awkward silence. 'You can see it tomorrow…I mean, whenever you next come to call.'

'Tomorrow will be fine. There is a concert of Handel's *Water Music* on at the Royal Theatre. I thought you and your stepmother might enjoy going. You did enjoy the theatre so much in Liverpool last March.'

'I promise not to flirt with any strange men

with my fan. I gave that up after I met you. Lesson learnt.'

A tiny smile touched his lips. 'You have our story down.'

'It is important not to make a mistake.' Sophie turned back to the paints. 'I've no wish to come undone over it. I've told the story so many times now that I almost believe it myself.'

'Do you have a subject in mind for this painting of yours or shall I pose for you?'

Sophie examined the carpet of the small sitting room. If he posed for her, he'd have to stay. A large chunk of her wanted him here, but the more prudent side knew he should go. She had given up being reckless years ago. And while Richard might say he was different, she had no desire to put him to the test. Once bitten, twice shy as her nurse used to say.

'It normally takes me an age to decide on the subject,' she said. 'I like to spend time arranging things and doing preliminary sketches. Paintings don't happen like that. They need to be prepared.'

'Do you draw people?'

'I used to.' Sophie gestured towards the pen-and-ink portrait of her stepmother that stood on a side table. 'I did that one the spring before I made my début. My stepmother was a poor sitter. She kept moving her hands and changing expressions. Most aggravating—the drawing took twice as long as it should have done.'

'You are very talented.'

'You're being kind.'

'Kindness has nothing to do with it. I merely appreciated your talent.' He nodded towards the paints. 'Another time, then. When you are more confident at drawing people. I promise to sit very still and not move a muscle…no matter how much my nose itches.'

'Perhaps.'

'No perhaps. I shall look forward to sitting with anticipation.'

Sophie's mouth went dry. And she privately decided the time would never come. The risk to her resolve was far too great. There would be too many opportunities for seduction. Richard might proclaim to be different from Sebastian, but she didn't want to tempt fate.

She hugged the paintbox to her chest. 'I will think about it, but your suggestion to paint the wax fruit is a good one. My stepmother has a silver bowl which will work admirably. Nothing too complicated to begin with.'

'I am counting the hours…' His mouth quirked upwards at her expression. Her cheeks burnt. 'Until the theatre. It is your decision if you need a model. Know that I am a willing volunteer, if required.'

'And I will let you know if you are ever required.'

'We understand each other.' He took the box from her nerveless fingers and placed it on the table. 'Don't worry, I shall show myself out. You get on with your painting.'

Sophie stood in the middle of the sitting room, staring at the paints for a long time. Why did Richard Crawford have to turn out to be kind? He was right. He wasn't like Sebastian at all. He was infinitely more dangerous.

Chapter Eight

'There you see, all done.' Sophie held up the still life of wax fruit in a silver bowl for Richard's inspection a few days later. Her eager expression lit the room with its glow.

He'd done the right thing coming here, instead of going to the club or sitting and fuming about his mother's spending habits. Somehow being with Sophie made all of this morning's annoyances fade into insignificance.

He took the painting from her and their fingertips brushed. A warm pulse shot up his arm. Demonstrating to Sophie that he was far removed from Cawburn was getting harder and harder when all he wanted to do was to take her into his arms and kiss her.

Rather than having his desire for her diminish through seeing her, it had grown. But more than that he looked forward to pitting his wits against her and talking to her about things which had nothing to do with his family or the other demands on his time. When he was with her, everything faded into insignificance.

'You are very talented.' Richard concentrated on the painting and regained control of his body. Sophie was not the sort of woman one seduced; she was the sort of woman one married. 'That painting is more than a simple bowl of fruit. It looks good enough to eat. And I love how the shapes complement each other.'

'It is fine, but the apple gave me trouble. The red proved harder to get right than I thought it would.'

Sophie moved closer to him and their shoulders accidentally touched. Richard kept his body rigid.

'I could never do something like that. I wouldn't even know where to begin.'

'I had a strict drawing mistress. Do you know how many different colours a simple shadow can be? They are not dabs of black paint.'

He shook his head. Even now, Sophie wanted to belittle her accomplishments. 'It is more than simple-rote, schoolgirl painting. There is something indefinable here. You must learn how to take a compliment, Sophie, or I shall be forced to pay you them until you do.'

Her eyes danced. 'How do you take a compliment?'

'You say thank you and don't attempt to deflect it or apologise for it or make it seem less than it is. All it takes is a thank you and nothing more.'

He put the painting down. Sophie needed to have her confidence grow. He could only keep making excuses to his mother about the need to ensure Hannah's engagement for so long, before awkward questions would be asked, and Richard knew he wasn't ready to share Sophie with his family. His relationship with Sophie had no bearing on his relationship with his mother or sister.

'I shall try to remember that.' Sophie gave a mocking curtsy. 'Thank you for the compliment about the painting.'

'Shall we practise to make sure you understand the concept? Your blue dress looks exceptionally charming today, Miss Ravel.'

'This is hardly necessary. I do know how to take a compliment.'

'I used to think your eyes were the colour of sapphires, like your ring, but now I see the colour depends on your mood. Midnight blue when you are angry right through the blue of a summer's day when you are happy.'

'You are being foolish. Cease this blather immediately.'

He took a step closer. 'I intend to keep paying you compliments until you show me that you know how to take them. I prefer your hair like this when it makes little ringlets of its own accord.'

Sophie wet her suddenly aching lips. Her entire being trembled. Where did he intend taking this game? Her dreams had been full of him lately but ever since the carriage ride, he had made no attempt to kiss her.

'Thank you,' she gasped out as he took another step closer, so close her skirt brushed his leg. Another step, and she'd be in his arms. What was worse, she wanted to be in his arms. She wanted to taste his lips again and see if they matched her memory of them.

'At last my fiancée shows some sense.' His eyes danced with a thousand different lights. 'Shall I continue?'

'No.'

He inclined his head and stepped backwards. 'I bow to your no and stop immediately.'

A tiny bubble of amazement burst through her. He'd obeyed her no. She hated that she wished she'd urged him to continue. She put her hand to her mouth, exploring the way it faintly tingled as if he had indeed kissed her. The trouble with Richard was that she liked him far too much.

To cover her confusion, she grabbed the painting and held it out.

'You may have the painting if you like it. I painted it with you in mind.'

He tilted his head and she caught a sudden flaring in his eyes. 'It is kind of you. I will treasure it. I don't think anyone has ever done something like that for me before.'

'A thank you for the paints and for getting me started on painting again.' Sophie clasped her hands together and hoped he'd think the redness of her cheeks was from the fire, rather than the awkwardness she suddenly felt. 'I hope you don't consider it too forward.'

'Forward?' His eyes widened. 'Perish the thought. I'm very touched and honoured.'

'It is funny how you don't realise you missed something until it comes back into your life and suddenly your life takes on a new meaning.'

He stilled. 'Have you decided to start painting people again?'

Sophie put a hand on her stomach to stop the butterflies. Somehow she knew she had to get the answer right. Because if she got it wrong, he'd go and she wasn't ready for that yet.

'I have only ever done pen-and-ink drawings, but some day, I will start using oils for painting portraits. I promise.'

'I live in hope, then.'

Sophie let out a breath. She had passed the test.

He reached for the painting and his fingers brushed hers, almost a caress. A little touch which could have been accidental, but she chose to consider it deliberate. 'You will go with me tomorrow to the cricket? The match is an important one.'

'I look forward to it.' Sophie held her body utterly still.

'Out with it, Sophie. What is wrong?'

'How could you tell that something was wrong?'

'You always develop a little frown between your brows. And you have glanced at the desk ten times since I arrived. What is on that desk?'

He had noticed that! Sophie forced her features to relax. She walked over to the little desk she used for correspondence and withdrew the letter which had arrived in this morning's post.

'I have had a letter from my solicitors. You

agreed to my terms for the settlement. No quibbling!'

'Your terms were the same as I wish for any bride.' He lifted an eyebrow as if daring her to say differently. 'I thought you would have made them much more onerous and demanded a massive allowance or something outrageous. Having complete control over your own money makes common sense.'

'My stepmother would have questioned it, particularly after I made the claim of undying devotion at the Assembly Rooms. She did look over the request I sent to the solicitors to make sure my interests were well looked after.'

He lowered his voice. 'When do you plan to tell her about it?'

Sophie chose to assume he meant the letter about the settlement, rather than the bigger question of their false engagement. Her stepmother simply would not understand. And she would not understand why Sophie had to keep on seeing Richard and how precious these moments were becoming to her. She'd start on about a blossoming romance and what a shame it was that Sophie had not agreed to a true engagement when she was asked, instead of being mealy-mouthed.

'About the settlement being agreed?' Sophie

tapped the letter against her hand. 'I had to show her the letter.'

'And is she insisting on that engagement party now the settlement is finalised?'

'She has agreed to wait until Robert and Henri return. Robert should look over the settlement first was my excuse. My stepmother thinks I'm overly cautious. You know how she adores you and the fact you agreed so readily to the settlement has only enhanced your standing. She refuses to hear a word against you.'

'Why did you tell her you wanted to wait?'

Sophie turned away from his burning eyes. If she looked at him, she'd be tempted to blurt out the truth. She enjoyed his company and wanted to prolong the time they spent together, but she knew it had to end. There wasn't a future for them. They were strangers, not friends and certainly not lovers.

She wasn't going back to the romantic fool who faced utter ruin. And she was determined to marry for love, real and lasting love rather than a fleeting illusion of romance. Lasting love happened quietly, not this sudden bolt of lightning longing she'd experienced in connection with Richard. It reminded her too much of how she'd felt with Sebastian—unsettled and unbalanced. Surely if it was love, she'd feel complete and whole?

She put the letter back on the desk. Her hand trembled. It was far too soon to think about love in connection with Richard.

'I had to tell her something, otherwise she'd have been penning invitations this morning rather than going out visiting. Needing Robert's and Henri's blessing seemed like a sensible excuse.'

He tapped his fingers together and his lips pursed. 'When are the Montemorcys expected to return?'

'In the early part of June, no later than the eighteenth. Lady Forbisher always has a ball to celebrate Wellington's victory at Waterloo and then there is the Stagshaw Fair on the fourth of July. Henri helps with the planning of that. We had a letter from Henri yesterday.' She kept her head up. 'The timing should be perfect. All the commotion will have died down. Our parting will go unremarked.'

'We shall have to hope that Montemorcy sees some reason to object, then,' he murmured.

'I'm sure he will,' Sophie assured him. 'Robert is quite protective. He was the one who saw through Sebastian straight away. And Henri is brilliant at matchmaking. She is sure to find a reason why we wouldn't suit if Robert doesn't.'

The words tasted like ash in Sophie's mouth. She wanted Richard to deny it was a good idea and that he intended to remain in Newcastle for the summer with her—in fact, that against all expectation he wanted to marry her.

'It is good to know how long we have left. Early June after Montemorcy arrives back and sees the terms. After he has withheld his consent, we part. Amicably.' His lips became a thin white line. 'It is what happens in these cases.'

A pang went through Sophie. He was right. 'It is the most sensible thing. And it has happened to other people. Our parting will hardly be remarked on. I promise you.'

'And if it is? How will you weather the storm?'

'I'll go to Corbridge with Henri and Robert to ride out any lingering tittle-tattle. I won't be judged there.' Sophie kept her head up. It would be the perfect place to recover from the ache she felt now that the date had been decided.

His eyes became inscrutable. 'Early June, then. It is good to know so I can make plans... for my return to London.'

Sophie brushed away the great empty hollow which opened inside of her at the thought of never seeing him again. 'But we have until then.'

The dimple in the corner of his mouth deepened. 'Yes, we have until then. Best not waste any time, Sophie.'

Richard stood on the pavement and looked back at the brown-brick house. The day which had seemed bright and cheerful when he went in had become gloomy and overcast, matching his mood. The first few splashes of rain fell on his hat and frock-coat. Richard ignored them.

He had an ending date for his friendship with Sophie. Early June. Somewhere deep inside him, he had known that this was going to have to end. Only he wasn't ready. The very prospect of not being able to spend time with Sophie filled him with horror.

He had no wish to be judged unworthy by some former guardian. The man could not even take care of Sophie properly. Richard wanted to know Sophie would be looked after as she deserved to be. Her so-called friends had not even seen that she did much better when she was painting.

There was no hope for it. In order to keep Sophie safe, he'd have to marry her.

He groaned as he remembered what she had

said when she refused his earlier proposal. Sophie wanted to marry for love and love was the one thing he couldn't offer. Love only led to heartache.

'I will find a way to marry you, Sophie Ravel, but I will not mouth lies.'

Was she truly ready to say goodbye for ever to Richard?

Sophie bit the top of her thumb and tried to concentrate on the cricket match unfolding in front of her. Richard was batting and doing a sterling job of knocking the ball all over the ground after their team had had a disastrous start. The cricketing whites suited his figure. She noticed many admiring glances from the other ladies as he strode out to occupy the crease.

Today was far worse than yesterday. Yesterday, she'd known it would happen some day in the future. Today was the start of the march towards when Robert returned and she parted from Richard for ever. Each moment with Richard seemed to take on an added intensity. It was as if some secret part of her wanted to store every second she had with him so she could remember them later.

Perhaps today, after the match when he

dropped her off, she would risk lifting her face up to him and seeing if his kisses were as exciting as her memory of them. She'd use the excuse of him winning the match. With the number of runs he'd scored, he was today's hero and heroes did deserve their rewards.

'Are you enjoying the match, miss?' a well-dressed woman about her age asked, bringing Sophie back to the game which was unfolding in front of her. Richard had just hit the ball for four more runs.

Sophie frowned. There was something vaguely familiar about the woman's exotic features, but Sophie felt certain they had never met before. She rarely forgot the shape of a face or the eyes. It would come to her in a little while where she knew the woman from.

'Yes, very much. And it is Miss Ravel, Sophie Ravel.'

The woman regarded the cricket bat which lay at Sophie's feet. 'Are you going to play?'

'My fiancé is batting now and I go in after if necessary. I haven't played since my school days so I hope I can bat well if I have to go in. It would be dreadful to make a mess of it as our team stands a chance of winning. But there is every chance I won't have to go in. Only ten more runs. Lord Bingfield did promise he'd arrange things so that I would not have to go in. And it appears he has.'

'I am Hannah Grayson.' The woman said the name like she should know it. 'My fiancé is playing for the other team. He is the bowler for this over. You know, the bowler who took all those wickets in the first few overs. Sir Ronald Ferguson. We became officially engaged last night.'

'Congratulations.' A pang went through Sophie. Miss Grayson seemed so happy and in love. She could well imagine how that engagement went. Nothing like her own pretend one. 'Have you known each other long?'

'For a year or so, but I never expected things to go so quickly. I thought we were simply friends, even though Mama had hopes.' Miss Grayson held out her hand where a diamond surrounded by garnets sparkled. 'Sir Ronald gave me the ring last night. It is completely perfect. I am ever so grateful to my brother. I owe everything to him. I had feared that this day would never come to pass.'

'Your brother?'

Miss Grayson bent her head and picked at her glove. 'He came up from London and sorted everything out. At first I thought he wouldn't be able to stay beyond a day and a night, but he

has. It turns out that Sir Ronald was the year
below him at Eton and that made everything
easier. And yesterday evening, everything fell
into place. The settlement, everything. I feel so
happy that I could embrace the whole world.
Isn't it marvellous how things work out sometimes? Love is a truly wonderful thing.'

'Yes, it is. I am very pleased for you.' Sophie
composed her face. Somehow Miss Grayson's
unbridled joy only served to underline the hy-
pocrisy of her own position. Getting married
should be because you were in love with someone, deeply and irrevocably. It should not be because society dictates you must marry a stranger
in order to save your reputation after an item
has appeared in a newspaper. And it should not
be because you want that stranger to kiss you.
There ought to be more.

'Do you have a brother, Miss Ravel?' Miss
Grayson asked as the bowler started his run up.

'I'm an only child. I've often wished for a sister, but never a brother. Alas, it was not to be.'

'I agree it would be pleasant to have a sister,
but I shall make do with my brother...for now.'
Miss Grayson's brow knitted. 'It is most vexing
that he remains unmarried. He truly is the most
perfect of brothers. I pray he finds a woman who
deserves him.'

'Maybe he will marry and you will get a sister,' Sophie said. Miss Grayson did seem overly keen about her paragon of a brother. She had to hope the mysterious Mr Grayson was worthy of such praise.

Miss Grayson's lips parted as if she wanted to say something more, but a great shout went up and the bowler appealed to the umpire, who nodded and raised a finger, signalling out.

'I fear, Miss Ravel, my fiancé has taken your fiancé's middle stump. You'll have to go in after all. A pity.' Miss Grayson gave a little clap of her hands. 'There is only one more wicket to go and then Ronald will have won the match. It is terribly exciting. I had never considered cricket to be anything but dull, but it isn't. Good luck, Miss Ravel.'

Sophie stood up and grabbed her bat. She swung it lightly to test her arm. She could do this. There were only five more runs required.

On the way out to the middle, she met Richard, who looked furious at making the mistake.

'Never mind, it was a difficult ball to hit,' she said. 'You played marvellously to get us so close to the number of runs required. Before you went in, I feared our side would lose by a huge amount. Now we are nearly level and poised to win, if I can avoid getting out.'

'Who were you speaking with?' he asked, his brows knitting together. 'Just now? Another recruit to the game of cricket?'

'A Miss Grayson.' Sophie swung her bat slightly, testing its weight. She was surprised that Richard had even noticed where she was sitting or whom she was conversing with. She had thought he would be totally focused on the game. Her heart gave a leap at the intelligence. Despite everything he had noticed her!

'Are you acquainted with Miss Grayson?'

'She has very recently become engaged and wanted to sing her brother's praises as he apparently enabled it to happen. I was the nearest person to hand,' Sophie explained. 'I suppose love will do that—make people overly inclined to speak to strangers.'

'I regret my mistake interrupted your conversation.' He stopped her bat swinging and adjusted the grip. 'You were marvellous to volunteer when Charlton failed to show. It has allowed the entire match to proceed. I never thought you'd actually have to bat.'

Sophie's heart did a little skip as she basked in his praise, but it put more pressure on her to do well. The last thing she wanted was to let him down. And she had known that taking part in the match was the only way she could spend time with him. If it had been called off, she wouldn't have an excuse to stay. She would have had to go visiting with her stepmother. The prospect had held little appeal, particularly as it would have meant less time to be with him.

'It is perfectly fine,' she said, tightening her grip on the cricket bat. 'I hope I don't make a mess of things. I would hate to think we will lose because of me.'

'You won't.' He put a hand on her shoulder and his eyes turned serious. 'Keep the bat straight and swing if you have to. Keep the bat low and the ball will fall harmless to the ground. There is only one more ball left in the over. Let Armstrong do the rest.'

'Thank you for the advice.'

'My pleasure. You will do wonderfully, Sophie.'

Richard allowed Sophie to walk out to the crease and then went towards where his sister sat, shading her face with a parasol.

'Hannah!' Richard glowered at his sister. He had known Ferguson was on the other side, but he had thought Hannah would stay at home with their mother, discussing plans for the wedding. He had given his approval last night and had simply assumed Hannah would be too busy to attend today's match. The last thing he had wanted was Hannah here when he was attempting to manoeuvre Sophie towards marriage. It was a delicate operation, but it was for Sophie's own good. The last thing he needed was his sister causing mischief.

'It is not like you to miss a shot,' his sister said with a faintly smug smile. 'Ronald clean bowled you. Took out your middle stump. When was the last time that happened? At Eton? Or before that? You see, he is the better cricket player after all. You shouldn't boast so much, Richard. It doesn't become you.'

Richard tightened his jaw. He had missed the shot when he saw his sister speaking to Sophie, against his direct orders.

'I thought you were not to speak to Miss Ravel until I told you that you could.'

Hannah pouted slightly. 'I wanted to see what she was like. I'd only had a glimpse of her at the Assembly Rooms the night she announced the engagement to everyone. I thought her wonderfully brave, no matter what Mama said.'

'And you should have told me that you intended on defying me over this cricket match. I would have found an excuse not to bring Miss Ravel.'

'But I'm pleased you did.' Hannah clapped her hands together. 'She is extremely beautiful, Richard. It is the sort of beauty which lasts rather than coming from a paint pot or cleverly dressed hair. And she was sitting on her own. I thought it couldn't hurt.' Hannah's teeth worried her bottom lip. 'It seemed opportune. I wanted to meet the woman who has made my happiness possible. I wanted to see if she was worthy of my brother!'

'Did you have to go on about your brother? We had agreed to keep everything separate for our mother's sake. Sophie needs to remain in ignorance. It is far too risky.'

Richard closed his eyes. Sophie provided a bright spot in his life, untainted by his parents' warfare.

Would she understand why he loved them both and wanted to maintain cordial relations with both of them, rather than choosing a side? They were both part of him. He did not want to upset the delicate balance that he now enjoyed. Neither did he want her used as a pawn in that war. He could not stand to see Sophie hurt by either of them.

He could be married to Sophie and protect her from the taint of his past. It was possible.

'Are you going to marry her, Richard, for real? She wants a sister.' Hannah gave a small sigh. 'I think we could be friends. It would be so romantic to have a double wedding.'

'A double wedding is an impossibility. Stop this foolish behaviour and think of our mother. You know my father will insist on being at any marriage of mine.'

'Then you mean to marry her. Mama was wrong. I knew you must love her.'

Richard watched Sophie face the first ball. Her blouse tightened, revealing her curves as she batted the ball away to safety.

She was secure now and should not have to face another ball if Armstrong did his job. Sophie seemed so eager to play her part in the match and he knew he didn't want her to be the one to make the team lose.

'Stop putting words in my mouth, Hannah! Simply because you are love-addled, it doesn't mean you need to see romance with the rest of the world. I explained about Miss Ravel's necessity. Nothing has altered my view.'

The last thing he needed was marriage advice from his baby sister. He wanted Sophie in his life. He wanted Sophie happy. Love made people unhappy and foolish.

'Stop being foolish!' Hannah whispered in a furious tone and put her hand on her hip. 'You wrong me and Miss Ravel. I was curious. You have been spending an inordinate amount of time with her. Far more than Mama or I expected when you told us of the plan. Every day seems to bring something more that you must do. No wonder it took so long to negotiate my settlement with Ronald. Both he and I despaired of you.'

'Allow me to conduct my relations with Miss Ravel in my own fashion. Please.'

Hannah's marriage arrangements had given him the excuse to linger without family interference. But Sophie had changed the rules and he no longer had time. He had made sure that Hannah's interests were looked after, now he intended to look after his own. Everything had taken on a new urgency because of his father's note which he'd received this morning. Against all expectation his father had decided to travel and inspect his son's choice of bride. He declined to give a date, but Richard knew he had a week, ten days at most, before his father appeared.

If Sophie truly did not want to marry him, he needed to break it off for her sake, but he did have hope his plan would succeed. Silently he damned Cawburn for all eternity for making her wary of men.

It wasn't love, not the sort of love that he'd seen his parents experience, but he wanted to protect her and keep her safe from harm. He did have feelings for her and they frightened him to death.

Now his sister had nearly ruined his delicate plans. Sophie needed to be cajoled into this or she'd bolt and he'd lose her for ever. He didn't want to give her the additional excuse of his family. He tolerated them because he was related to them, but he was under no illusion—they were an acquired taste.

'Go away, Hannah. Keep your nose out of my business.'

'I shall go back to my seat now if you are going to be horrid,' his sister said, sticking her nose in the air. 'You failed to pay me the slightest bit of attention.'

'Do! And next time, keep your solemn promise.'

Hannah stalked off without replying.

Richard sank down in the chair and contemplated the scene in front of him. Sophie stood at the non-bowling end, her straw hat pushed back on her forehead, poised to run if the occasion called for it while Armstrong faced the new bowler.

A smattering of applause rippled through the ground as Armstrong ran one run. At a moment's hesitation, Sophie ran the other way. Silently he willed Armstrong to take another, but Armstrong motioned for Sophie to stay where she was.

Sophie nodded and banged the bat on the ground, signalling she was ready for the next ball.

The bowler's run took an inordinately long time. Richard clenched his fists. All Sophie had to do was hit a single run and then allow Armstrong to face the next four balls.

She swung and missed, but the ball carried on harmlessly to the wicket keeper. Richard silently vowed that the next time she offered to play cricket, he'd refuse. His nerves couldn't stand it. She glanced over to him and he gave an encouraging smile. Sophie had done a good thing with volunteering, but should he have allowed it? What moment of madness had he experienced?

He had never considered that she'd actually have to bat. A humiliated Sophie would hardly be conducive to seduction.

The bowler lifted his arm.

The ball came in at a slow curve and looked like it, too, would miss her stumps.

'Leave it alone, Sophie,' Richard muttered under his breath. 'Just survive.'

Sophie lifted her bat and swung.

The crack of the bat hitting the ball echoed around the ground.

Richard watched in amazement as the ball arched out over the field, finally landing some feet on the other side of the boundary.

A huge cheer went up from the crowd. Richard leapt to his feet.

Sophie had done it! She had hit a six and scored the winning runs.

He ran out to the crease along with the rest of the team.

'We won!' Sophie shrieked happily. 'And I can't believe it. We really won!'

'Thanks to you.'

He took the bat from her and tucked it under his arm before catching her hands. She circled around him, her face lit with happiness. It was all he could do not to kiss her thoroughly in front of everyone. His Sophie had won the match. She'd stepped up and played the game, beautifully.

'The bowler thought I was a helpless female

and sent me an easy ball.' Sophie gave an infectious laugh. 'But I was determined not to let the side down, particularly not after you had done so much to get us in the winning position.'

'Where did you learn to swing like that?'

'At school. That ball reminded me of the sort of delivery Miss Denton used to give the new girls. I knew I could do it and I did!' Sophie gave a happy sigh. 'I really did.'

'You should have told me that you were a crack shot.'

'I told you that I used to play at school. It is why I knew how to use the frying pan.' A mischievous smile lit her face. 'The third time I hit Sebastian was just like I hit that ball. Thwack!'

'Makes perfect sense why he retreated,' Richard said with mock gravity.

She laughed, a happy unaffected laugh, her face glowing with pride at her accomplishment. He wanted to swing her up in his arms in front of everyone and kiss her soundly. She had come so far in the past few weeks. Cawburn hadn't destroyed her. He fought to keep his arms at his sides.

She ducked her head and spoke to the ground. 'You have no idea how competitive girls can be at sport.'

'I can well imagine.'

Before she replied, the team came up and surrounded her, blocking his view of her face. Their cheers rang out throughout the ground, but Richard wanted to murder each and every one of them. Sophie should be his and his alone. And he would do everything in his power to claim her.

Chapter Nine

Sophie sighed happily, leaned back against the horsehair seat in Richard's carriage and closed her eyes as the carriage started off from the cricket ground in Jesmond.

The day had gone perfectly from start to finish. She knew it wasn't strictly proper, but she had adored having the rest of the team crowd around her, congratulating her on her skill at batting. Mr Armstrong had asked her to play the next time. Sophie declined with a laugh, but it felt good to be asked. Richard had been very silent while this was happening, glowering in particular at Mr Armstrong as if in truth he were a jealous fiancé, instead of a pretend one.

She gave a sideways glance at Richard. Was it possible to fall in love with someone after only a few short weeks? Or was it simply the heady romance of the moment? Finally, after so many years, to be free of the guilt and the shame of that one night?

It would be easy to start to depend on Richard, but it also would be a huge mistake. Once Robert and Henri returned, Richard would go out of her life for ever. All this pleasantness would be mere memories.

'I was sorry not to say goodbye to Miss Grayson,' she said, putting the thought from her mind. 'I looked for her after the match, but she had gone.'

'Who?' Richard sat bolt upright next to her, suddenly alert.

Sophie shivered and made a show of straightening her gloves.

'The lady I told you about when I met you on the way out to the crease. She was pleasant and bubbly. She had just become engaged to the bowler who took your wicket, the one I hit for six.'

'Ah, the one with the brother. You told me about her when you went to the crease.' There was a new note to his voice, something she couldn't quite put her finger on. 'Was there some reason you brought her up again?'

'Yes.' She turned towards him and leant forwards. His eyes watched her much as a cat might watch a mouse. Her hand toyed with the collar of her blouse and his eyes followed her hand as if he wanted to touch her there. An awareness of him filled her.

A sudden recklessness filled her. The fearful Sophie would have ignored it, but the new Sophie, the one who dared play cricket with gentlemen and win, wanted to test her theory. He was not indifferent to her. He had been jealous earlier.

'I wondered if her brother was at the match. Do you think anyone could be as good as Miss Grayson painted this man? Such a paragon of virtue and apparently extremely handsome,' she added for good measure, embellishing the story.

'Does it matter what he looks like?' Richard's face became very stern. 'Speculation does no one any favours. You of all people should know that by now.'

'You never know.' Sophie toyed with her gloves, straightening the seams, rather than looking at him. Every fibre of her being was aware of him and the way he glowered. He was jealous, she realised with a start. 'They live in Newcastle. We must travel in the same social circles. I wish I could figure out why I thought at first I must know her from somewhere. I felt we could be friends. It is all most peculiar.'

'Leave it, Sophie. You are unlikely to encounter this lady again…if you haven't encountered her before.' His voice held a certain finality. Sophie twisted her engagement ring. It was amazing how it felt part of her now. She had become accustomed to wearing it. She gave a soft sigh. But she had no right to it, not like Miss Grayson and her ring. Hers was a lie from start to finish, doomed to end in three weeks at the outside.

After today, she must refuse his invitations or else her heart would be seriously involved. And he wouldn't be jealous. Jealousy only happened if feelings were involved.

'I suppose you are right,' she said as a pang ran through her. No more conversations. No more gentle teasing. No more cricket matches. 'I was simply curious. It intrigued me, that's all. To have a sister that devoted. She swore that the only reason she was engaged was down to him.'

Richard's voice became even colder. 'I am sure he is not worth wondering about.'

She turned towards him, surprised. Normally he encouraged her to talk about people and make observations. 'Is there some problem? You were quiet during the celebrations afterwards.'

'I don't like the thought of you wondering about men when you are engaged to me.'

He regarded her with a fierce expression. Sophie's heart thumped and her lips tingled. He was jealous! Truly jealous of an unknown man, simply because she'd expressed an interest in that man. Her earlier instincts were correct. A heady sense of power coursed through her veins. He did feel something for her. Maybe they would not have to part for ever. Maybe it could blossom into something more. Maybe the romance was real, instead of pretend.

She wanted him to kiss her. Thoroughly and completely. Here in the carriage where no one could see. She wanted to see if his kisses were different when feelings were involved. And he would if she pushed him a bit further. The knowledge thudded through her, making her limbs feel weak.

She felt as if she was playing with fire, but that only served to make her feel more reckless. She could do anything she set her mind to. She had hit that six and won the game!

One single kiss to end a perfect day. She was safe with Richard. She trusted him to stop when she said so and she did know the boundaries.

The knowledge thrummed through her. She loved him and she wanted to pretend that she was worthy of experiencing romance in the same way Miss Grayson had. She wanted to prove once and for all time that she wasn't like those names Sebastian had called her. She wanted to believe for a little while that this romance was real. She could risk one kiss without endangering her reputation.

She tilted her chin in the air and lowered her lashes.

'Strictly speaking we are not engaged nor are we ever likely to be. We are merely using it as a convenience to stop untoward comment. Therefore I can speculate all I like. My heart belongs to no man.'

The blood raced through her veins and she hoped that he would not see her blatant lie. But she knew she had to provoke him.

He gave a soft curse and pulled her firmly into his arms. His lips lowered and captured hers.

Where his other kisses had been gentle and coaxing, this one was possessive and demanding. It seemed as though he wanted to brand her. A warm thrill went through her and she yielded up her mouth to his, opening under his onslaught, tasting the interior of his mouth. Their tongues tangled, retreated and then met again.

The warmth became a wildfire and she knew

she wanted more than this one kiss. Her body desired his touch. She arched forwards, bringing her arm about his neck and holding his head against hers as their mouths continued to do battle.

His arms pulled her tight, knocking her straw hat down to the floor. He rained little kisses on her face, nibbling and caressing her as if that one touch had unlocked the floodgates of passion. With each new touch, her heart beat faster and she knew she had to have more. She had been wrong to think that one kiss would satisfy her.

Sophie dug her hands in his hair and felt its silky smoothness against her fingers and brought his mouth back to hers. She opened her mouth and took him fully inside, and suckled, allowing her instinct to guide her.

Her breasts grew full and strained against her corset, causing her blouse to choke her. She tugged impatiently at it, seeking relief from its constriction, squirming against Richard's chest. He clasped her to him, preventing her from moving.

'Please,' she whispered. 'My blouse, it's choking me. Far too tight.'

'Allow me to help.'

'Yes.'

His hand roamed down her back, stopping on

the tiny buttons and then skimming upwards.
Her body arched forwards.

'Please,' he growled in her ear. 'Let me.'

All she could do was nod. His hands started
to undo the blouse. Her blouse immediately loosened and he slipped his hand under the fabric,
sending little licks of fire coursing through
her body as he stroked her skin and his mouth
tugged at her earlobe. Her body arched forwards.
This was what she had been longing for—his
touch. It felt so right and necessary.

His fingers moved ever lower, reaching her
breast. One finger brushed her nipple, turning
it to a hardened point. With the other hand, he
pushed the material down on to her arms so that
the tops of her breasts were exposed.

Slowly he lowered his mouth, placing tiny
kisses on her throat until he reached her breast.
He tilted the breast so that the dark-rose nipple just peaked out and captured it, running his
tongue over it. Again and again he circled until
it hardened to a tight point.

She moaned in the back of her throat as stars
exploded around her. Her body surged upwards
and she knew she had to have more. She wanted
to feel his skin beneath her fingers. She wanted
to see if her dreams were real.

She reached out and stroked his chest. Her

hands went to his neckcloth and started to undo it. She wanted to see if the strong column of his throat was as soft as his face.

Instantly he froze. His hands went to hers and stilled them. He lifted his head and looked at her with dark passion-filled eyes.

'No,' he said in a ragged voice. 'Say it, Sophie.'

'No?' she whispered. Surely he couldn't mean to stop. Her body wanted—no, needed his touch. She wanted to touch him like he had touched her. 'Why not?'

'Just say it. Like you mean it. You must, Sophie!'

'No! Richard—'

He put two fingers against her aching lips and shook his head, before flopping back against the cushion. 'Because I refuse to have your first time be a frantic coupling in a carriage.'

Sophie looked down at her naked breasts. They puckered slightly in the cold air now that his mouth wasn't on them. Exposed. Lewd and wanton. All the words she'd been called before.

She quickly crossed her arms over them. The delicate fabric of the blouse tore, a loud ripping sound which seemed to signal her reputation was equally torn and shredded.

She struggled to get the words out. 'My first time?'

His eyes were heavy-lidded with passion.

'You do know what passes between a man and a woman, Sophie.'

'Yes, of course.' Her cheeks burnt. It was all the worse for the gentleness of his tone. He thought her completely ignorant in the ways of men. Another man would have taken advantage of her, but not Richard. She straightened her shoulders. 'We whispered about it at school, and one of the girls had *Aristotle's Compleat Masterpiece.*'

'How did she get it?'

'She had borrowed it from her father's library and sneaked it back after the Christmas break. We passed it from girl to girl until Miss Denton found it and destroyed it. She would have expelled the girl, but her grandfather was an earl.' Sophie gave an uneasy laugh. Talking made it easier to forget what she had nearly done, how she was truly wicked rather than good. Her last few years of keeping herself aloof had been for nothing. She forced a soft laugh which sounded far too throaty. 'You would not have believed the uproar.'

'But you read it first. You were not the sort

of girl to allow an opportunity like that to slip between her fingers.'

Sophie gave a reluctant nod. He seemed to know her young self so well. 'It was full of astonishing information. I wanted to know. Thinking back, it probably was one of the reasons why I was such easy prey.'

'You have a good instinct, Sophie. It is better to know than to be frightened.' He reached out and pulled her over to him so that her head lay against his chest. The racing thud of his heart resounded in her ear. 'You did the right thing. Cawburn took advantage of you and your good nature. Never stop believing that. You are delightful, innocent and very much a lady.'

She started to sit up, but he gently held her there with one hand, while the other moved her blouse up over her shoulders, straightening her costume with almost impersonal expertise.

'Shush now, let me put you right. Nothing happened here that can't be fixed. I am to blame, not you.'

His fingers neatly did up her back. He was probably used to playing the ladies' maid, Sophie thought miserably.

He knew how this game was played and she had only heard rumours and read the book. She knew the theory and none of the practicalities. She should feel better that he accepted the blame, but all she felt was hollow and depressed. Her inexperience had stopped him, not her virtue.

She'd hate herself later, but right now, even the impersonal touch of his putting her clothing to rights made her thrum with desire. She'd spent years denying what she was and now she knew.

When he had finished, he set her from him. His face was very serious, far more serious than she had ever seen it before.

'If we continued on,' he said in a low voice, 'I would have been unable to stop. I was barely able to control myself as it was. You do understand how hard it can be to stop when two people desire each other, don't you?'

'I suppose you say it was all my fault. I should never have goaded you.' The words tasted bitter in her mouth. He was going to behave precisely like Sebastian Cawburn. She had been wrong to think any differently. It was all her fault for allowing the romance to go to her head. She couldn't be trusted. 'And I should be grateful for your restraint. My behaviour must disgust you. It falls so far short of what is socially acceptable.'

He placed two fingers over her mouth and shook his head.

'I want you, Sophie,' he said slowly and patiently. 'I have wanted you since the first time I held you in my arms. I want you more than I have ever wanted a woman. But not here and not like this. I want it done right. There is far too much at stake.'

'You want me?' she whispered. Her heart gave a little leap. She didn't disgust him. He desired her. But desiring her didn't mean he wanted to marry her or even that he cared about her.

'Desperately.' He took her hand and placed it on the front of his trousers. He was rigid beneath her palm. Her traitorous fingers itched to linger and trace the line of him.

Sophie jerked her hand back as if it had burnt her. She was all the words Sebastian had snarled at her—wanton, a cock-tease and worse. She had the soul of a loose woman. She had fought for years, trying to deny it, but she'd proved it in this carriage. She'd allowed her heart to overrule her common sense. She would have to take steps. They would have to end today.

'I suppose you want me to thank you for your forbearance then, for resisting your baser instincts,' she said, tears brimming in her eyes. 'It was an act of singular virtue. It won't happen again. I have learnt my lesson.'

'Thank me for what?' Richard asked, remorse

and regret swamping his senses. Sophie made
it sound as though he was a saint. He was far
from that.

He had gone further than he wanted, but the
result would be the same. There could be no
objections to their marriage…from anyone. He
could make sure that she stayed in his life. He
had wanted her to have a choice, but now she
had none. He had to keep her off balance and use
the desire she felt for him to achieve his goal. He
knew the power of seduction and had sworn not
to use it against Sophie, but he saw no other way
of securing her agreement in marriage.

'For saving me and reminding me of what
could have happened here.' Sophie made a helpless gesture with her hand. 'I will hate myself
enough as it is later. I thought I was better than
that, but obviously I was wrong. I overestimated
my own virtue. We will have to end after today,
never be alone again. I thought you should know
I do appreciate the way you have protected me,
even from myself.'

'I think you want me as well.' He forced his
voice to continue on as if she hadn't spoken. Her
virtue did not stand a chance against his seduction. He'd known that since the first time they
kissed. Now, he'd broken his promise. He was
seducing her, but seducing her into a marriage,

a marriage which was not the sort she wanted. He could not promise love. He didn't believe in it. The very thought of it scared him to death. To love someone was to be abandoned when you needed them the most. When given a choice, those he'd loved had chosen someone else.

His heart thudded so loudly he thought she must hear. Sophie had no choice if she wanted to remain within society—she had to marry him. Just now he'd taken every other option from her.

Because of her desire to appear virtuous, she wouldn't abandon him, even if she found out what he was truly like. Even if she found out that his mother had not wanted him and his father wasn't interested in him beyond what was required of his duty.

It bothered him that a small piece of him wanted her to have a choice. For once he wanted someone to choose him, but he also knew he wasn't prepared to take the risk. He'd deal with the consequences later. He'd trust Sophie's desire to appear virtuous would outweigh any need to escape from the marriage.

'There are two people in this carriage, Sophie. You kissed me back, more than dutifully kissed me. There was passion in your kiss and I heard your cry when I suckled your breasts. You enjoyed it. But you deserve better than this for your first time. You deserve white sheets and a closed door. You deserve time, rather than frenzy. It needs to be done properly, Sophie.'

'It was wrong of me. It won't happen again.' Sophie stared straight ahead, not meeting his eye. 'No one has to know.'

'You are wrong there. You and I both know and I have little desire to forget.'

Tears brimmed in her eyes. It took all of his self-control not to pull her into his arms. But he had gone too far already. He had to make certain she would be his. He refused to risk losing her. Once her former guardian returned, the objections to his suit would overwhelm her desire for him. He had to act now. He had to be ruthless about it.

'But we can be strong,' she whispered.

'This thing between us is growing. It is not diminishing.' He lifted her hand to his lips. 'Say you feel it as well and it is not just me who is waking every night in a hot sweat with your name on my lips and the dream of you in my arms.'

Sophie knew he was right. The ache in her middle had grown and she knew she craved his touch. For the past ten days, she'd woken with her hand between her legs, a nameless ache in her middle and Richard's name ringing in her ears. Every night she promised herself that this time she'd dream of something else and she never did.

During the day, she found herself hoping that he would call unexpectedly and reliving each one of his accidental touches when he was not there. She had taken to sketching the shape of his eyes, the way his hands looked when they held his cane and the curve of his mouth, most especially the curve of his mouth.

She wanted to feel ashamed about what she had done in the carriage, but she found it was impossible. He made her feel womanly and desirable. He was right. She might be wicked, but he was totally different from Sebastian. He had stopped it before she was utterly ruined. It had been him to pull back, not her, and she'd know that to her dying day.

She shook her head and tried to get control of her wayward thoughts. There were so many reasons why they needed to end it today, before the unthinkable happened and she was utterly ruined. But she could not bear the thought of never seeing him again, never hearing his voice or having his lips against hers. But he had said nothing of marriage.

'I suppose it is best that no one discovered us.' She waited for his agreement.

'And if I say that I want you in my bed? I want to spend hours exploring your body? I want to see your golden hair spread out against white-linen sheets. I want to see what moonlight does to your skin. I want to wake up in the morning and have your face be the first thing I see.'

'It can't happen.' She forced her shoulders to relax. The picture he painted was doing strange things to her insides. He had only mentioned desire, she reminded her rebellious heart. And she knew where that led. She refused to go back to that room where she felt unclean and sordid, even for Richard. Silently she bid the picture goodbye. A deep empty well opened within her. Richard Crawford was precisely like Sebastian Cawburn and she'd be wrong to forget that. She'd refused his first offer, had insisted on this sham and why would he ask her again, particularly now when he knew what she was like? 'You are wrong to ask me.'

'It can happen.' He leant forwards and smoothed a tendril of hair from her forehead. 'It can, Sophie.'

'How?' she whispered from aching lips. 'How can it? If I do that I will be outside society and I refuse to behave that way, even for you, Richard. How can you ask this of me, knowing all that, knowing my background?'

'You wrong me.' He gathered her in his arms and pressed his mouth to her hair. 'There is only one remedy, Sophie. We must marry.'

She leant back against his arms and tried to ignore the sudden leaping of her heart. He wanted to marry her! He was asking her again. She quashed the thought. Men like him dealt in some day, not in reality. They were back to where they had started. 'You mean in due course. Some day. Easy words, but you are asking me to take an unacceptable risk.'

He laced his fingers through her hand. 'No, I mean as soon as possible. A special licence. I take full responsibility for what happened here and I would never insult you by making you my mistress. My honour gives me no alternative but to make you my wife...if you will have me.'

'A special licence?' Her heart thudded. Richard was utterly serious. And despite her actions, he was prepared to behave honourably. She'd wronged him in thinking he wasn't safe in carriages. It was she who wasn't, but this time it had worked out.

'Neither of us is made of steel. The next time, we might not be so lucky and we might be discovered. The choice would be taken out of your hands. Either marriage to me, or confess to your stepmother on your own and you know she will look at your state of undress and make the logical conclusion.'

'But…but…' Sophie tried to think of a logical reason while her heart soared. Richard was right. They could be married by a special licence. Given Richard's family background, there would be no problem in getting a licence. He wanted to truly marry her. He felt the same way about her. He had to. She put her hand to her head. Against the odds, he had proposed a second time. If she refused, there would be no third time.

He placed a gentle kiss on the corner of her mouth. The touch was filled with possibility. 'Say yes, Sophie. Put me out of my agony. Or let me go, but don't keep torturing me in this way. Say yes, Sophie, and come into my bed. Be my wife, please.'

She knew in that instant she couldn't allow him to go, even though he had not mentioned finer feelings or love. He made her feel alive. If he went, the world would be a miserable place. She had to take the greatest risk of her life. She had to believe in the romance. She had to do it or face a lifetime of wondering what might have been. He might not have said anything about his finer feelings, but she had to believe in them.

She wanted to believe in this improbable romance.

'Yes,' she whispered back. 'We will marry as soon as possible.'

'Sophie! What on earth has happened to you?' Her stepmother's outraged voice greeted Sophie the instant she walked in the door. And she knew Richard's ministrations as a lady's maid had failed.

As she caught sight of her hair, her ripped blouse and her overly kissed mouth in the hall mirror confirmed her hunch. There was no hiding what she had done. She was only thankful that Richard had immediately ordered the carriage to start moving again and that he had simply held her hand all the way back home.

'Congratulate me, Stepmother.' A huge bubble of excitement coursed through Sophie's veins. She cleared her throat and straightened her shoulders. 'I'm proud to announce I am getting married to Lord Bingfield.'

'I know you are getting married. When Robert and Henri return from the Continent. It is all decided.' Her stepmother clasped her hands together. 'You told me this not three days ago when the news that the settlement had been reached. I'm so grateful that Henri will be able to help with planning the engagement party. It should be the pinnacle of the summer's entertainment. An autumn wedding will do.' Her stepmother walked around Sophie. 'I want to know what has happened to you! If anyone saw you...well, they'd think the worst. Did the carriage turn over? You look as if you have been through a hedge backwards.'

Sophie was grateful for Richard's hand in the middle of her back. He was there, supporting her. They had discussed in the carriage about the best way to tell her stepmother. While Sophie had wanted to tell her on her own, Richard refused to hear of it. They were doing it together or not at all.

'We are marrying as soon as practicable, Mrs Ravel,' Richard said in a tone which allowed for no opposition. 'I will see the Bishop after I leave here. There will be no problem with obtaining a licence.'

'But the settlement, the party after Robert and Henri arrive, the society wedding. The wedding breakfast.' Her stepmother started to fan herself. 'I want it to be special...for Sophie. Everyone is sure to want to be there.'

Sophie's insides twisted. All of her white lies to placate her stepmother were coming back to haunt her. *But would it have been any better if she'd known the truth?* a little voice inside her nagged.

'Sophie! Are you going to answer me?'

'Sophie and I—' Richard began, but her stepmother turned towards him, fury contorting her face.

'Pardon me, Lord Bingfield, but I want to hear my stepdaughter's answer. It seems from the look of her that she has been up to mischief and I want to know how deep this mischief runs! Sophie, what have you done? Did you go to the cricket match? Or did you go to an inn? Are you breeding?'

'Mrs Ravel!' Richard thundered.

Sophie gave Richard's hand a squeeze. She'd have to play this out. To confess to her stepmother what she had just done and why a marriage was now imperative, particularly as the engagement had been a false one, was impossible. Her stepmother's hysterics was the last thing she wanted to face.

'The settlement is more than adequate and stop using Robert's approval as an excuse.' Sophie fixed her stepmother with her eye. 'Richard's solicitor agreed to all my demands and you know they were designed to protect mine and Father's fortune. I showed you the letter from the solicitors. Robert and Henri will understand. We don't truly know the date they intended to return. Everything else like the wedding breakfast and a large wedding is mere frippery.'

Her stepmother opened her mouth several times, but no sound came out.

'Even if they did intend to come back in early June, they might be delayed for all sorts of reasons,' Sophie argued. 'I don't see any reason to wait any longer. Sometimes you just know when the time is right. And Richard agrees with me.'

'But the party? I wanted everything to be special for you. You are to be a society bride. This sudden headlong dash towards marriage sounds like a very hole-in-the-corner affair. People will talk. They will look at your waist and count.'

'Let them.' Sophie tilted her chin in the air. 'I've nothing to hide. Let them whisper and titter if they must, but I haven't done *anything* to be ashamed of.'

Richard's hand tightened over hers. She was grateful for the touch. She'd been foolish to worry that they weren't well acquainted. They would be spending the rest of their lives together and Richard appeared to understand her so well.

'We shall have to have a ball to celebrate the wedding when we return from the wedding trip. Problem solved. Right, Richard?'

'I feel certain my father would approve of

such a measure, Mrs Ravel,' Richard said in a smooth voice. 'We should have two. One in Newcastle and one at Hallington to introduce Sophie to the neighbourhood. After all, she will be the Marchioness of Hallington one day.'

Her stepmother beamed with pleasure and Sophie knew Richard had promised precisely the right thing.

'And London, let there be a ball in London.' Her stepmother clapped her hands. 'It will be the talk of the autumn season.'

Richard squeezed Sophie's hand tighter. It amazed her that he seemed to instinctively know the prospect of a ball unnerved her. 'That will be for Sophie to decide. But before any of that happens, Sophie and I will marry. We see no point in waiting. I expect you to attend the wedding.'

Her stepmother's ribbons trembled. 'You are eloping?'

'We will be married by special licence as soon as possible. I intend to see the Bishop of Durham this evening. If he is unwilling, I will travel down to Canterbury tomorrow and get permission from the Archbishop himself. At the very worst we will be married in two days' time.'

'What I don't understand is the sudden need

for haste!' Her stepmother's eyes narrowed and she examined Sophie's waist.

Now it was Sophie's turn to be outraged by what her stepmother was thinking. She crossed her arms and glared. 'Stepmother.'

'I want Sophie for my bride; I am hardly likely to take her for my mistress. I value her too highly.'

Value. The word thudded a warning through Sophie. She dismissed it. Value was close enough to love.

'Your stepdaughter has not been dishonoured, Mrs Ravel. You have my word on it.'

Sophie could hear the unspoken 'yet' in Richard's voice. She swallowed hard, knowing how close they had come in the carriage and whose fault it had been. It could so easily have been a forced marriage. As it was she had had a choice and she had chosen Richard. She loved how she had felt alive in his arms. Her entire body thrummed with the memory.

Sophie held out her arms and willed her stepmother to give in. 'Please say you will be there. Help me make my wedding a joyous occasion. Give me your blessing.'

Her stepmother threw up her hands in capitulation. The tension flowed out of Sophie. She had won. 'But the wedding breakfast. Sophie's wedding dress?'

'You had best start preparing it.' Richard's eyes twinkled. 'There is not a moment to lose. Once I have the licence, I will marry Sophie in whatever dress she happens to be wearing.'

'And I am more than happy to wear my white ball gown. We can easily fashion a veil. There is a mountain of tulle lace left from my latest ball gown. I will look like a fashionable bride, Stepmother.' Sophie gave her stepmother a hard stare. 'I will not disgrace you or my late father, but I will be married as soon as Richard can arrange it. The alternative is unthinkable.'

Her stepmother turned bright red and hurried from the hall.

Richard's laugh boomed out. He caught her in his arms and hugged her to him. 'That went well. Better than you feared. Your stepmother will be at the wedding.'

'Thank you,' Sophie said, letting out a breath. He seemed to understand her so well. 'You made it easy. I didn't know what I was going to say to her and how to confess about what nearly happened in the carriage.'

'There is nothing to confess. We were engaged and now we are getting married. It is the natural order of things.' He placed a soft kiss on her lips. Her entire being tingled with anticipation. She looped her arms about his neck, inviting him to deepen the kiss, but he gave a slight shake of his head. 'The next time I see you I will have the licence and we can be together, properly.'

A quiet thrill filled Sophie. She had left this morning thinking that she should end their acquaintance and she'd come back a nearly bride. The quickness of it made her head spin.

They were right not to wait. The alternative was far too dangerous. This way they could say that there was no dishonour and that they chose to marry, rather than being forced into it.

She leant back against his arms, memorising the planes of his face and the way a lock of hair flopped over his forehead. Later she intended to draw him from memory so she could have a memento of today.

'Is everything all right, Sophie?'

Her smile widened. She could tease him now. 'Then you had best get the licence and I will see about this wedding breakfast you require. Send me a note when you know.'

He nipped her chin. 'The only thing I require is you in my bed as soon as possible. As my lawful bride.'

Chapter Ten

'Richard, what is going on? Hannah returned practically in tears because of your cruelty this afternoon. How dare you!' His mother's voice assaulted Richard when he walked into his rooms later that evening.

Myers gave him an apologetic look, but Richard merely smiled at his valet. He patted his coat pocket which held the special licence. Nothing was going to disrupt his happiness, not even his mother and her accusations. Sophie would be properly his tomorrow. He had done it. Sophie would belong to him. His refuge from the world would be secure.

As he had suspected, the Bishop of Durham had been more than happy to oblige the son of the Marquess of Hallington and had even offered to perform the ceremony tomorrow morning at eleven. Before he left the Bishop, Richard penned a note to Sophie to be ready and sent his coachman off to Sophie's house to deliver it.

Tension flowed from his shoulders. Sophie would know now what tomorrow would bring. Things had worked out better than he'd hoped this morning. He had succeeded—even his mother and her accusations of cruelty towards his sister could not change his future.

He looked forward to initiating Sophie tomorrow afternoon in the art of bedsport, but first he had to deal with his mother.

'Congratulate me, Mother, I am going to marry.'

His mother's face pursed like she had just swallowed a sour plum. 'To the common chit whom you have used as a decoy when you were negotiating Hannah's marriage? But how? Why? You have barely spent any time with her beyond your duty.'

'To Sophie, yes.' Richard frowned. His mother had no right to speak of Sophie in that fashion. And he had kept his visits with Sophie private. Sometimes his mother was a worse snob than his aunt. 'You will like her when you meet her. You will find her an admirable daughter-in-law. There is nothing common about Sophie at all.

You will see why I married her once you are acquainted with her.'

His mother raised an eyebrow. 'I have heard from your sister that Miss Ravel is a classic Beauty with a friendly unaffected manner. However, Hannah is no judge of character. I thought we had agreed—there is no need to actually marry the girl. If a woman wishes to ruin herself, allow her. You did the honourable thing. You proposed, she refused. You have squired her to a few amusements, but you were well chaperoned.'

'She has accepted my offer. My second offer.'

'This woman was merely the excuse you were going to give your father if he required an answer.'

'You chose to believe that, Mother. I saw no need to correct your assumption.'

'Are you telling me that there was more to it?' His mother paled visibly. 'What have you done, Richard? How did she trap you?'

'Mother, my relationship with Sophie is none of your business.' Richard breathed deeply. His mother had never met Sophie. She could not possibly understand why he needed to be certain that she would remain in his life. He wasn't even sure he understood. He only knew that he had to have her. 'Why did you allow Hannah to go to the match today? I asked you to prevent it.'

'She wanted to. Ronald wanted her there.' His mother ran a finger along the oak table. 'I don't see why you had to take rooms here in Granger Street. Your man does not clean properly. You could have stayed with us. It would have been good to have you there when you were needed, rather than me having to seek you out.'

Richard gave a faint shudder at the thought of staying any length of time with either of his parents. With his father, they were at least able to be in separate wings. His mother's house on Charlotte Square was a reasonable size, but not overly large. And given his impending marriage, these rooms would have to do as a bridal suite. He withdrew the licence from his coat pocket.

'I will be married tomorrow, Mother, and that is the end of it. Remember, Sophie is *my* chosen bride and address her civilly. Otherwise don't bother.'

'May I come to the wedding or am I to be forbidden as unfit for society? My father was a baronet. And now every door is shut to me.' His mother slammed her fists together. 'Why? Because of your father and his vindictive nature.'

'I haven't told Sophie about you and Hannah yet,' Richard admitted between clenched teeth.

Trust his mother to hit on the nub of the problem. His plans had moved at a breathtaking rate after Sophie melted in his arms. He had to trust Sophie would understand why he hadn't told her before the wedding. 'Events rather overtook us. If there was any trapping to be done, it was me who pushed. I want her for my bride. You who followed your heart and abandoned your family surely must understand this?'

His mother digested the news with difficulty. 'Do you love her?'

'What does love have to do with it?' He refused to discuss his feelings for Sophie with his mother of all people! They were far too new and raw. He had never felt like this about anyone before. All he knew was that he wanted her in his arms for always. He also knew he'd forced the marriage, rather than trusting Sophie to make the right decision.

'I know what it is like to be in a loveless marriage, Richard. I suffered dreadfully. You have no idea how it can suffocate you. I thought I'd go mad if your father mentioned his pigs again.'

He crossed over to the desk. 'My father has written. The letter arrived this morning. He is coming to Newcastle. I have no idea when he will arrive. I thought you should know. He is apparently prepared to leave his pigs to meet Sophie.'

His mother went white and she staggered over to the sofa. 'You swore this wouldn't happen. He never travels up here. He knows I am here. Whatever am I to do? Do you suppose he knows about Hannah's impending marriage? Could Parthenope have heard a whisper? That woman is a menace! She has always aided and abetted your father.'

'He wants to meet Sophie. He makes no mention of you or my sister.' Richard's mouth twisted and he clenched his fist. He'd been the one to taunt his aunt at the At Home. Now, he potentially had both his parents thinking Sophie was beneath him. 'I suspect my aunt did not send a favourable report. And I do not intend to have any of his interference in my marriage.'

His mother nodded as she withdrew a handkerchief and dabbed her eyes. She gave a shuddering sigh before she continued. 'Perhaps you are wise. It is best your bride meets your father without knowing about your sister or me.'

'Why? I would have thought Hannah would want to go to my wedding.'

'Your bride-to-be is the one who was supposed to be keeping your engagement quiet, but before twenty-four hours were up, she announced it to the packed Assembly Rooms in a very dramatic fashion. If she meets your father, she might suddenly take it into her head to blurt out about Hannah and her engagement.'

'There were circumstances beyond her control.'

His mother gave a faint shudder. 'Can you trust this Sophie with the secret? With your father in the same city as me? After all these years? Don't you care about your sister and her happiness?'

'Mother! You are speaking about the woman who will be my wife. If I didn't trust her, I would hardly marry her.'

His mother raised her hands in supplication. 'Let me get your sister properly married first. After that, your father can't touch her. Please, for Hannah's sake. I've told you how vengeful your father is. How he hounded me and wouldn't rest. How he refused to hand over any of my dowry. He will destroy Hannah out of sheer spite, if he realises the true reason why you travelled up here. I know he will. Is this such a little request to ask of you?'

Richard pressed his lips together. The excuse would serve. The last thing he wanted was Sophie having to deal with his mother's unwarranted snobbery on her wedding day.

On the way back from the Bishop's, he had stopped at John Ormston shipping agents on the quayside and booked two first-class tickets to Hamburg, reserving the best cabin. Sophie and he could spend the summer touring Germany and Austria, taking the waters in various fashionable resorts. For Sophie, he'd brave the crossing. The agent promised as-smooth-as-glass sailing at this time of the year. They could return in the autumn, in time for Hannah's wedding. It would give his mother enough time to realise Sophie was his wife, rather than a woman who could be snubbed.

'I agree, Mother. I will tell Sophie everything eventually...when the time is right, but she will dance at my sister's wedding.' He glared at his mother. 'It will mean you and Hannah will not be able to come to my wedding.'

Tears glimmered in his mother's eyes. 'I knew I could count on you to understand, Richard. It means I fulfil my final promise to my beloved and see our daughter properly settled. It has been a worry and a bother for many years. Hannah's future must come first. You will explain that to this bride of yours. You have a title and an inheritance. Dear Grayson's daughter has nothing but her beauty and sweet nature. She must make this match.'

Richard nodded, knowing his mother had made a choice, the same choice she had made years ago when she had chosen bringing up Hannah over maintaining any contact with him. Her excuse was that he was his father's heir and his father would never have allowed him to go. His mother could never understand why he kept in contact with his father after knowing the truth about how she was treated. But his father was his father and he loved him for his eccentricities and for the way he had been there when Richard needed him as a boy.

'Happy to oblige.'

Sophie stood next to Richard before the high altar in St Nicholas's church, waiting for the ceremony to begin. She grasped the tiny nosegay of baby's breath and rosebuds, which her stepmother had managed to procure in time from the florist, tightly to her bosom and drew a quick breath. Yesterday at this time, she had just agreed to play in the cricket match, and today she was a properly attired bride.

Everything seemed to happen at such a speed, once she received Richard's note that the wedding was set for eleven this morning because of the Bishop's commitments.

Jane, her lady's maid, had been up until the

early hours making sure the ball dress was properly altered and the veil securely attached to her newest straw bonnet. When she looked at herself in the full-length mirror just before going downstairs, she had to agree with Jane's assessment that she was fashion-plate perfect. It might be a rushed wedding, but the bride would not disappoint the crowd.

Sophie wrinkled her nose. Not that there were many gathered when she arrived in her stepmother's carriage.

The large Gothic interior of St Nicholas's church loomed around her. Cold and silent. Her footsteps had echoed when she walked to the altar. Besides her stepmother, Jane and Richard's valet, the church was empty of witnesses.

'Are you all right?' Richard asked in an undertone. 'You appear pale.'

'I think my corset is one notch too tight, but I won't lock my knees and faint. I've no desire to collapse at my wedding like my friend Judith did.'

'I will catch you if you faint.'

'I believe you would.' Sophie pasted a smile on her face. Richard was here and that was all that mattered.

The Bishop began to intone the words of the

service and Sophie turned to look at her bride-groom and make a memory.

Richard stood upright with a very serious expression on his face. He answered the Bishop in a loud ringing voice, whereas Sophie found it difficult to utter the words above a whisper.

'Those whom God hath joined together let no man put asunder.'

The Bishop's words as he concluded the ceremony sent a shiver down Sophie's back. And the enormity of what she had just done hit her. For better or for worse, she had married Richard Crawford and was now Lady Bingfield.

Until a few weeks ago, they had been strangers. Not like Henri, who had known Robert for years before they married, or even Cynthia, who had known her new husband for a year before they eloped. All she knew was that she had to do it or face ruin. She couldn't bear the thought of not seeing Richard again and she couldn't trust herself to stop the next time. She was so glad that Richard had given her a choice.

She would make it for better, she decided. She would be a good wife.

Richard raised her veil and placed a chaste kiss on her lips. The gentle touch did much to settle her nerves. He did want her as his wife.

'It is done,' she said, looking into his burning-gold eyes.

'Let no man put asunder,' Richard replied with a determined set of his jaw. 'We are properly married, Sophie. No one can remark now. Shall we go and have the wedding breakfast your stepmother prepared, even though I'd prefer to get straight to the wedding night?'

Sophie's cheeks heated as his warm voice did things to her insides. 'You mustn't say such things, even in jest.'

He lowered his voice as his hand squeezed her waist. 'But I am thinking them. Know that I am counting the minutes until I get you alone and in my bed.'

'Hush! My stepmother will hear and she was up nearly all night making the wedding breakfast. She even made her famous seed cake.'

'I am honoured. I will eat a slice and then we shall make our excuses. Your stepmother will understand.' He started to escort her down the aisle. 'Neither of us is hungry for food.'

'What is going on here?' a loud overbearing masculine voice thundered at the back of the church. 'Richard, I went to your rooms and they said you were at church. Is this harum-scarum affair your wedding? And this woman—is she the common chit your aunt wrote me about?'

Sophie halted. She looked up at Richard, whose face had gone thunderous before becoming a mask of urbanity.

'The Bishop finished not a moment too soon,' Richard murmured. His hand tightened on Sophie's elbow. 'My father has arrived and is his usual charming self. Shall we go and greet him before he bellows the church down?'

'Did you know he was coming to Newcastle?' Sophie whispered, an uneasy feeling creeping up the back of her neck. Richard had known his father wouldn't approve of the match.

'I knew he had plans to travel to Newcastle. I didn't know when he'd arrive.'

Sophie stared at her new husband. He had deliberately kept his father's imminent arrival from her. What else had he hidden from her? 'You should have said.'

'What, and risk giving you or your stepmother a chance to delay the proceedings?' He gave a short laugh. 'Not likely. You are hard won, Sophie. I want my prize. I want you in my bed and this is the only way I could get you there.'

Hard won. Her heart did a little leap, but a niggling doubt filled her. Did he think his father would object to her, was that why he'd rushed the marriage? He had given her a choice, hadn't he? 'But your father…'

He pulled her closer and whispered in her ear, 'Remember you are my wife, Sophie. There is nothing my father or anyone else can do about it. You are Lady Bingfield now. You are my chosen bride. It matters not a jot what my aunt or indeed my father thinks of you. It only matters what I think.'

Sophie bit her lip. Richard made it sound as though she was somehow likely to be found wanting by Lord Hallington. Her pedigree might not be top drawer, but she was hardly a pauper. Her father had wanted her to marry into the aristocracy. She had had the right sort of education. She wasn't some governess or vicar's daughter, but... All the memories of feeling inadequate and that people were whispering behind their hands at her during her first Season came flooding back.

She regarded the red-faced Lord Hallington. Despite his high colour, she could see the family resemblance. She would have known that he was Richard's father anywhere. They shared the same facial structure and their eyes were the same colour. She tried to breathe. This was not how she had envisioned spending her first few moments of married life, confronting an irate father-in-law and trying to convince him that she was the proper person to marry his son, when she knew she had behaved very improperly. She knew the true reason for the haste.

'Meet your new daughter, Father,' Richard said, putting his hand about Sophie's waist as his gaze warred with his father's. Lord Hallington was the first to look away, defeated.

'You have married the chit!' he growled. 'Do you know what your aunt wrote about her and her family? Parthenope did not mince her words. Do you know how her father made his money? How he got his start?'

'Hardly a chit, Father, Sophie is my bride. Be civil,' Richard said, giving his father a hard look. He could happily murder his aunt. 'I have no idea what sort of report my aunt wrote, but I assure you that Sophie is *my* choice. I am the one who married her. My aunt had nothing to do with it. The sort of woman she approves of leaves me cold. As Sophie's father died years ago and I never met him, I can offer no opinion on his manners, but I've been increasingly impressed with Sophie's gentility and civility. Her stepmother is one of the kindest souls I have ever met.'

His father's frown increased. 'You would say that!'

'Sophie is now Lady Bingfield and my wife.

She shares my status. I married her because I wanted to. I was determined to have her.'

'Just as you were determined to have that other chit, the one who died, the one who had you sent down from Oxford. Marry in haste, repent at leisure as my dear mother used to say.'

Sophie went cold. She'd known Richard had been sent down from Oxford, but he'd never said about wanting to marry anyone. How many other things had Richard kept from her? How well did she really know her husband?

'I see little point in bringing up ancient history, Father, and as I only received your letter after I made the appointment with the Bishop, your assumption is incorrect.'

His father spluttered something incoherent.

'If you wish to cause mischief, you may leave,' Richard continued. 'Now, you may begin again and give my bride proper congratulations or you turn around and go. I do not care which.'

He waited, barely clinging on to his temper. His father should know better. The last thing he wanted was to have a fight with his father on his wedding day, but he would protect Sophie.

His father's shoulders sagged and he appeared to age, but his face remained an unnaturally red colour. Richard braced himself for the next onslaught. Silently he thanked his guardian angel that his mother and sister were not here. When his father was in these moods, there was no reasoning with him. It was only after the colour receded that some semblance of normality returned. His father always regretted his actions, but that was not the point.

'Welcome to the family, Sophie,' his father said, holding out his hand. 'You must forgive my rough speaking. Lately I have been spending much of my time in the company of pig keepers.'

'My father's passion is pig-breeding,' Richard explained between gritted teeth. His father's bad grace was clearly evident with the way his mouth curled. He had to hope that neither Sophie nor her stepmother had noticed the rudeness. 'It is why he rarely travels far from Hallington. It rules him.'

'That is not true, Richard,' his father protested. 'I went to the Great Exhibition last year in London. I wanted to see the improvements in pig farming that the Americans had. Excellent farmers, those Americans. They truly know their pigs.'

'Did you see anything else?' Richard enquired. 'Be honest, Father.'

His father puffed up his chest. 'There wasn't time. I had to get back to my pigs. Your aunts wanted me to attend some ball. I hate balls.'

'I am not personally acquainted with any pigs,' Sophie said slowly. 'Therefore, I have much to learn. Hopefully we can have a good conversation about pigs later. I am sure they are very fascinating creatures. And sometimes I am sure they are better and more honest company than some in society.'

The red receded from his father's face and Richard knew Sophie had said precisely the right thing. His father always calmed down when he spoke of his pigs. To him, the pigs were the most important thing in the world.

'My dear, they are completely fascinating. Far more intelligent than most people.'

'You must come to the wedding breakfast, Lord Hallington,' Sophie said with a very pretty curtsy. Richard silently blessed her for being understanding. He was hard pressed to think of anyone else who could handle the situation so well.

His father raised an imperious eyebrow and looked at Richard with a disdainful expression. 'Am I invited to my only son's wedding breakfast?'

Richard's fist balled and he fought against the urge to deny the request and tell him to leave immediately. It would only end badly with both of them shouting. He refused to air his dirty linen in public. It was the last way he wanted Sophie to remember the moments after their wedding.

He struggled to find the right words which would tell his father that he was unwelcome if he persisted in this behaviour, but held the thinnest veneer of politeness. His only hope now was that Sophie remained unaware of how incredibly rude his father was being.

'Of course you are invited,' Sophie said with a perplexed frown. 'You are Richard's father and his nearest relation. Now you are mine. Had we known that you were expected today, we would have waited the ceremony for you.'

Unexpected tears came into his father's eyes. 'Truly? You would have waited for me?'

'You failed to give a time or date of your arrival, Father. You have no one to blame but yourself,' Richard said, silently blessing the fact that Sophie had not known about his father's intended arrival. He could not have taken another night without her in his arms. 'You must become more modern and consult a train timetable before you write your letters.'

His father gave an incommunicative grunt.

Richard barely restrained himself from shaking him.

'Lord Hallington, I'm Dorothy Ravel, Sophie's stepmother.' Mrs Ravel bustled up and did an extravagant curtsy. Her many ribbons and flounces quivered.

His father looked taken back at the vision of ribbons, flounces and violent clashing colours which was Mrs Ravel.

Richard wanted to shake him for not seeing the good heart which beat underneath. He was going to react like his aunt and mother—condemning the Ravels for having too fine of a manner for their station before actually knowing them.

Mrs Ravel's voice might not be cut-glass, but she was Sophie's stepmother and now his mother-in-law. She deserved more respect than a curled lip. Surely his father had to see that there was no point in making matters worse and saying the words out loud where other people could hear?

'You must come back for the wedding breakfast,' Mrs Ravel said from where she remained in the curtsy. 'I'm sure dear Bingfield had no idea of your arrival. You must be famished. I have made my famous seed cake. I found it wonderful for restoring the late Mr Ravel after travelling.'

His father's eyes gleamed for an instant before his mouth turned down. 'Seed cake? I am partial to seed cake, if it is properly made. You can't get the sort I had as a child these days. More is the pity.'

There was a defiant tilt to Sophie's head and her eyes flashed dangerously. 'My stepmother's seed cake is famous throughout Northumberland. She has won a number of competitions with it, including the blue riband at Stagshaw Fair last year. You should try it before you dismiss it out of hand, Lord Hallington.'

Richard glowed with pride. His father had not succeeded in cowing Sophie, despite his fearsome rage. His father's mouth opened and closed several times, but no sound emerged.

'I find any sort of shock is better dealt with a drop of Marsala and piece of seed cake,' Mrs Ravel said in a soothing voice. 'It is what my late husband, Sophie's father, used to swear by.'

'With an invitation like that, how can I refuse?' His father inclined his head and his eyes began to twinkle. 'Particularly when it is given by two such charming ladies.'

Richard's neck muscles relaxed. Crisis averted. He silently bid farewell to his plan of taking Sophie away to the Alps for their wedding trip straight away. A few days' delay while his father remained in Newcastle. He could not risk having his parents meet and not being there to deal with the fallout. His father was unpredictable at the best of times, and his mother might give way to hysterics. It would be wrong to expect Hannah to cope on her own.

He kicked himself for having given the promise to his mother to delay telling Sophie the full truth. But a promise was a promise, even if it was an unwise one. He could not break it without informing his mother first.

'You must ride back in my carriage, Lord Hallington. The newlyweds need a bit of privacy. Now, you will advise me… What sort of clothes will dear Sophie need in her new position? I have not had time to sort out the trousseau. And a future marchioness needs to be a leader in fashion, rather than a follower. I am sure you understand, Lord Hallington, the necessity.'

Mrs Ravel hustled his astonished father away, leaving him alone with a white-faced Sophie. Her hand clutched her nosegay as if she were drowning and it was the only thing which could save her. His father had badly shaken her. He struggled to control his anger at his father and recapture that feeling of pride and anticipation he had had when they finished their vows.

'Shall we go to this wedding breakfast?'

Chapter Eleven

Sophie bit back her questions about Richard's past until they were in Richard's carriage. Safely out of earshot of anyone else. The last thing she wanted was the humiliation of having to ask for explanations for things her new husband should have told her about *before* they married. She had her pride.

When they had come out of the church, a light rain had started to fall, but a small crowd had gathered, waiting for them. She thought she'd seen Hannah Grayson hurrying away with a heavily veiled woman and somehow it made things worse.

Yesterday, Miss Grayson had been so happy about her upcoming wedding and all the plans. It was sure to be a big society affair with lots of friends and relations, much as Robert and Henri's had been.

There could not be a greater contrast with her hurried hole-in-the-corner affair with barely anyone attending. She had never considered her wedding would be like this, particularly not with her bridegroom's father demanding an explanation as to why Richard had married so quickly.

There could be only one conclusion. Lord Hallington had intended to stop this marriage, just as he had stopped another marriage. If he had arrived sooner, would Richard have even married her? Would she even have been in that carriage with him?

A small knot of misery formed in the pit of her stomach. Moments before she'd been so happy and excited to be married to Richard. Now she realised that she knew very little about him. She knew small things like how passionate he was about cricket and what a brilliant dancer he was, that he took his tea black, but she didn't know any of the truly big things, particularly how he'd conducted his previous relationships. She'd waited and waited for him to talk about the scandals in his past, or indeed anything significant about his childhood, but he hadn't. He hadn't even given her a subtle opportunity. And now they were married. Rather than marrying a friend, she'd married a stranger.

'When were you going to tell me about your father's imminent arrival in Newcastle? Before or after the wedding trip?' she asked in a deadly calm voice, the sort she only used when she was very upset. The taste of unshed tears slid down the back of her throat. She looked up at the roof and blinked rapidly. She absolutely refused to cry on her wedding day. Her wedding day! She was supposed to be happy, not feel as though she had been kicked in the stomach by a horse.

'My father sent a note saying he intended to travel to Newcastle. He failed to give a date or time, merely that I should expect him.' He put an arm about her shoulders, but she shrugged it off. 'I am a grown man. I refuse to wait attendance on him.'

'People don't travel like that, not these days,' Sophie protested as her mind reeled. What was it that Richard wasn't telling her? She had always hated it when her father was alive and he had kept things from her. She'd always vowed it would not happen to her again. She didn't need protecting from anything, particularly not his family. 'There are timetables and schedules. People send letters. The post takes a matter of hours.'

'My father is remarkably old-fashioned about such things, as you will discover. This is possibly the first time he has ever taken a train.' He covered her hand with his, but she withdrew it. 'In the past he called trains the devil's creation and stoutly refused to consider boarding one.'

The back of Sophie's neck prickled. Old-fashioned. Was he also old-fashioned about the sort of woman he wanted his son to marry? She wanted to be a credit to Richard, not drive a wedge between him and his father. 'You know your father best.'

'You must believe me, Sophie.' He put his hands on her shoulders and turned her to face him. His face bore a pleading expression. 'I truly didn't expect him to arrive today. There have been times in my life that he has promised to arrive, but some crisis with his pigs has prevented him. I have given up expecting him to do things because I want him to be there. And I did want to marry you as soon as possible, rather than waiting for my father who might not appear. My aunts always came to Montem Day at Eton with a picnic for my cousins, but my father never managed, despite saying he would. Do you know how hard it is to wait for someone to appear and then for them not to show up because their prized sow has given birth to piglets?'

Sophie's heart bled for the younger Richard who had wanted his father and had been overlooked for a load of pigs. Her father might have been busy, but he'd always been there when she had needed him. She couldn't imagine the pain and humiliation Richard must have felt.

'I didn't know. My father always made time for me…after my mother died.'

'My father has said on numerous occasions that he will never go to Newcastle. You heard my aunt at your stepmother's At Home. I refused to wait any longer for you in my bed and in my life.' He raised her hand to his lips. 'I refused to give you an opportunity for delay and you wanted this marriage to happen quickly as well. You agreed to it.'

'I suppose.'

'I'm selfish, Sophie.' He put his hand to his heart. 'One of my worst faults. I admit it, but can you blame me? You are too great a prize to risk.'

Sophie gripped her flowers tighter. She had spent her entire life trying to be genteel and refined, and Richard's family didn't think she was. Any more than Sebastian had or indeed some of the truly refined girls at school. 'But you were going to tell me about your aunt's verdict.'

'Any report my aunt made to my father matters not a jot to me. I told her so at the At Home.'

He gave a heart-melting smile which sent a shot of warmth coursing through her. Sophie struggled to ignore it.

His aunt's verdict might not have mattered to him then, back when the engagement was false, but would it matter one day? His aunt's report had mattered to his father.

'I have the wedding trip all planned,' Richard said, seemingly oblivious to her concerns. 'We are going to Hamburg and then we will travel to the Alps. For you and your dreams, I will travel on the sea. You would not believe how efficient shipping agents can be when you explain it is for a wedding trip and are willing to pay. It is where you said you always wanted to go. I shall pose for you in an Alpine meadow. You can paint and then we shall see where it leads.'

Sophie's heart did a little leap. He did remember the dream she had abandoned after the Sebastian incident. It was more than the painting. She bit her lip, torn between her desire to see the Alps and the knowledge that her father-in-law had indeed travelled all the way up from Hampshire to Newcastle. And if Richard was to be believed, taking a train for the first time in order to meet her and see if his aunt's judgement was correct.

She drew a shuddering breath and felt stron-

ger. There was little point in crying over what
might have been. 'We may have to postpone the
wedding trip. Your father is here now. It seems
churlish to leave. Can you work up your courage
again to brave the sea? I promise to hold your
hand all the way.'

'You have a very sweet nature, Lady Bingfield.' He raised her hand to his lips. 'Very
sweet indeed. My father was a foul-tempered
brute today, but he is my father. He can be very
charming when he makes the effort. It will mean
a lot to him if we stay.'

'We can go later in the year. It will be all the
more pleasant.' Silently Sophie resolved to win
Lord Hallington over. She would prove to him
that she was a worthy daughter-in-law, rather
than the sort of woman he thought her to be.

'You are sitting far, far too far away from me,
Lady Bingfield.'

Sophie sat up straighter and concentrated on
her nosegay. If she allowed it, he would change
the subject and she might never learn anything
more about him. It was important that she know.
The true extent of her ignorance frightened her
and the knot of misery seemed to be growing
larger.

'Was it true what your father said about you

marrying someone else?' she asked around the hard lump in her throat.

'I hardly intend to spend my wedding day discussing other people, but I made my vow never to be the knowing instrument of Putney after I learnt of Mary's tragic death in an accident.' He made a cutting motion with his hand. 'I was young and had been just sent down. Mary's family decided not to wait and married her off before I had a chance to return. Mary had been resisting the match before. He was a friend of Putney's. Mary decided to escape the marriage and died in a canal-boat accident. Her sister said that she was on her way to me. How much of that was true I didn't know. I resolved never again to knowingly let that happen.'

'I'm sorry.' Sophie closed her eyes. His insistence that his first proposal was a real one now made sense.

'Whether or not I'd have married her is pure speculation. It didn't happen. I can truly say that of all the women I have met, you are the only one who has tempted me to put my head in the parson's noose.'

'My friend Henri lost her first husband shortly after they married. For years she refused to even look at another man.'

'The state of my heart had nothing to do with

my reasons for not marrying.' Richard's features appeared carved out of stone. 'I have seen the problems firsthand when your heart rules your head. I had not met anyone I wanted to marry until I met you. All of the women I became involved with did not tempt me, Sophie. Several of them tried.'

Sophie looked at her nosegay where the tiny pink roses stared up at her in mute rebuke. He had not claimed any finer feeling. She had simply assumed. She had wanted to marry a friend for love and she'd married a stranger for desire. And the stranger was highly experienced, whereas she had no experience in these matters.

'Your father didn't approve of me. It is why he came up.' Sophie tightened her grip on the nosegay and hoped he'd understand and give her some measure of reassurance. 'Your father seemed so angry at the wedding. I have never seen anyone go red like that before.'

'Once he gets to know you properly, he will approve wholeheartedly. Trust me on this. I know my father and what he wants for me. You are precisely what I require in a wife and that is what is important.' He leant over and kissed her forehead.

Sophie tried to hang on to his words and use them to quieten the hard knot in her stomach.

What he required in a wife. They were not precisely words of love, but it would have to do. For now. But he seemed to be holding something back, something vital, and it niggled at her insides. 'I will attempt to remember that.'

'Now, are we going to enjoy the day, our wedding day, or are we going to spend the time discussing people and events that have no bearing on our future?'

'That went better than I had hoped,' Sophie said as they left the wedding breakfast in Richard's carriage. She had changed from her wedding dress into a smart bottle-green dress with a matching tailored jacket. Her tiny pillbox hat with its dyed green feather and the beaded gloves completed the outfit. She thought it set off her blonde hair admirably. The warmth she had seen in Richard's eyes when she came down the stairs with her crinoline imported directly from Paris slightly swinging to reveal her ankles encased in half-boots made the time she'd spent getting ready worth it.

The tiny hard knot in the pit of her stomach faded.

Contrary to her earlier fears, Lord Hallington had proved remarkably charming at the wedding breakfast and had gone out of his way to be kind to her stepmother, even going so far as to compliment her on using wax flowers rather than the real thing. Apparently Lord Hallington had recently developed a passion for collecting china pugs, but her stepmother had a number which he had not seen before.

'Did my father say how long he was staying in Newcastle? He merely told me that he was staying as long as necessary. I want to start the wedding trip as soon as possible. I have promised you the Alps and you shall have them.'

Sophie laughed at Richard's expression. It had been obvious to her at the wedding breakfast that Lord Hallington adored his only child. He had simply been upset at the suddenness of the marriage and hungry. Once he had eaten a bit, she could see where Richard had acquired his charm from.

'He has taken rooms at the Neville Hotel on my stepmother's advice. He said nothing to me, but from what I understood from my stepmother when I changed into my going-away dress, it will be a week or two, possibly three.'

'As long as that?'

'He plans to visit his mother's grave. My stepmother has undertaken to be his guide as he is now family.' Sophie tapped her finger to her chin. She should have remembered what Lady

Parthenope had said on the first night about visiting her mother's grave. It provided the perfect explanation as to why Lord Hallington was uncomfortable in Newcastle. 'That must be the reason he never visits here. The memory is far too painful for him.'

'I am thankful that he had enough sense to realise that he would not be a welcome addition to our rooms.' Richard wrapped his arms about her and pulled her close. 'I am postponing the wedding trip on his account. I'm not postponing anything else.'

'You shall have to take me to your grandmother's grave so I can pay my respects.'

He loosened his arms and a surprised expression crossed his face. 'I will find out from my father where it is.'

'Don't you know?' Sophie asked in dismay.

'Until my aunt said something the other day, I had forgotten—if I had ever known. My grandmother died before I was born. I know its general location.'

'It would be a good thing for me to visit it.' Sophie forced a smile. 'Something to discuss with your aunt when I next meet her.'

'I do refuse to discuss the dead, departed and most particularly my aunts on my wedding day, Sophie.'

The tiny hard knot returned with a vengeance. Her husband was a stranger. She had thought she'd known, but could she count on him in a crisis?

She reached up and brushed her lips against his. 'I'm sorry.'

'That's better.' He gathered her to him again and returned the kiss, nibbling her bottom lip. 'I have wanted to do this all day.'

'Do you think it is too early? The sun hasn't set. What will the servants think?'

He put his hands on either side of her face. 'Promise me never to be shy with me, Sophie. You are beautiful and I want to unwrap all the layers of your clothes and feast on your magnificent body.'

'My stepmother sent Jane on ahead, so that she'd be there with my things, waiting to help me get ready. We have everything planned.'

'Your stepmother and your maid have no place in our marriage bed.' He put his forehead against hers. 'It is well that I told Myers that the entire staff were to have the afternoon and the evening off. He will ensure your things have been safely put away, but no one remains. You will have to allow me to be your maid for tonight.'

Sophie gulped. 'We will be entirely alone.'

'What passes between us, Sophie, is strictly private. No audience needed.'

Rather than glancing at his face, Sophie toyed with the beaded portion of her glove. She wasn't sure if she should feel pleased or distinctly shocked. He made it seem as though it was an everyday occurrence. And for him perhaps it was. She didn't want to think about all the other women he must have known. She had to wonder if Myers was used to disappearing when Richard brought his new mistress back to his rooms. Not mistress, she corrected her thoughts. She was his wife. 'Is it normal for married people to behave this way?'

'Normal people be damned! It is how I want to behave.'

Sophie folded her hands together primly. 'I merely asked. I didn't want to provoke comment. I know how servants talk and gossip. I was brought up to respect convention.'

'There won't be, not about that.' He took her hand and slowly removed her glove, finger by finger. The gold band gleamed against her naked flesh. 'People do not pry into the bedroom of married people, Sophie. Our marriage will be on everyone's lips for a few weeks. Can your conventional soul withstand that?'

'Yes.' She put her hand on Richard's cheek

and felt the soft bristles against her palm. 'I have never done this before.'

'We are both new at marriage.' He turned his face to her palm and kissed it. 'We shall grow in it together.'

His words sent a soothing balm over her jangled nerves. He might be infinitely more experienced in the ways of love than she, but he had never been married before, either. This was the start of a new life for the both of them. It was something they could share together.

'It is a good thought.'

Sophie started to lean towards him. The carriage jolted to a halt and the coachman opened the door. Instantly she sat bolt upright. Richard got out first and turned back to her with his hands outstretched.

'Are you ready?'

'Ready?'

'I intend to carry you over the threshold.'

'You don't have to. I must weigh a ton. I ate far too much of the seed cake.'

'You will be as light as a feather. I want this to be perfect.'

'Very well. You may carry me.'

He put his arms about her and she looped her hands about his neck. Sophie noticed the servants filed out after the door had been opened. Richard had arranged everything to perfection.

Richard carried Sophie into the bedroom. Myers and Jane had done their work well. The severe masculinity of the room had been transformed with vases of flowers, flickering candles and Sophie's nightdress, prettily arranged with ribbons. A cold repast of cheese, apples and bread sat on a small table beside the small coal fire. Everything ripe for seduction.

He could not have planned it better.

'Shall I put you on the bed?' he whispered in Sophie's ear.

'I'd prefer to stand.'

'Would you mind telling me why?' he asked, slowly lowering her to the floor. He had to hope that Sophie's stepmother hadn't filled her head with silly notions about propriety. When Sophie had insisted on changing and her stepmother followed her up, Richard had known what was coming—the talk about doing your duty and allowing a man to take his pleasure. Always have the light off and other nonsensical rules. It was little wonder she had seemed distant in the carriage, bringing up all manner of topics for discussion. Her stepmother had probably scared her half to death.

'Why, Sophie, is it necessary for you to stand?' he enquired softly when she bowed her head.

'You have to be careful when you sit in a crinoline. They have tendency to fly up and expose everything.' Sophie gave a feeble laugh. 'It took me ages of practising before my stepmother would allow me out of the house. And you have to know where your skirts are. Fanny Hubert suffered terrible burns to her legs when her skirt caught fire. Luckily, I remembered to shout roll like Henri had taught me or it could have been far worse.'

'Why wear it if it is so dangerous?'

'Because it weighs so much less than six petticoats.' She laughed and placed her finger against his lips. 'And here I thought you were more than adequate as a maid.'

'I'm obviously out of practise.'

'Then we must hope you do a good job of it tonight.' Her hands went to her tiny hat. 'I expect you to be neat and tidy or Jane will grumble.'

'I will be what I am,' Richard growled, reaching for her. 'And your maid will mind her manners about you or she will have to find another situation. But since you asked so prettily, I will do my best to keep your clothes neat.'

Sophie's heart gave a little leap as he quickly

divested her of the jacket and undid the back buttons of the dress. The cool air licked her shoulders as she stood in the centre of the room dressed only in her crinoline, corset and combination.

He walked all around her.

'It is a cage.'

'It hooks at the back.' Somehow the knowledge he had not encountered a crinoline before made everything easier. The enormity of what was about to happen hit her as he carried her into the bedroom. She wanted to please him and all she could think about was that awful night four years ago.

The last thing she wanted was Richard getting angry with her. She wanted to be perfection and drive all thoughts of other women out of his mind. She wanted to match the picture he had painted in her mind yesterday, but she'd never done anything like this before.

'Step,' he commanded, releasing the crinoline and pushing it down over her hips. His hands caressed her hips, sending tiny licks of fire throughout her body, driving all thoughts of the other time away. This was different. This was Richard and she desired his touch.

He undid the hooks of her corset and sent that tumbling to the ground as well. Without giving her time to think, he lifted her up again and gently laid her on the bed.

'I prefer slippers to boots, Sophie,' he said, undoing the laces of her half-boots and easing them off. 'And I don't care about fashion, I want you to be able to breathe.'

'I like to look fashionable.' Sophie lifted her hands and removed the pins from her hair, allowing it to tumble about her shoulders.

'You look utterly delectable.' He moved her hair and kissed her neck. 'Even better when you are undressed.'

He undid his neckcloth and quickly took off his shoes, coat and shirt but left on his trousers.

Sophie realised with a start that he wasn't wearing anything underneath. His skin gleamed golden in the candlelight.

The bed sagged when he sat down next to her. His hand stroked her hair, sending a tingle down her spine.

The hard knot of misery had vanished to be replaced by something new and exciting.

She reached up a hand and stroked his cheek. 'Hello, husband.'

Instantly he rolled over on top of her and she felt the full hard length of him.

He bent his head and kissed her. Their tongues

met and parted. The wildfire which had spread through her yesterday, reignited, blazing hotter and more out of control because she knew what was coming. Her nipples tightened and her back arched, demanding more of him.

His mouth left hers and trailed down her throat, lower and lower until he reached her breasts. Rather than moving the material away, his tongue drew lazy circles, turning it translucent, so that her nipples showed a dusky pink.

She squirmed and her drawers rubbed against the apex of her thighs, sending a fresh wave of pleasure throughout her body.

Her head thrashed backwards and forwards on the pillow, but still he continued to suckle through the cloth. Her breasts grew full and ached.

'Please,' she gasped out, tugging at his shoulders. 'Please.'

He lifted his head. 'Allow me to pleasure you, Sophie. It makes me happy. I have dreamt about this. We are man and wife. Nothing is forbidden.'

'I know,' she said in a small voice. 'I want to do it right.'

'Relax.' He ran his hand down her flank, before placing his fingers at the apex of her thighs. The new sensation sent pulses of warmth through her. Her body bucked and she knew she wanted more. She wanted to feel all of him.

'We are overdressed,' she whispered.

He started to undo her combination, but the buttons stuck and he ripped it.

'I will buy you a new one,' he murmured, nuzzling her ear as his hands slipped off his trousers. 'You are more beautiful than I dreamt. Allow me to explore you.'

She gave a nod.

His hand returned to the apex of her thighs and slipped in between her nest of curls, parting her folds. The action sent fresh waves of pleasure throughout her body.

His silken warmth covered her. She ran her hand down his hard muscular back, marvelling. She cupped his buttocks and held his against her, lifting her hips to meet his.

The tip of him nudged her.

'I'm sorry,' he breathed in her ear. 'This will hurt. There is no way around it.'

He positioned himself and drove deeply between her thighs.

The pain and burning instantly blotted out all the earlier pleasure.

Sophie froze, shocked. She'd expected a pinprick of pain, not this burning sensation. A tiny cry of 'no' emerged from her throat. She tried to close her legs and her body bucked upwards, driving him deeper, making it worse. She beat her fists against the mattress in frustration. She had wanted this to be perfect. She wanted it to be like her dreams.

'Shush, it will be fine. Trust me. It was necessary, but now I will make it better.' His voice came through the pain and the panic subsided.

She forced her body to lie still and concentrated on the bed hanging and trying to breathe slowly.

He was deep within her, unmoving. She noticed the small things—how his chest felt against hers, how the candlelight highlighted the planes of his face and the way his fists were clenched as if he was under some nearly overpowering urge. She ran an experimental hand down his back, but he still didn't move.

His lips brushed her temple. 'There, it wasn't too bad. I had to break your maidenhead.'

'Is that all there is?'

He raised himself up on his elbows and his mouth curved up in a sensuous smile. 'Do you want more?'

She wrinkled her nose, considering. 'Yes, please. I liked the first bit very much, but not what just happened.'

He began to slowly move within her. 'We shall have to see if we can get you to enjoy this bit as well. Relax and open your legs wider.'

She tried to and he moved his hips slowly, going deeper, then retreating as his mouth returned to hers. The gentle movement reignited the fire within her. Her hips lifted in time with his, matching him.

The movement became faster and more intense, but she was swept along on a wave of intense pleasure.

Finally he drove hard and cried out before collapsing on her.

She put her arms about him and held him, glorying in being one with him, her body alive with new sensations. Richard was right. It would have been foolish to wait any longer. She was pleased he'd insisted on their marriage.

'Thank you,' he said, placing a kiss on her temple.

'For what?'

'For being you.'

'How can I be anyone else?'

He rolled off her and started to move away.

'Where are you going?' She held out her hand. Her entire body seemed to be remade and he wanted to leave her.

He returned with a damp cloth. 'We need to clean you up.'

She looked down and saw the blood on her thighs. Her hands went to hide it. 'I'm no longer a virgin.'

'You are truly my wife.' He nipped her chin. 'And well worth waiting for.'

He moved her hands and wiped her thighs. The cool cloth contrasted with the burning, soothing her. Her hips moved upwards, seeking the relief. He slowed the movement of the cloth and stroked her gently. The heady longing returned and she knew she wanted his hands on her. She wanted him inside her again.

When he had finished, he gathered her in his arms and held her. She felt him grow hard and knew he wanted her again. The thought gave her a heady sense of power.

'All gone.'

'Do you intend to do it again?' She hesitated. 'Please?'

He gave a brief laugh. 'Unfortunately you are too sore. We have the rest of our lives and I intend to teach you all the ways it is possible to have pleasure.'

She wriggled. 'I believe I shall like that very much.'

* * *

Much later, Richard lay with Sophie in his arms. It had taken more self-control than he thought possible to avoid taking her again.

He had done the right thing in marrying her. He was not going to become like his father, overly possessive and jealous, driving her away. He wasn't going to fall in love with her at all. He was going to look after her and protect her. The way he felt about her and having her in his life frightened him.

Richard stiffened. His father. With mental apologies to Sophie, he released her and rolled away from her warm body.

He needed to tell his mother about his father's arrival and plans such as he knew them. It was not something which he could put in a letter. He had to see his mother and suffer the hysterics, but then he'd be done.

He ran his fingers through Sophie's hair. It was better to keep Sophie out of any fireworks. She didn't understand the problems and the way both parents had used him when he was little. The last thing he wanted was for her to be hurt. He'd promised to keep her safe. He could not ask her to take on this burden.

'When we are in the Alps, Sophie, and we

know each other better,' he murmured. 'Then I will explain. I'm sure you will understand.'

She murmured softly in her sleep. He took it for a 'yes'.

Chapter Twelve

Sophie awoke, naked and alone in the large bed. The sunlight flooded on to her face. Her only ornaments were her engagement ring and the thin band of gold Richard had placed on her finger yesterday. It took her an instant to think where she was and why. Her body ached with muscles she didn't know she had. She reached out a hand to touch Richard. Even though she could see the imprint of his head on the pillow, the space beside her was cold.

She glanced about the bedroom. Someone had cleaned up the candle wax and the uneaten meal. Her dress and underthings no longer lay on the floor and her robe was neatly folded at the foot of the bed. A small fire blazed in the grate. But Richard was nowhere to be seen.

Something inside her shrivelled. She reached for the robe and slipped it on. What had she expected—that Richard would watch over her while she slept, transfixed by her beauty? That he'd be so enamoured of her charms that he wouldn't bear being separated from her?

Her mouth twisted. All of her doubts and fears from yesterday came crowding back in. Had she done the right thing by marrying this quickly? Did she truly know the man she had married? The man who promised passion, but never mentioned his finer feelings?

Marry in haste, repent at leisure.

She had certainly married in haste. She hadn't even given herself time to think. And Richard had never claimed anything more than desiring her. Was desire enough to build a marriage?

And she was stuck here until Richard returned, unable to dress herself without assistance. Silently she cursed the twenty-four hooks of her corset and the fifteen back buttons of her going-away dress. The other dresses she'd packed were just as bad. Without assistance, she was as helpless as a babe in arms.

Sophie swung her feet on the floor. 'Hello? Is anyone there? Richard! I'm awake.'

Jane hurried in. 'Oh, I hope I didn't wake your ladyship with my tidying earlier.'

Sophie's throat closed. Jane, not Richard, had tidied the room.

'You are back.'

'Mr Myers and I arrived back from the hotel early this morning. I could hardly allow my lady to be on her own on the morning after the wedding.' Jane's plain face broke in a wreath of smiles. 'I need to have my lady looking her best for her new husband.'

'You tidied everything up?' Sophie's face flamed.

'There wasn't much. Your clothes hadn't been properly hung and the fire needed cleaning and restarting. The master said that I wasn't to disturb you, that you needed your sleep.' Jane bit her lip. 'I dropped the shovel as I went out, but you slept for another hour.'

'You have done nothing wrong,' Sophie assured her, trying to peer around Jane, hoping to see if Richard would suddenly appear, having heard the murmur of voices.

Her maid's shoulders sagged. 'I am so glad. I want to be a good maid, your ladyship. I want to serve you well, particularly now you are a viscountess and will some day be a marchioness. I never thought I'd be a maid to such quality when I first entered service.'

'Is his lordship here?'

Jane shook her head quickly. 'His lordship went out over an hour ago. He didn't tell me or Mr Myers where he'd be going.'

'Did he say when he'd return?'

'I doubt he will be long. He thought you'd sleep as you had such a big day yesterday with the wedding and all the preparations. You were such a picture, my lady. A fairy princess bride could not have looked finer.'

Sophie silently blessed Jane for not remarking how odd it was that a man should leave his bride on the morning after their wedding night.

'I suspect he has gone to see his father.'

'I shouldn't like to speculate.'

'We are not going on our wedding trip until his father departs from Newcastle.'

'Do you know where you are going?'

'The Alps, I believe.'

'Mr Myers and I are to go on the trip.' Jane clapped her hands. 'I have always wanted to go abroad. The delay will give us time to get you a proper wardrobe. One fit for a peeress!'

Even her maid didn't consider her a fit person to be Richard's wife.

Jane began detailing the sort of costumes Sophie needed, from walking dresses to ball gowns and parasols for keeping the sun off. Sophie lis-

An Ideal Husband?

tened with half an ear and tried to ignore the tiny hard knot in her stomach.

If Richard had not returned by the time she finished breakfast, she would go to her stepmother's rather than sitting around here, waiting. She'd use the pretext of sorting through the wardrobe she'd left and seeing if any of it was suitable. She wouldn't go and see Lord Hallington until Richard was with her—that would be prying. She didn't want Richard to think she was checking up on him or becoming a shrewish wife, but if she remained here, waiting, she'd go mad.

'There you are, my dear,' her stepmother called out from the sitting room.

'I…I came back for some of my things,' Sophie called back.

'Is dear Richard with you?'

'No, I believe he went to see his father.'

'His father is here, dear, taking tea with me in the small sitting room. Neither of us expected to see you today. But I am ever so pleased you called. We have something to ask you. Can you spare a moment?'

Sophie's stomach knotted. Richard wasn't with his father. He had gone somewhere else. The knowledge thrummed her. 'I…I…'

'No doubt Richard will be along as soon as he discovers where his father is. You will have time for a cup of tea.'

Sophie breathed more easily. Her stepmother thought that they had just parted. The last thing she wanted to explain was how she'd woken up alone, without even a note. And Richard was sure to come here once he had finished whatever he was doing. Staying in those empty rooms would have given her time to panic. This way she could begin her acquaintance with her father-in-law properly.

'I am sure he will be,' Sophie said, going into the small sitting room.

Her stepmother and father-in-law were sitting in front of a fire. A variety of china pigs were placed in front of her father-in-law and it was obvious they had been discussing their respective collections. Her stepmother probably wanted to know where one of the china pigs was. Sophie attempted to remember if any had broken lately.

'What is it that you wanted to ask me?' Sophie asked, opting for a bright voice as her stepmother passed her a cup of tea.

'Where did you say you and dear Richard met?'

The back of Sophie's neck prickled. The story was foolproof, but somehow it didn't seem right to lie any more to her stepmother or her father-in-law. They deserved the truth, but Richard might want to be there when she explained fully.

Sophie mentally sighed. She had to play for time. She placed the cup down with a clank. 'We met in Liverpool last spring. I was there for the ship launch. You remember, Stepmother, the ship launch. It was such a big occasion.'

'That's what I thought. We were there on the nineteenth of March.' Her stepmother gave a smug smile. 'I consulted my diary. You enjoyed the play very much.'

'Yes, it was…it was that evening when we went to the theatre that I first encountered Richard.'

'Impossible!' Lord Hallington thundered, banging his fist down.

'Impossible?' Sophie clasped her hands together and looked to the door, hoping Richard would appear. 'No, no, I assure you it was then. Richard could not get me out of his mind. It was why he journeyed up to Newcastle and we became engaged. Things progressed more quickly than either of us imagined, but why wait?'

Sophie included her father-in-law in her smile. She was proud of her explanation.

'The nineteenth of March is my birthday, my dear. Richard was at Hallington for the entire week. In fact, he stayed ten days,' her father-in-law said in a firm voice. 'Perhaps you are remembering the date incorrectly.'

'Hornswoggle! The nineteenth was when we were in Liverpool,' her stepmother declared stoutly. 'It was the only time we were away from Newcastle, except to go to Corbridge for Christmas and the New Year. And the one short excursion to Carlisle Sophie made when I had a cold. I have shown you the diary.'

'Do you have an explanation, Sophie?' Lord Hallington asked. His brows lowered. 'How could my son be in two places at once?'

'Yes, I want to hear it.' Her stepmother pinned her with her gaze. 'We have been arguing over this for more than an hour.'

Sophie sank back against the sofa, suddenly sick. She had to tell the truth without Richard being there. She had no choice.

'We didn't meet in Liverpool,' she whispered.

Lord Hallington gave her stepmother a triumphant glance.

'Where did you meet if it wasn't Liverpool?' her stepmother asked in a deadly quiet voice. Even her cap radiated disappointment. 'I think I deserve that much, Sophie.'

'We met the night Cynthia Johnson eloped,' Sophie said in a rush.

'But that… But you said…' Her stepmother's face crumpled and she fumbled for her handkerchief. 'How could you, Sophie?'

'I know what I said.' Sophie handed her stepmother her handkerchief. 'I am ever so sorry, Stepmother. It wasn't supposed to come to this. We…we never planned to marry. The engagement was false, but the marriage isn't.'

'You had best explain from the beginning, young lady,' her father-in-law thundered as her stepmother wept. 'You have caused your stepmother considerable distress.'

'I will be happy to.' Sophie glanced over her shoulder and prayed that Richard would arrive to rescue her. 'Shall we wait for Richard's arrival? It will be better if we are both here.'

'No, I don't think we shall,' Lord Hallington said with a severe frown. 'I take it that you are truly married? Your marriage was not some sort of attempt to trick everyone again for your own purpose?'

'Of course they are married.' Her stepmother pointed towards the door. 'If you are going to make outrageous allegations, Lord Hallington, you may leave. Dear Richard is my son now. Sophie is properly wed and there isn't anything you can do about it. Anyone with half a brain can see how much in love they are!'

'We are truly married.' Sophie winced. She wanted to kiss her stepmother for being such a romantic and so loyal. She was going to have to hope her stepmother would understand. But love didn't come into it, not on Richard's part. And some day, when she'd shown him that she was worthy to be a marchioness, it would be different. She had to believe that. Out of unpromising starts, happiness could be found.

'Sophie, start from the beginning. Start with the night you met. Lord Hallington and I need to hear the truth.'

Lord Hallington started to say something, but her stepmother hushed him.

'Sophie will tell us everything, Lord Hallington. I find it best in these situations to allow Sophic to explain in her own time. My stepdaughter is normally a truthful person. I am sure there is a logical explanation. After all, they are married and the settlement agreed to everyone's satisfaction.'

Seeing no other option, Sophie began to explain, starting with the ball and how Richard had saved her. She skated over the kisses they had shared and the incident in the carriage where Richard had acted honourably.

'In any case, what does it matter now?' Sophie finished. 'Richard and I are married and everyone is happy. All is well that ends well.'

Sophie choked back the 'in love' part. She loved Richard or rather the Richard she thought she knew, but she had no idea about his feelings for her. He had only married her to satisfy his notion of honour. Was he starting to regret his actions already? She wished he was there and then her doubts might vanish.

'Do you know why Richard was in Newcastle to begin with?' Lord Hallington asked, drawing his brows together.

'What does it matter why Richard was here? He stayed to help out Sophie and they fell in love.' Her stepmother gave a happy sigh. 'Harum-scarum to begin with, Sophie, but ultimately one of the most romantic things I have heard in years.'

Richard's father looked less convinced.

'Do you know, young lady? Until I had his letter, I was unaware that he had ever visited this city. He was supposed to be in London.'

Sophie kept her head up. Richard had never said why he was at the ball that night. It hadn't seemed important. 'He was undoubtedly visiting friends. There are several men he was at Eton with on the cricket team.'

'But why keep it from his father?' Her step-mother rapped her finger against the diary.

'Richard is a grown man. He doesn't live in his father's pocket and have to explain where he is going and who he is seeing. Perhaps the invitation was sudden,' Sophie replied evenly. 'I know he stayed only to help me out. The events at the Assembly Rooms meant he could not just disappear. He was quite clear on that point. He had a score to settle with Sir Vincent. That was the only reason he stayed. Then there seemed to be no reason to wait after the settlement was agreed.'

'I wonder why my son failed to mention his journey? He went out of his way to make me think he was in London.'

'Perhaps he knew that mention of the city upsets you.' Sophie took a deep breath. 'Your son loves you, Lord Hallington. He knows your mother is buried here and that is why you don't visit it. Surely after all this time, you can visit her grave.'

Lord Hallington frowned. 'That is not why. Newcastle is where my former wife lives, or rather lived.'

Sophie's mind reeled. Richard's mother. The woman who had caused a huge scandal. If his mother was in Newcastle, surely she would have attended the wedding? 'Richard's mother? He never mentioned her. Does he know?'

'The divorce was a bad business. I had Marguerite agree never to speak to him as a condition of the divorce. I couldn't risk my son being hurt the way I was. The woman is a she-devil.'

'Funny, Richard has never mentioned his mother,' her stepmother said. 'Did he mention his mother to you, Sophie?'

'Only in passing,' Sophie answered truthfully as her stomach knotted. Richard would have said something about his mother. He had no reason to hide his mother from her and he didn't know his father would appear at the wedding, unless... Sophie refused to allow her mind to go there. Despite what his aunt thought about her lack of suitability, he had married her.

'I am sure he would have done, Sophie, if his mother was the reason for being in Newcastle,' her stepmother said soothingly, handing Lord Hallington another piece of seed cake. 'You have upset Sophie by implying differently, Lord Hallington. Do you know if your son and your former wife are in contact with each other? Do you even know for certain that she resides in Newcastle now? People do move about so these days, not like when I was young.'

'I have no idea.' The colour in Lord Hallington's face subsided. 'I don't want him being hurt. I can forgive most things, but I can't forgive what that woman did to my boy. How could a mother treat her child like that? Even now it makes my blood boil and the doctor has told me it does nothing for my heart.'

'Did you ever tell him why you didn't want him in Newcastle?' Sophie asked, curious.

'Of course not!'

'Well, then, you are making mountains out of molehills,' Sophie argued. Her stepmother was right. Richard would have confided in her something so important as his mother living in Newcastle. 'Think about the consequences if you had accused Richard of it.'

Privately she decided that when they returned from their wedding trip, she'd make an effort to find the woman and see if she wanted her son in her life. She knew that if either of her parents were alive, she'd want to see them. She loved her stepmother dearly, but it wasn't the same. Her mother might have died when she was just a little girl, but she still had memories of her gentle hand on her brow and the way her rose scent hung about her. It would be a good thing to do, she decided, feeling virtuous. But until she discovered where his mother lived, she wouldn't say.

'You are right, my dear. It is no wonder that Richard decided to act so quickly. He knew a good thing when he saw it.' Lord Hallington mopped his brow with a spotted handkerchief. His high colour had receded, but a sheen of sweat shone on his forehead. 'What a blessing it is to have you in my family. I hope we can become good friends. I have longed for a daughter for...for a long time.'

'I hope so as well.' Sophie took a cautious sip of her tea while she glowed internally. She'd won Lord Hallington's approval and her stepmother understood. Everything was going to be wonderful once Richard arrived. She put a hand to her throbbing head...if he arrived.

'What is going on here?' Richard asked from the doorway. Her heart did a crazy leap and she remembered how he'd kissed her so thoroughly last night. 'Did no one think to invite me to the family party?'

Sophie gulped. Richard had arrived at precisely the wrong moment. 'I was just explaining how we met.'

'In Liverpool?' His face seemed to be carved from stone, but his eyes flickered between her and his father.

Sophie stood up and linked her arm with his. 'The true circumstances.'

The colour drained from Richard's face. 'Did you volunteer the information, Sophie?'

'The nineteenth of March is your father's birthday.'

'I know when my father's birthday is.'

'The ship was launched on the nineteenth,' Sophie explained evenly, willing him to understand the problem. 'My stepmother noted it in her diary.'

'But you said late March.'

'In my world, the nineteenth is late March.'

Richard put a hand to his throbbing head. His quick visit to his mother and sister had turned into a disaster of epic proportions. His mother had flown into hysterics, making all sorts of wild accusations about his father and what he'd do to her and how Sophie was sure to be a she-devil. In the end, he had gone for the doctor, who sedated her with laudanum. Richard waited with a terrified Hannah until his mother slept and then had left for home.

All he had wanted to do was to sink deep inside Sophie and forget the trauma. He wanted to enjoy further awakening Sophie's passionate nature and making her truly his own.

He had hopes that Sophie would have remained asleep while he was away, but she was nowhere to be seen and neither was there a note.

The rooms were devoid of life. The pit of his stomach roiled. Abandoned again. Always. It hurt that he cared when she cared so little.

Luckily Myers had returned from shopping for the ingredients for his black boot polish and volunteered the information that Sophie and her maid had gone to her stepmother's to get more clothes. Richard had not stopped to change his neckcloth, but had hurried off.

Now, rather than collecting Sophie and departing with all speed, he had to cope with more trauma—his father and Sophie's confession. There had been no need to check the date of the Liverpool launch before. It hadn't been important.

'I hadn't realised the launch was on the nineteenth,' he admitted as evenly as he could. 'The nineteenth is my father's birthday. I always spend that day with my father.'

'So Lord Hallington informed my stepmother. They were in midst of an argument about it when I arrived.' Sophie held out her hands. Her blue eyes were wide and pleading. 'You can see why I had to tell them. My stepmother thinks it very romantic what you did. Apparently it is just like in one of her novels.'

He was suddenly glad that Sophie knew nothing about his mother or Hannah. She would have been unable to resist telling his father and then all hell would have broken loose and Sophie would have been hurt, used as a pawn or worse. His parents were his burden, not Sophie's. He had made her marry him. She had not asked for the craziness of his family.

He ran his hand through his hair and peered more closely at his father, searching for signs of his temper. One hysterical parent on the day after his wedding was enough, two were unthinkable. Against the odds, his father appeared happy with the situation, far happier than he'd seen his father in a long time.

'You did admirably, my boy,' his father said. 'I can see why you decided to remain in the north, and why you married Sophie so quickly. You were always headstrong, but a good woman is hard to find.'

'You approve?'

'Yes, I approve!' His father clapped his hands together. 'I'm utterly impressed and astonished. Despite the unorthodox meeting and courtship, you managed to find the sort of woman I have always wanted for you. Your aunt as usual wrote a load of blathering nonsense. I should have guessed. No sense about pigs, none whatsoever about people!'

'Then you won't mind if I take my bride away

now?' Richard put a hand on Sophie's shoulder and felt her flesh quiver under his fingers. Today could be redeemed. 'We did only marry yesterday.'

'We entirely understand,' Mrs Ravel said with a beatific smile. 'I was surprised to see Sophie here. I would have thought you'd depart on your wedding trip today. Sophie's father took me to Paris and then to Venice.'

'When do you leave for your wedding trip, Richard?' his father asked.

Richard froze. This was his chance to get his father to leave without causing a scene or alarming Sophie.

'Richard and I have decided to postpone the wedding trip so that you will have time to get to know me,' Sophie said before he had uttered a word.

His father's eyes widened. 'I had no wish…'

'But we do.' Sophie darted forwards and gave his father a kiss on the cheek. 'It will mean so much to both Richard and me. You are part of my family now. And you travelled on a train for the first time. Trains can be rather overwhelming. The noise, the dirt and the steam.'

Tears came into his father's eyes. 'Bless you, child. I will look into taking rooms. There is much to admire about this city. I haven't been here since I was a young man. The pigs will have to do without me for a while. My new daughter requires me.'

Richard forced his jaw to relax. His father had never done that for him—put him ahead of the pigs. Sophie with her impulsive invitation had just closed the one bright hope in his life—that his father would leave Newcastle quickly. His father would now stay and his own problems had grown. Somehow he had to figure out how he was going to protect Sophie and keep her from being used as a pawn.

'What do you think you were playing at, Sophie?' Richard exploded the instant he shut their bedroom door. 'Leaving like that! No note. Nothing.'

Sophie dropped her reticule on the ground. She had known something was wrong by his silence on the journey back and the way he'd marched into their bedroom. True, he'd been charming at her stepmother's, but he had insisted they leave immediately after he'd finished his cup of tea, not even waiting for Jane and her dresses.

'I don't know what you are talking about.' Sophie crossed her arms and readied for war. He'd been the one to be out when she awoke.

'You failed to leave a note.' He ran his hand through his hair. 'I had no idea where you were when I returned.'

Sophie tapped her foot on the ground. All the hurt and anger from earlier rose within her. He dared to complain about her absence when he couldn't be bothered to be there when she woke! She was the one who should be angry, not he. He should be on his knees in abject apology, rather than demanding explanations. 'You also failed to leave a note. I had no idea where *you* were. I refuse to wait around in rented rooms, hoping you might put in an appearance before nightfall.'

His mouth twisted. 'You decided to serve me back?'

'No, I let Myers know where I was and when I expected to return.' Sophie stuck her chin in the air. 'I needed my dresses which button down the front. I refuse to be stuck somewhere naked simply because all my clothing requires the assistance of a lady's maid.'

She waited for him to accept the truth.

He glared at her. 'Did you have to tell my father about how we met?'

'I had little choice.' Sophie met his gaze with a furious one of her own. 'I could hardly lie to him. You saw how it was. Undone by a date. It had to come out sooner or later. The truth always does. My stepmother took it very well and your father as well.'

'Who else will learn of the truth?'

Sophie rolled her eyes. 'I suspect I shall have to tell Robert and Henri. My stepmother is sure to tell them in any case. They and their children are like family.'

'Shall I take a notice out in *The Times*?' he enquired in a cutting voice. 'It will save time.'

'Once you meet Robert and Henri, you will love them.'

'I prefer to make my own judgement about people. You swore only a few days ago that this Robert of yours would find fault with me and my suit.'

'Yes, but we are married now.' Sophie pressed her hands against her temples. She had only said that when she had been certain he had no desire to marry her. Everything had changed. 'It no longer signifies. They know what society demands when people are compromised. Ultimately, all they want is to see me happy. They will be delighted that you did the right thing.'

He reached out to her, but she ignored it and stood there with crossed arms. She refused to ask him where he'd been. He should tell her and explain why he had left her for so long this morning.

An Ideal Husband?

'This is all wrong.' He reached out again and pulled her into his arms. He rested his chin on the top of her head. 'That's better. You were too far away. Can we start today over, please? I missed you more than I thought I would.'

'I would like that,' she said. Being in his arms made everything better. He'd missed her or perhaps just her body. It had to be enough. She would make him proud of her accomplishments. She'd show him how truly worthy she was and he'd start to truly care for her. He might not love her now, but she could make love grow...if she had enough time.

'I didn't expect to see your father,' she said, concentrating on his waistcoat rather than looking him in the face. 'My dark-rose gown has easier buttons and requires no crinoline. Jane wants my wardrobe to be fit for a peeress, but I'd rather be able to dress myself. Surely both can be managed?'

'I like your way of thinking, Lady Bingfield.' Richard's eyes glowed with appreciation as he ran his hands down her back.

They had that, Sophie realised. They desired each other. It would have to be enough to build her marriage on. She couldn't suddenly wish for undying love when he had never pretended more than desire. She had to hope his feelings for her would grow. Right now, his touch was wakening the ache in her middle.

She gave her mouth up to his mind-numbing kiss. When he kissed her, she knew everything would be right with the world.

Much later when they lay in bed together, Sophie's head against Richard's chest and her body faintly throbbing, she glanced up at his face and he seemed to be far away, concentrating on the bedpost rather than on her face.

'You haven't heard a word I said.'

He placed an absentminded kiss on her hair. 'Was it important?'

She shook her head. Her question about his childhood could wait. 'What were you thinking about?'

He put his hands behind his head. 'My father took the truth about our meeting well though. Better than I had hoped. It was a simplistic, but fatal error. I never thought about his birthday.'

She ran her hand down his chest. 'We had different expectations when we decided the story.'

'I could tell he likes you.' His hand stroked her hair. 'He does have excellent taste if you can get him to talk about something more than pigs.'

'You did want him to stay. He seemed sad earlier. I couldn't quite put my finger on it.' Sophie shook her head. Now was not the time to bring up the intelligence about his mother. Not after their quarrel had just mended. She had hated how her insides felt during their last one.

'You were completely right. I was being selfish. I wanted to start our wedding trip as soon as possible and didn't think my father would want to stay as he normally hates being away from his beloved pigs.'

'He puts his son above his pigs.'

'I live in hope, rather than expectation.' He gave a pained smile. 'Thank you for putting duty before pleasure. We will go once my father decides to depart, but it won't be long before the pigs need his attention. I want a proper wedding trip with you this summer. I positively insist on it.'

'We are still together and we will get to the Alps this summer.' She placed a kiss on his chin. 'I'm looking forward to painting you properly. A sunlit Alpine meadow will be the perfect backdrop.'

'Shall I be naked?'

'Richard!'

His eyes danced and he ran a hand down her flank. 'I keep forgetting how truly innocent you are, Sophie. Only if you desire it. Otherwise, I shall sit very still, dressed in my best hat, coat and trousers while you paint. The very proper husband for my Lady Bingfield to paint.'

Truly innocent. Sophie's heart gave a little pang. She should never forget how experienced he was. He was used to women who knew how to do all sorts of things. The cruel words Sebastian had shouted through the keyhole circled around her brain—*Men tire of innocence very quickly.* How could she ever hope to hold Richard, if she remained innocent? How could she hope to keep him from being bored? She wanted to use the desire to bring finer feelings to the marriage. She had to show him that she was worthy of taking her place beside him, so that he wouldn't regret his impulsive act of honour.

'Sophie? You appear awfully serious? Is something wrong? You have forgiven me, haven't you? I won't allow you to wake up without me again. I promise. I had no idea that it would upset you so.'

She pushed her doubts away. In Richard's arms, everything was perfect. 'Nothing is wrong. How could it be with you here?'

Chapter Thirteen

The sooner they left Newcastle, the better, Richard decided three days later. The last thing he wanted was for Sophie to encounter his mother. Rather than getting better and reconciled to the marriage and asking to meet Sophie, his mother had written to his aunt, requesting the report on Sophie.

Richard had considered something was truly wrong with her when she sent a cryptic note and so he had hurried over there this morning, only to be greeted with a litany of Sophie's imagined faults.

With Sophie attempting to create a wardrobe fit for a viscountess before they left for the wedding trip and generally showing nervousness, the last thing she needed was his mother picking petty fault. He wanted to throttle his aunt, but knew he ultimately was to blame for goading her that day.

He refused to allow anyone to hurt Sophie or twist her into something she wasn't. He wanted the passionate woman, not the mask she'd shown to the world when they'd first met. But there was no point in explaining this to his mother. Instead he had made his excuses and left.

Richard marched into his rooms with his aunt's poison burning a hole in his pocket. He would write his aunt an uncompromising and long-overdue missive about *her* behaviour and afterwards he'd consign the so-called verdict to the fire. Sophie need not worry what his family thought of her.

He stopped, confronted with the delectable sight of Sophie in her robe.

'What are you doing back here, Sophie?' Richard tilted his head, searching for signs of distress. 'I thought you had fittings for your new wardrobe all morning and were then going to have lunch with your stepmother.'

'I came back earlier from my stepmother's.' Sophie waved an airy hand. 'There was little point in me staying. My stepmother agreed with me. A woman's place is with her husband when they are first married, rather than gossiping.'

He raised an eyebrow. 'Is that so? Did you happen to see my father? Has he decided when he is leaving?'

'Next week. The tickets are all booked.' Sophie gave a little twirl, allowing her robe to slip a little. She had to hope her scheme was working and that Richard did have a little regard for her beyond desiring her in bed. But everywhere she turned these days, it seemed people conspired to make her feel awkward and as if she was a disappointment. She wanted to be the perfect bride. She wanted to show Richard that his trust in her was not misplaced. 'I have given the servants the afternoon off.'

His glance became appreciative rather than the glower he'd worn when he first came in. 'Is there any reason why?'

'I thought I could paint you. Get started on the portrait. It might not be an Alpine meadow, but I thought the bed would do.'

Dark passion flared in his eyes. 'You want to paint my portrait now? What has brought this on?'

'Now!' Sophie put her hands on her hips. If he went, she'd never regain the courage. She had everything planned in her mind. She'd seduce him and then she'd explain about the dinner party she'd planned. She knew having a dinner party before they had done the rounds of the At Homes wasn't strictly speaking the done thing, but she wanted to show Richard and his father that she was a capable hostess. 'Myers said that there wasn't anything you had to be doing. I laid careful plans, Richard.'

He pressed his lips together and then his face cleared. A wicked glint came into his eyes, warming her. And she breathed a sigh of relief. This was going to be easier than she'd feared. 'Never let it be said that I don't do what my lady requests, particularly when it is prettily put. Do you want me in my coat and hat for this portrait of yours?'

'I would like you to sit over there on the bed.' Sophie's limbs trembled. He was doing as she asked. She walked over to the easel and picked up a brush.

'You want me seated, not reclining.'

'Whichever way is more comfortable. But you need to keep still. Don't move a muscle. I want to capture you. When it is finished, I want to hang it over our drawing-room mantelpiece. Today I want to do a preliminary study and see if you can withstand the rigours of sitting.'

The dimple flashed in the corner of his mouth. 'I assume you will insist on entertaining the worthy.'

'Precisely. I've no wish to shock.'

Sophie drew a rough charcoal sketch of Richard's head and shoulders. She did intend to paint his portrait eventually. It would give her a chance to get to know him better, but this afternoon was about more than simply painting. It was about showing Richard that she could be inventive in their love-making.

'And you intend to paint all afternoon?' he asked after a few moments' silence in which she sketched the outline and gave a rough indication of how his hands ought to go.

'Is there some problem with this?'

'My nose is starting to itch. How am I supposed to scratch if you don't want me to move?'

Sophie smiled and reached for her brush. The request she had been waiting for. She walked over to where he sat. 'I believe I have a solution.'

She leant forwards and stroked his nose with the brush. 'All better?'

He gave a slight nod rather than reacting as she expected. 'Trying not to move as my wife ordered.'

She pursed her lips. This might take longer than she thought unless... She allowed her robe to slip as she started to turn away. His hand caught her sleeve.

'Where are you going? Other parts of me itch.'

'Do they?'

He nodded. 'All over. It is deuced uncomfortable being a model. You should have told me when I volunteered.'

'Then I shall have to see to them.'

'With your brush?' His voice held a husky note.

'I use it when I am painting and don't want to get paint on my nose.' Sophie used the brush to caress his cheeks and forehead. 'You see. Nice and soft.'

His eyes closed. 'More, please. Remember you told me not to move. I've no intention of spoiling your...portrait.'

Her hands worked at his neckcloth and discarded it. She gently stroked down the strong column of his throat, before working on his collar and the collar studs.

His coat proved a bit more problematic to remove. And he kept true to his word and didn't move a muscle, allowing her to undo the buttons and pull off the sleeves.

With a sinking heart, she saw his shirt sleeves were fastened with intricate cufflinks. Richard's clothing was every bit as fiddly as her own.

'Next time I paint you, I think I shall have to

take your advice and have you in fewer clothes. I can always paint the clothes in later.'

'I am taking your instructions to heart, but I do have the most terrible itch.' A faint smile touched his lips. 'You are not drawing now.'

Sophie drew her brush along his collar bone. 'You know how this game is played.'

'I'm a good guesser.' He pulled her against his chest. 'Is it all right for me to move now? Truly?'

She gave a nod. 'It is safe. I reached a stopping point on the portrait.'

'I promise to be the most obliging of models, but it is best to do a little at a time. It saves on the itching...' He took off his shirt and vest, leaving his skin gleaming golden. She put out a hand and touched the warm muscle.

He fell back on the bed so that she straddled him. His hands reached up and cupped her breasts. His thumb slowly rubbed her nipple, making it become a hardened point. Sophie gasped. He bucked upwards and his arousal teased her.

'What are you wearing under this robe?'

'Nothing,' Sophie admitted. 'I wanted to see how it would be for painting.'

'A novel approach—having the artist undressed and the model clothed.'

'I can be unconventional as well as conventional.' She brushed her lips against his mouth.

'Have I ever complained, Sophie?' He caught her face between his hands.

Sophie bit her lip. He had not complained, but she felt him slipping away from her.

Rather than answering him, she concentrated on the next stage. Her hands went to his trousers and undid them, allowing his erection to spring free. Without waiting, Sophie opened her legs wider and positioned herself. She moved her hips back and forth, feeling the engorged tip of him rub her as the ache grew within her and then, very slowly, she lowered herself down on him, calling the rhythm for once.

Much later, Richard lay with a sleeping Sophie curled beside him. With a gentle hand, he smoothed a lock of blonde hair from her face.

Sophie had the unerring knack of knowing what he needed without him even having to tell her. With her curled into his side, he could almost allow himself the luxury of believing that he could protect her and keep her safe. That he would have chosen this marriage if she knew everything about him.

He watched her stir and realised his feelings for her had grown, rather than diminished. But the only reason she was in his bed and his life was that he'd used her desire for virtue. Sometimes it felt as though he was waiting for the whole house of cards to fall.

'Mmmm,' she murmured, giving a stretch. 'That was pleasant.'

'Pleasant?'

'Wonderful. It may take me an awfully long time to get that particular portrait done.'

'I'm happy to pose whenever you like.' Richard sobered. 'You said my father has set a date for leaving.'

'A week on Monday. He has booked his train ticket.' Sophie raised herself up on her elbow. 'We are going to give a dinner party, Richard, on the Sunday. For your father, my stepmother, Robert and Henri. I have sent the invitations. I was sure you wouldn't mind. Robert and Henri arrive back two days before your father leaves. It seemed opportune. My stepmother and your father agreed readily.'

Richard went cold. He wasn't ready to meet Sophie's former guardian and his wife. He wanted to have more time to bind Sophie to him, rather than encountering the two people who would find fault with him. 'Shouldn't you have asked me before you sought assurance from my father and your stepmother?'

Her nose wrinkled. 'The letter from Henri arrived while your father was at my stepmother's. It seemed like too happy of a coincidence not to organise a dinner party. I am sure my stepmother will be happy to host the party if you don't feel we have room here.'

Richard ran his hands through his hair. Dinner parties with his father were to be endured, particularly when his father decided he could comment on the food with impunity. He could see the disaster unfolding before his eyes. His father behaving badly, Sophie in tears and these friends of Sophie's judging him. He shuddered. 'Sophie, a word of advice—if you want something big, ask a man before you ask his father.'

'I did mention giving a dinner party for Henri and Robert this morning.'

'You did?' Richard searched his memory. This morning he had been distracted by his mother's latest note about her finances and her request to see him immediately. 'The only thing you asked me about was another new dress. You always look well turned out, Sophie, and you are spending your own money.'

'Before that. The dress is for the dinner party.'

Richard rubbed his eye. The dull ache in his head returned. 'I don't recall, but I believe you.'

'Then it is a no.' Her lips turned down. 'I'd hoped…'

He flopped back against the pillows. It was wrong of him. He wanted to keep what passed between Sophie and him private. This was their kingdom. Dinner parties and At Homes belonged to a life after they returned from the wedding trip, when he could be sure of her. But Sophie was right. His father needed a proper send off. He could endure the Montemorcys, knowing that once his father was gone, he would have Sophie to himself for weeks on end and no family to bother him.

He turned over on top of Sophie and caught her wrists, putting them above her head. 'You wrong me.' He nipped her chin. 'It is a yes. Have your dinner party. Buy your gown.'

She kissed him back. Enthusiastically. 'I knew you'd understand.'

'Is everything under control?' Richard asked on the morning of the dinner party.

Sophie looked up from measuring the place settings. 'Everything is fine. I have borrowed my stepmother's cook and the menu is all agreed. Jane and Myers are dealing with the flowers.'

'Why the ruler?'

'A trick Henri taught me.' She set the ruler

down. Since the afternoon she had started painting Richard, something had changed between them. She had to hope that he understood how important it was that this dinner party went smoothly. She wanted to demonstrate to Robert and her stepmother that she was now an adult. Her dinner party would positively radiate virtue. They would see that despite the hastiness of the marriage, she was happy. And she was happy... most of the time.

'Surely Myers can do that.'

'It is best to do things myself if I want perfection.'

'Perfection isn't always possible.'

'With planning it can be achieved.' She nodded towards where two long red candles stood in brass candlesticks. 'I love how the red and the brass go together. Candlelight is far more pleasant for a party of this nature than gas.'

'I shall leave you to the last-minute preparations, then, as you have things well in hand.' He picked up his hat and gloves.

'Are you going out? The party is going to start in a few hours. I thought...I thought you might want to go over the choices for port.'

'There are a few things I need to complete before we go on our wedding trip. They shouldn't take long. Myers can solve any question with the wine. It is one of the reasons I hired him as my valet.'

Sophie pasted on a fake smile. It was there again, that withdrawing. Her stepmother had warned her—men don't like to hear about domestic bother. 'Of course, how foolish of me not to have thought Myers would know.'

'I will be back before the party starts. We will greet your guests together.'

Sophie sat watching the final splutter of the last red candle. The remains of the disaster were clearly evident.

Five plates with food—barely touched, and one plate without anything—spotlessly clean.

Richard, despite his easy assurance, had not returned in time for the start of the dinner party or its conclusion. A boy had delivered a note halfway through from Richard explaining they should start and that he'd been unavoidably delayed. He had no idea when he'd return, but he hoped it would be shortly.

She had Myers start serving the food, hoping against hope that each noise outside was Richard returning. But he hadn't, not even when the clock struck ten.

Everyone offered to stay and wait with her,

but she refused them all. The humiliation was far too great.

Henri, as she was leaving, squeezed Sophie's hand and told her that she always had a place with them.

Lord Hallington muttered about horse whips and how his son ought to know better. He offered to take her straight to Hallington the next morning if she wished.

Sophie kept the tears back until after they had all gone. She had calmly gone through his desk, hoping she'd find a clue as to his whereabouts. She hated herself for doing it, for being the sort of suspicious wife she'd always sworn she'd never be.

She happened on a letter with her name scrawled halfway down, detailing all her faults. Exhibitionist tendencies, overly refined, no taste. The final page was missing as if for some reason Richard had changed his mind about sending the letter to this Marguerite, his confidante.

It was one thing to worry and another thing to see it in black and white. She'd always worried what others thought of her and now she knew what her husband thought. If it had not been for his honour, they would have never married. It was ironic. She had spent the past few years keeping away from men like Richard because of their lack of honour...

She put her head on her arms and cried. Richard had demonstrated what he thought of their marriage and her. She had tried so hard. In spite of the letter, she still cared about him. She wanted to know he was not hurt or in trouble.

'I'm sorry, Sophie. I will make it up to you. I promise.'

She looked up and saw him standing in the doorway. His eyes were red ringed and tired, his normally pristine clothes mussed as if he'd stripped them off and put them on again. There were blotches which looked like dried tears on his shirt front. She wanted to murder him for scaring her like this. She wanted to scream at him that she wasn't too fine for her manner or suffering from an overdose of gentility or given to making an exhibition of herself. Or the half-a-dozen other phrases that had been listed.

Sophie stood up and scrubbed her eyes with the back of her hand. 'Sorry does not even begin to cover it.'

'Let me hold you.' He held out his arms and beckoned to her. 'The thought of holding you has been the only thing which has kept me going through the last few hours.'

'Really?' Sophie crossed her arms and moved

so that the table was between her and Richard. Her desire for him had been how all this trouble started. If she hadn't kissed him in the carriage, they would never have married. She'd still have her self-respect and illusions. 'You have a funny way of showing it. There again, I don't suppose you truly wanted to be here and see me make a disgrace of myself with an excess of courtesy.'

Sophie picked out one of the more hurtful phrases from the letter and waited for his reaction.

His hand dropped to his side. 'I brought you something, a token of my affection. And I wanted to be here...to make sure...'

'To make sure what? That nothing went wrong? That I didn't disgrace your name?' Sophie tapped her foot on the ground. Affection? She wanted more than affection. Affection was for pets and mistresses. She was his wife. She had wanted his regard, if not his love. 'I don't want anything from you. And I don't need your help. I managed the dinner party without you. I managed my life without you before we met.'

'I bought you a necklace.' He held out a slender box. 'A necklace of sapphires to wear at the dinner party. You could never disgrace me, Sophie.'

He placed the open box on the table and the

jewels winked up at her in the dim light, mocking her.

'You see, they match your eyes.'

Her stomach twisted. He'd brought her jewels, but he couldn't be bothered to show up for the dinner party, something which was important to her. She wore his ring, but he treated her like a mistress and a not very important one at that. She had thought he might come to love her and appreciate her social skills.

'Do you think I am little better than a courtesan? To be bought off with presents? I am your wife, Richard, regardless of who my father was or—'

'I know who you are, Sophie,' he said in a deathly still voice. 'I want to explain. The necklace is an important part of the explanation. When I was at the jewellers, Hannah caught up with me.'

'Hannah?' Sophie wanted to throw up. Richard was speaking of a woman she barely knew in intimate terms. 'Hannah Grayson? The woman I met at the cricket? You know her well enough to call her Hannah?'

She sat down heavily. Her entire world crumbled about her. She had thought Sebastian was bad, but Richard was far worse. Stupid, naïve Sophie for believing Richard could be different.

Once a rake, always a rake. First the letter, now this. She should have trusted her head, rather than her heart. She'd stupidly believed that she had enough love for the both of them.

'Sophie. It is not what you think.'

'How do you know what I think?' She stared at the jewels. 'Do you even care what I think?'

He winced. 'I do care, Sophie. I care very much. You are my wife. It is why—'

'It is why what? I found your letter to some Marguerite detailing my faults. How many women are in your life besides me?'

'Hannah Grayson is my sister, Sophie, and Marguerite is my mother, but I have never written any letter. Why were you looking through my things?'

Sophie put her hand over her mouth. His sister! His mother! Why hadn't he told her that he had a sister? Why had he hidden it from her? Particularly in the carriage when she had teased him about Hannah Grayson's brother? 'You are the brother who enabled the engagement, the one Miss Grayson is so proud of.'

He gave an uneasy laugh. 'Hannah wasn't supposed to be there or I'd never have taken you there that day.'

Sophie went cold. He wanted to keep his sister from her. 'I wasn't to know? About your sister being in Newcastle? Ever? What was wrong with me?'

'Can you let me finish? Nothing is wrong with you, Sophie. You were an unasked-for complication in my ordered existence.'

'An unasked-for complication?' Sophie put her hands on her hips as outrage poured through her. He made it seem as though she was a burden! 'I am sorry to make your life more difficult. You didn't have to marry me. You were the one who insisted because of what happened in the carriage.'

He raised an eyebrow. 'I wasn't planning on meeting you when I came to Newcastle. I came up to vet my sister's fiancé. My mother worried. I wanted to make sure that Hannah would be looked after properly and I know how men can take advantage of women, particularly when they fail to have adequate settlements. Then I met you and certain events followed.'

The news crashed through Sophie. Before Richard arrived she'd been furious, worried and scared for him. Now, she was simply numb. Not only had he kept his sister from her, but his mother as well. If ever she needed proof that he didn't have any feelings for her, this was it. She struggled to frame the words. 'Why did you keep them a secret from me? Why didn't you trust me? Why were you ashamed of me?'

Richard gave an apologetic smile. 'My mother is terrified of my father. She worried that something might happen when she heard that we were marrying. She has become quite irrational and hysterical. She chose not to come to the wedding and I hardly wanted to give you an excuse to delay. You see, Sophie, there is a logical explanation. It is not what you thought. Imagine what would have happened if she'd been at the wedding when my father showed up. In the end, it was a minor miracle. I wanted that day to be perfect for you.'

He looked at her with lidded eyes. Even now, he wasn't trusting her with the full story. His mother had chosen not to go to the wedding because she felt Sophie wasn't good enough.

'You were ashamed of me? Is that why you wrote that letter?'

'My mother can be overly proud. She has no cause to be.' Richard rolled his eyes. 'She and my aunt are like that. She wrote to my aunt asking for her opinion, once we were wed. The letter you found was my aunt's reply, detailing what she wrote to my father after I goaded her. Now you see that this is all a tempest in a teapot.'

'No, it is far worse. You didn't trust me. You

still don't trust me. You married me without trusting me. You only married because we had to, because I forced the issue by kissing you.' Sophie struggled to take a breath. Her insides were torn to tiny shreds.

'There were two of us in that carriage.' He gave a half-smile. 'I was hardly reluctant. And as for not telling you about my mother…well, my father arrived. You tell secrets readily and without meaning to. I don't blame you, Sophie, but they just seem to spill out of you. I selfishly wanted to concentrate on my marriage, rather than having the drama of my parents.'

'I tell secrets!'

'Look at how our engagement was announced to all and sundry at the Assembly Rooms, how you proclaimed it was a love match.'

'You know the circumstance.' Sophie ground her teeth. Of all the accusations, that was the most unfair. She prided herself on her ability to keep secrets. 'My quick thinking destroyed Sir Vincent.'

'I never said you did it deliberately, merely that you found it difficult to keep secrets.' Richard's tone became overly reasonable. 'Secrets spill from your lips at the earliest opportunity and then someone else has to deal with the consequences. I didn't want to deal with these consequences.'

'Do they really?' Sophie narrowed her eyes. She wanted to shake him hard. He knew nothing about her! She prided herself on being able to keep important secrets. She would never deliberately tell anyone anything which would harm them or make them upset. Above everything, it showed how mistaken she'd been to marry a stranger. 'Richard, I kept the truth about our engagement from the woman who brought me up until after we were married and I was confronted with a glaring lie. I kept the truth from my guardian and his wife. And I share everything with Henri.'

'You share everything with an unknown.' He slammed his fists together. 'There, I rest my case. Precisely why I didn't tell you. I know what my parents are like.'

'You are seeking to justify the unjustifiable.' Sophie's mouth tasted like ash. He hadn't even listened to what she was saying. Neither did he care about her feelings. 'And you obviously don't want to know me very well. I thought we were friends, Richard, but we are merely strangers who shared a bed. You should have trusted me with this. Instead, you allowed me to blunder about, not knowing what was happening or why you were distant.' Her limbs started to tremble. In another moment, she'd break down and cry. She absolutely refused to cry in front of him. 'What else have you kept hidden from me? I loved you, Richard.'

The words hung between them. Sophie covered her mouth. She hadn't meant to confess her love in that way.

'That is unfair, Sophie. Bringing love into it to suit your purposes.' He gave a half-smile and held out his hands. 'I did marry you. I do want you, Sophie, as my life's partner. Being with you has been an oasis of calm in my life. I'm selfish. I know that, but it was done to protect you.'

'Shall we be honest, Richard? Finally? You married me because you could not have me any other way. Because you wanted me in your bed, but your sense of honour meant that you had to marry me. This was about sex and desire, pure and simple on your part. But I'm not a mistress. I thought I was your wife.'

'You are making wild accusations. You are overtired.' He put out his hand. 'I married you because I wanted you in my life. My whole life. I planned on telling you about my mother and sister when the time was right. I wanted to enjoy you without my family causing problems for just a while longer.'

His pity at her love somehow made it worse. She hugged her waist. 'No, you only wanted me in your bed. I suppose some should say that I should be grateful that you gave me your name. But you didn't want me in your life, not really. You were ashamed of me.'

He winced when she said the words, but he did not say anything. He allowed his hand to drop to his side. And she knew her words had hit their mark. She waited for him to deny it, or say something that would fill the great yawning gap where her heart had been. 'You were the one who wanted to show me off like some prize you'd won. You were the one who planned a dinner party without asking me first. Why is it so important to you what other people think about you and your life?'

The silence became deafening and she knew she had her answer.

'I'm going, Richard. I refuse to stay here in this sham of a marriage.'

'You can't abandon our marriage.'

'You already abandoned it. You never gave me a chance. You were not interested in me.'

'Don't you want to hear why I was late?' he whispered in a ragged voice. 'Hear me out before you make your decision. Once you know, you will understand.'

'I doubt I will ever understand. You are ashamed of me. You only married me because you have your code of honour. I hoped it might be love, but it wasn't.'

'Listen, Sophie, before you judge. Please. I never wanted my family problems to concern you. It is not you I am ashamed of, but my family and the way they act.'

Sophie struggled to control her temper. She was married to him. All her instincts screamed that she should grab her valise and go. If Richard touched her, there was every possibility she'd melt. 'Why were you late?'

'My mother took an overdose of laudanum. I had to get the doctor. I had to make sure she was going to live. Otherwise our trip would have to have been postponed again. Hannah was beyond hysterical. You do understand why I had to stay.'

'Why did she overdose?'

'You would have to ask her.' He ran his hands through his hair. 'I had told her about the dinner party and that my father would be leaving in the morning. You and I were going to the Continent. I would see them again when I returned and that I hoped she'd enjoy getting to know you then. I left and went to the jewellers to pick up that blasted necklace for you.'

'I didn't want a necklace. I never wanted a necklace.'

'I wanted to give it to you, to mark our first dinner party. I wanted it to be something you would always remember.'

'I shall always remember it.' Sophie clenched her fists. 'I tried so hard. All I wanted to do was to show you that I was worthy of being a viscountess. Quite frankly, that doesn't matter any more. I am who I am and I like me. I am through with tying myself in knots for anyone, most especially you!'

'Have I ever asked you to?'

'But you are ashamed of me. I read the letter…'

'I meant to burn that after I wrote to my aunt, telling her a few home truths. But I have been so angry about it that every time I sit down to write, I can't.'

He held out his arms as if he expected her to walk straight into them, lay her head against his chest and forgive him.

Sophie put her hand to her head. 'It doesn't change a thing.'

'Sophie!'

She forced herself to turn her back and walk to where she had placed her valise. She'd packed it this afternoon in readiness for the wedding trip, a trip which was not going to happen now. A huge lump formed in her throat. She swallowed hard and, when she felt in control of her emotions, turned to face him.

'The only thing you wanted to share was sex, Richard. I refuse to have a marriage based on that. Desire always fades without something real and solid behind it. You are right. I was in a dream of love. I have woken up and discovered that I am worth it. It is why I am leaving now. I am going to spend my life living it as it was meant to be lived, rather than existing and hoping for a few crumbs of praise from you.'

'I forbid it.'

Sophie kept her back ramrod straight. The old Sophie would have crumbled, but Richard had given her her self-respect back. She knew now what she wanted and why she wasn't going to settle for this second-best marriage. 'You can forbid nothing, Richard. Not any more.'

'Where are you going?' he asked in a ragged voice.

'Where I am safe,' Sophie answered, knowing he'd never guess what she planned on doing or where she was going. She would start living her life on her terms now. 'Where no one cares what my reputation is or what title I have, but what they do care about is me.'

Chapter Fourteen

Richard stood in stunned silence. Sophie couldn't really be about to leave him. Not Sophie, not when he needed to forget about today. He wanted to hold her as she lay sleeping and look into her face. But mostly he wanted her there, beside him, talking to him about little ordinary things and worrying about little details that most people never even noticed. She was his refuge from the storm which had engulfed him. He needed her.

'Don't go,' he whispered. 'Stay with me, please. I…I care about you. I need you.'

The sound of the quietly clicked door echoed through the now-empty rooms. He wandered through the rooms aimlessly, leaving the bedroom until the last. It was as if all the light and joy had been sucked out of them.

Beside the bed, he sank down to his knees and buried his head in his hands. Tears flowed down his face. Sophie had gone. She had walked out of his life. And she would not be back.

His gut ached as if it had been torn out and roughly stuffed back in. A great black emptiness filled him. Sophie had abandoned him.

This black emptiness was far worse than when, as a boy of seven, his mother had left him with Hannah in a small glade while she ran away with her lover. When the light had faded and it was clear that no one was coming for them, he had carried the crying toddler back to Hallington and told her that he would look after her. He found his father in the study, drinking. His father had engulfed him and Hannah in a big bear hug, and told him that they would be a family together.

However, one day a few months later, he had returned from a ride to find the nursery empty. He'd gone again to the study and asked his father where his sister was and had his ears boxed for his trouble. He was never to mention his sister or mother again, his father declared, going into the first of his fearsome rages. Richard had gone back to his room and cried himself to sleep. It was the last time he had wept.

Two weeks later, he was on his way to Eton and his father had always had an excuse as to why he couldn't be there. Richard had pretended at first he didn't care and in the end he hadn't cared. He wanted to think it would be the same with Sophie, but he knew that was a lie. He'd always care. He'd always want to know where Sophie was and that she was happy. Sophie was as necessary as breathing to him.

Richard looked up at the bed and grabbed a pillow. Her faint scent of lavender and citrus clung to it but it made the ache worse and he put it from him.

'Sophie!'

The word echoed around the chamber, mocking him.

Would she have gone so quickly if she cared for him? He'd been right to keep from confessing how much he needed her in his life and how much his happiness and well being depended on her. She didn't care about him, not truly.

He started to get up, but an abandoned book under the bed caught his eye. He reached out and brought Sophie's sketchpad out.

He flipped through it. Page after page was filled with sketches of him. The first ones were hesitant and obviously done from memory early in their relationship. Later in the book, she must have drawn him while he slept. His favourite was him asleep with his face turned towards her. She had sketched his back and the way the coverlet had slipped to his waist.

Each line of the drawing screamed how much she cared about him. A tiny light flickered in the black emptiness deep within him and he knew the truth he'd been avoiding. She cared for him, deeply and passionately, and he'd refused to see it before, preferring to think that she was in love with new sensations because it meant he did not have to face his own feelings for her. He didn't want to give her the power to hurt him and in doing so, he had hurt her—deeply and irrevocably.

Richard closed his eyes, knowing he had killed whatever glimmer of love she had for him. He should have trusted her with his family, with his whole being, because she was his life. He was the one who had wronged her, dreadfully wronged her. There had been no marriage to leave, because he had not been prepared to give of himself.

He tore the drawing from the book, carefully folded it and put it in his pocket. It was a slim hope.

'I will get you back, Sophie, and I will spend my life showing you my finer feelings. I will show you that I know where you are going. I will always be there for you if you want me. And I do want you to stand beside me. If you need me to say words, I will, but I am scared.'

He put his hands to his eyes. Where had she gone? She had accused him of not knowing her and not caring. He had to prove that he did know her, far better than she thought.

He would find her without anyone else's help but he had to do it quickly.

'I want to see Lady Bingfield, Mrs Montemorcy,' Richard said, keeping his voice steady as he stood on the doorstep of the imposing country house in Corbridge that afternoon. 'Please tell her I am here.'

It had taken him several hours and a painful interview with his father, where he'd been accused of all manner of things when he confessed that Sophie had left him. Richard had not given him the true reason, but he had persuaded his father to stay until he found Sophie. His father had given him twenty-four hours. The instant he left his father, he knew where Sophie must have gone.

All the way to Corbridge on the train, he had

prayed his hunch was correct. But if it wasn't, he'd keep searching. He refused to give up.

The slender brunette stared daggers at him. If looks could kill or maim, the formidable Mrs Montemorcy's certainly would.

'There is no such person as Lady Bingfield.'

He knew then what Sophie and the Montemorcys intended—an annulment. Difficult, but not impossible and the last thing he wanted.

Heart thudding in his ears, he held out his hands and begged, 'I would speak with Sophie. Your friend Sophie. Let me speak to her, please.'

She tilted her head to one side, assessed him and found him wanting. 'And if she doesn't want to speak to you?'

'I am her husband.'

Mrs Montemorcy's eyebrow shot up. 'That remains to be seen.'

Richard's stomach clenched. He was expected to go, but he refused to give in to expectations.

'Sophie! Sophie! I will stand outside this house and scream your name until you come out. You decide. But you never need to hide behind anyone's skirt. You simply need to tell me to go away. But it has to come from you.'

'You are making a spectacle of yourself, Lord Bingfield. Cease it at once!'

'I want my wife, Mrs Montemorcy. I want to

speak with her. I want to know she is safe.' Richard held out his hands and willed her to agree. 'My wife's well being is very important to me.'

'You presume much, Lord Bingfield.' Mrs Montemorcy started to close the door.

Richard stuck his hand and foot in the doorway, blocking her. Sophie was there.

'All I want to do is talk with her. Sophie is fully capable of telling me to go to the devil, Mrs Montemorcy. You know that as well as I do. Sophie has no need of protection from you, from anyone.'

'If you speak to her and she tells you to go, will you go? Quietly?'

'Yes, I will go,' Richard said, bowing his head, giving in.

'Henri, it is fine. You can stop standing guard over me.' Sophie came out from behind her friend. 'Richard is right. I am a grown up. I fight my own battles now.'

Richard's heart lurched. Her eyes were mere slits, practically swollen shut from crying; her nose was red and her hair hung about her shoulders like snakes. She had never looked more beautiful to him. He wanted to throw her over his shoulder and hurry away from there. He wanted to kiss her feet. He forced his body to remain completely still and devoured her with his eyes.

'Sophie,' he said.

She gave a reluctant nod. 'I'm here. Say what you like, Richard.'

'You may speak in the drawing room, unless you wish to converse outside where all might hear,' Mrs Montemorcy said.

Richard kept his eyes on Sophie. She might be capable of fighting her own battles, but he wanted to be there for her. He had to hope that she wanted to help him fight his battles. 'It is Sophie's choice.'

'We can risk the drawing room.' Sophie took two steps into the house before stopping and fixing him with her eye. 'But, Richard, if you try anything, anything at all after I tell you to go, Henri's footmen will throw you out on your ear.'

'I understand.' He gulped a breath of life-giving air. Silently he prayed, as he had not done since he was a young boy in that wood, that she'd listen and understand what he was truly saying. He was going to bare his soul and hope.

Her legs like jelly and her head throbbing, Sophie staggered into Henri and Robert's drawing room. The last person she had expected to see today was Richard, but he was here. Her trai-torous body wanted to go to him and be held, but that was how the trouble had started in the first place.

She took a steadying breath. It was the shock of seeing him.

If he came at all, she had expected it to be within a week's time after he'd managed to get the probable destination out of her stepmother. She had expected her stepmother to be more closed-mouthed. She'd given Robert her assur-ance of that which was why he had stayed in Newcastle at his office, rather than travelling to Corbridge to be here with her. She should have remembered that her stepmother had a soft spot for Richard.

'Remember, Sophie, I am here if you need as-sistance.' Henri gave Richard a hard look. 'And my husband will return shortly.'

'My wife is perfectly safe with me,' Richard said firmly. 'You have my solemn word.'

Sophie motioned to Henri to go. With one last troubled glance backwards, Henri left the room. Sophie forced her shoulders back and waited.

Richard said nothing. He simply stood there, looking at her with a haunted expression as the silence grew and threatened to suffocate her.

'I suppose it is my stepmother I can thank for

you finding me so quickly.' Sophie pressed her hands together to keep them from trembling. 'She has a romantic soul, but she has gone too far this time. There was no need for it.'

'I have not seen your stepmother today. In fact, I have not seen her since the day before yesterday. You wrong her and me if you think that.' A muscle jumped in his jaw. 'I knew where you must have gone. And if you had not been here, I would have kept on searching until I found you. There are things which need to be settled between us.'

Sophie's eyes widened. She rapidly sat down. He'd known where she'd run to. He hadn't seen her stepmother. 'How did you find me? How did you guess?'

'When we first conversed after the item appeared in the newspaper, you said that if things became very bad, you would go to Corbridge. Once here, I learnt where your friends lived.'

'You remembered that?' Sophie trembled. It was when she'd been so sure that Richard hadn't cared for her. *If he didn't care, why remember?* asked a little nagging voice in the back of her mind. She quashed it, just as during her train journey here she'd quashed it every time it spoke up, reminding her about the little things Richard had done. Richard had wronged her. She be-

lieved in a person who did not exist and it was
time for her to stop believing in fairy stories
and romance.

'I try to remember everything about you, Sophie, because you are necessary to me.'

Necessary to him. Sophie put her hand to her
mouth. 'Why did you come here?'

'I took the second train this morning and
came to find you. I need your help, Sophie, and
I need it urgently. I am sorry that I can't pander
to your tender sensibilities and allow you to revel
in your hurt, but this matter refuses to wait.'

'You need my help with what?' she asked,
narrowing her eyes suspiciously. Pander to her
tender sensibilities, indeed. Of all the nerve! 'I
will end this interview right now if you wish
to be rude.'

'I need you to help put things right. I can't do
this on my own, Sophie.'

'Things are never going to be right between
us,' she said. 'I made that perfectly clear last
night and I am even clearer on it today. We can
never go back to what we had or what I thought
we might have. I have done a lot of thinking.'

He paled at her words. 'Hear me out, Sophie.
We are married. Lawfully man and wife. I never
wanted it to be like this. I intended to protect

you and keep you safe. I thought I could fight your battles for you.'

'I know our legal status to my cost. Robert has already pointed this obstacle out, but things can be done.'

He flinched as if she had struck him with her hand.

'All I ask is this one thing and I will let you go if that is what you want.' He bowed his head. 'I will even help with the annulment, false pretences or whatever is the most expedient. I will play the villain, if the law requires, but first I require this one thing of you.'

Sophie's insides trembled. Richard was not going to try to hold her to the marriage. He was going to let her go. He probably wanted her assurance that she wouldn't sell her story to the papers or some such nonsense.

She wanted to break down in fresh tears again, but she had cried herself to a standstill already. It was worse, somehow, seeing him again and knowing that his arms had given her comfort before. She'd never again be able to lay her head on his chest and listen to his steady heartbeat. And, despite everything, she loved him and cared about him.

'What is this one thing?' she asked between numb lips.

'I want you to listen to my story and then I want your advice on how to proceed.'

'My advice?' Sophie hated the way her heart leapt. 'You have never wanted it before. You kept things from me, rather than asking me.'

'I am asking now.' His voice became ragged. 'Please. You are my last hope, Sophie. No, that's not right. You are my only hope.'

Sophie sank down on the sofa. 'I will listen.'

'My mother left Hannah and I in the woods when I was no more than seven and Hannah was a toddler, barely able to walk on her own.' Richard's voice held little emotion. 'We were supposed to be on a picnic. The first picnic of the summer, just my mother and her two children. Three of us left Hallington that day, only two returned. My mother ran away with Hannah's father.'

Sophie stuffed her hand into her mouth. It was far worse than she had imagined. How could any woman leave her children alone and defenceless in a wood? 'How did you get back? Did your father find you? How long were you there?'

'Once I realised no one was coming, I carried Hannah all the way home as my mother had taken the governess's cart. Someone had to take responsibility.'

There was a wealth of information in the

stark sentences. Sophie could easily imagine the frightened boy left alone with a crying toddler, far from home, expecting help and having none come. Despite his reputation for scandal, Richard always tried to protect those who were weaker than him. It was why that woman Mary's death had affected him so badly.

She wanted to gather him in her arms and tell him what he'd done that day was a brave and wonderful thing. But she hardened her heart and stayed still. He should never have treated her in the manner he did.

'How...how could she do such a thing?' she asked instead.

'Hannah's father was my mother's lover before she married my father. He abandoned her for Australia and she married my father in haste. My father adored the ground my mother walked on. She found him old and fusty. She spent money doing up Hallington like it was water and gave extravagant parties while my father became ever more absorbed in his pig-breeding. Eventually Grayson returned and the affair started again. My sister was born nine months after he returned.'

'Hannah is your mother's love child?' Sophie closed her eyes.

'My father acknowledged Hannah as his own and then, when she was two…this happened.'

Sophie remembered the tears in Lord Hallington's eyes when he said that he'd always wanted a daughter. 'You had better tell me everything so I can understand. If I don't understand, I don't see how I can give proper advice.'

She listened carefully as Richard explained about the divorce and his father's conditions. How his mother had chosen Hannah and her lover had formally adopted her. How he'd learnt not to depend on his father appearing at any function and that he'd had to fight his own battles. Finally Richard spoke about how he always made sure that he was never hurt like that again and how if any of his mistresses wanted to leave, he let them go. He ended things before he became involved. How he never offered twice.

Sophie pressed her lips together and knew he'd broken his rules for her. More than once. Her heart fluttered, but she simply nodded her head and waited for him to finish.

'I thought I would keep my heart safe, but when you left last night, I learnt that simply denying feelings doesn't stop them from happening. When you walked out, you took my heart with you. You didn't mean to.'

'What do you want from me? Your heart

back?' Sophie clenched her hands and knew she had made a decision. Every woman Richard had known had abandoned him. She had done exactly the same thing when she didn't know about his past. But now she did and she knew he was worth fighting for. 'How can I give your heart back when I didn't know I had it?'

'It belongs to you now. It has belonged to you for longer than I dare admit.' Richard bowed his head and his shoulders slumped. 'What I wanted from you was for you to listen and you have. I will go now. I wanted you to know that I am here for you if you ever need me. And I have decided that there is no longer any purpose in trying to keep my parents happy.'

Sophie knew she had this one chance to make their marriage into the sort of marriage she wanted, rather than one that others might want for her.

'I am coming with you. I need you to need me and I think you need me by your side and in your life.'

His eyes opened wide and his mouth dropped open. 'What?'

'After you leave here, you are going to see your father and tell him the truth about why you were in Newcastle to begin with and what you wanted to accomplish. Then you are going to see your mother with your father and get him to give her a promise that he won't ruin Hannah out of spite. She believes his promises because he is like you. He always tries to keep his promises.' Sophie's heart thudded. She had to get this right. 'And if I am there, it will make life easier for everyone, particularly you. You shouldn't go into battle without your heart.'

He gave a shadow of his old heart-melting smile. 'Precisely, but why are you willing to do this?'

Sophie held out her hand. 'You could do this on your own, Richard, but it is easier if you have someone who will stand shoulder to shoulder with you. Your parents are difficult people. Your father will bluster and thunder. Your mother may fly into hysterics. They both need to see that you are not on your own any more. They both failed you when you were a boy. You never failed them. You don't have to put things right for them, but if you want to, I will be there at your side.'

'Sophie!'

'Your mother in particular needs to see that we stand together. That no one can drive a wedge between us. She needs to see that she is not losing a son, but gaining a daughter. And she is having no part in our marriage or the marriage of her daughter.'

He stepped towards her. 'What…what are you saying about our marriage, Sophie?'

Sophie drew in her breath. This time he had to believe her. But even if he didn't, she'd go on telling him until he believed.

'I'm saying that I love you, Richard, and, even if your scheme doesn't work and your parents behave badly, I will stand by you and make sure that Hannah's match happens. She is my sister now. She doesn't need to have her life ruined by selfish people who should just grow up. Just as you don't deserve it, either.' She stood up and held out her arms. 'I learnt something today. Life is better when someone believes in you and I believe in you, Richard.'

'You mean to stay married to me?' He caught her hand in his.

'Until my dying breath.' Sophie bowed her head. She wanted to get the words right and explain. 'I was angry and hurt last night because I didn't understand what you were doing. You wrongly kept me in ignorance and, rather than asking, I leapt to conclusions. I don't need protection from anyone, Richard, as long as I have you by my side. I don't care what other people say about us as long as we please ourselves.'

'Always.' He folded her in his arms and put

his head against hers. 'You'll always have me. I believe in you, Sophie.'

'I know that now.' She gave a little hiccupping laugh. 'I never thought you'd come out to Corbridge or face Henri down. Some people might think it isn't much, but I know you. I know what you have been through and what you believed might happen, but you still came and you were willing to fight for me. You fought for me when I tried to hide behind my experience with Sebastian. You showed me that it didn't define me. I defined me.'

He squeezed her hand. 'I do love you, Sophie. I simply was afraid to say the words before. Until you came into my life, I didn't know what happiness could be.'

'And I was too afraid to see the signs of your love. They were there but, until I started trusting me, I didn't think I was worthy of your love.'

'I forced you into our marriage. I rushed you before you were ready.' He put his hands on either side of her face. 'I seduced you, ruthlessly and cynically seduced you because I had to be certain of you. Do you forgive me?'

'Why, Richard? Why did you do it?' Sophie whispered.

'Because I needed you in my life, every part of my life. You complete my life and make me whole.' There was a new humble note in Richard's voice. 'I wanted to make sure you could become the person you were meant to be and the only way to do that was to have you by my side. Or at least that was what I told myself. It wasn't until you walked out that I knew I married you because I needed you in my life and for no other reason. You are necessary to me, Sophie, as necessary as breathing. Hopefully, some day, I will be necessary to you as well.'

'You are already necessary.' Sophie looked into his eyes. 'Robert and Henri's return was a fig leaf for my pride because I thought you would not ask me to marry you again. I remembered what you said on the night we met. I knew I loved you when you brought me the painting materials and then insisted I use them.'

'You were very late to fall. I know I started to love you when you refused my invitation to waltz on the first night. Any other woman and I would have walked away, but with you, I knew I couldn't. I wanted to be part of your life.' He gave a crooked smile. 'I took advantage of you in the carriage. I had promised I wouldn't, but the temptation was far too great. I had to know you would be in my life and I played on your need to be seen to be good.'

Sophie gave a throaty laugh. She had been

so intent on assuming things that she had failed to consider the obvious. Richard married her because he wanted to. Not because society demanded it, but because he desired it. 'I was easy to seduce. Love will do that to a woman.'

He smoothed her hair back from her forehead. His eyes looked deeply into hers. Sophie wondered that she had missed the deep love which shone out. Now that she knew where to look, the love was clear to see. 'If I had asked you to marry me without seduction, would you have done?'

'Ask me. Ask me now and I will give you the answer I would have given then.'

'Will you marry me, Sophie? Will you spend the rest of your life with me?'

'Always.' Sophie lifted her mouth to his. 'I will always marry you. I will always stay at your side. Not because society demands, but because you are the keeper of my heart and I want to be there.'

* * * * *

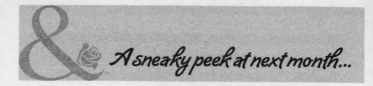

A sneaky peek at next month...

HISTORICAL

IGNITE YOUR IMAGINATION, STEP INTO THE PAST...

My wish list for next month's titles...

In stores from 3rd May 2013:

❏ The Greatest of Sins – Christine Merrill

❏ Tarnished Amongst the Ton – Louise Allen

❏ The Beauty Within – Marguerite Kaye

❏ The Devil Claims a Wife – Helen Dickson

❏ The Scarred Earl – Elizabeth Beacon

❏ Her Hesitant Heart – Carla Kelly

Available at WHSmith, Tesco, Asda, Eason, Amazon and Apple

Just can't wait?

Visit us Online

You can buy our books online a month before they hit the shops! **www.millsandboon.co.uk**

0413/04

Special Offers

Every month we put together collections and longer reads written by your favourite authors.

Here are some of next month's highlights— and don't miss our fabulous discount online!

Australia
OUTBACK FANTASIES

Margaret WAY · Barbara HANNAY · Leah MARTYN

On sale 19th April

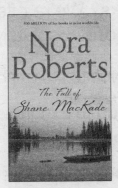

300 MILLION of her books in print worldwide

Nora Roberts

The Fall of Shane MacKade

On sale 3rd May

THE CORRETTIS

Sins

CAROL MARINELLI · SARAH MORGAN

On sale 3rd May

Save 20% on all Special Releases

Find out more at
www.millsandboon.co.uk/specialreleases

Visit us Online

0513/ST/MB414